Indelible Ink

A Deena Riordan Novel

Matt Betts

Indelible Ink © 2015
by Matt Betts

Published by Dog Star Books
Bowie, MD

First Edition

Cover Image: Bradley Sharp
Book Design: Jennifer Barnes

Printed in the United States of America

ISBN: 978-1-935738-74-9

Library of Congress Control Number: 2015943133

www.DogStarBooks.org

Praise for Indelible Ink

"Dark, imaginative, and thrilling, Indelible Ink is part urban fantasy, part crime novel, and completely enthralling. A first-rate adventure from the ever-reliable pen of Matt Betts."
—Tim Waggoner, *Dream Stalkers*

"Women assassins, guns, black magic and government conspiracy; what's not to love about Matt Betts' latest novel, Indelible Ink? Grab a copy now, before the powers that be decide you can't be trusted with the truth."
—Tom Barlow, *I'll Meet You Yesterday*

"Matt Betts doesn't seem to know all writers get put into a box. He ignores genres and boundaries and simply writes what his imagination wants. His stories are what make reading fun."
—Greg Hall, *Everyone Hates a Hero*

"This urban fantasy has a strong female slant that I enjoyed, and the quirky character of FEI Agent Pel is one of my favorites. Betts' use of the 'ink' and monstrous power it holds is intriguing and quite unlike anything I had read before. Deena is one tough fighter that I wouldn't want to come across in a dark alley, or in a Starbucks either, for that matter. In case of impending apocalypse, I want her on my side."
—Mercedes M. Yardley, author of *Nameless*

"A thrilling, clever, and quick paced fantasy!"
—Ellen Ann, NY Times Bestselling Author

"Mysterious powers and perpetual mayhem rip through this secret world where guns are bad, but something worse can lurk beneath the skin."
—Nayad Monroe, Editor *Not Our Kind*

"Betts's horror caper has its charms, including the portrayal of Deena's changing mind-set as she grows younger and then older again, and a sniper whose hallucinations of his mother, mentor, and childhood teddy bear constantly berate and insult him."
—*Publishers Weekly*

Dedication

To Dad for putting books in my hand when I was a kid, and for continuing to hand me great books today.

To Mom for cheering me on no matter what.

Acknowledgements

I can type away on a novel all I want, but I can't do everything myself. Once the writing is done, there are many, many people that get involved in preparing the book for publication, and I'm thankful for each and every one.

Thanks to Mike Liddy for not being bitter about getting killed in my first book, and for giving me awesome notes on this one (I promise you'll get to be the hero one of these days).

Huge thanks to Heidi Ruby Miller and Jennifer Barnes for taking my first novel at Dog Star Books. Thanks also to Jennifer for all the hard work and guidance on *Indelible Ink*. Thanks to the whole team at Dog Star and RDSP who got it ready for publication.

Thanks to my Nemesis, Mercedes Yardley, for the impetus to keep writing better and writing more. And writing *more better. YOU'RE the Doofenshmirtz.*

Thanks to the Naked Wordshop for giving me an incredible education in writing, publishing, editing, storytelling and general awesomeness. Ninjas make it all better.

And thanks to my family. None of these stories get told without your help. I love each of you to the moon and back. No… all the way to the Milky Way and back.

Foreword

I've known Matt Betts for over a decade, and he continues to be one of the friendliest, most enthusiastic, and magnanimous writers in the business. I suspect his unending good humor is simply a by-product of a great family life…and writing what he loves, even if it never fits neatly into one genre. That passion is evident in a myriad of short stories and in *Odd Men Out*, his debut novel that I acquired for Dog Star Books as one of the flagship titles to launch the entire imprint back in 2013. Now his affection for storytelling bleeds through here in *Indelible Ink*.

This latest addition to the Betts-verse is a spectacular brew seasoned with urban fantasy, science fiction, and horror. No surprise, considering his literary inspirations range from Seanan McGuire and Patricia Briggs to Elmore Leonard. These expansive influences inform his work and bring Deena and Harper's story alive through crackling dialog and quick pacing. "Leave the boring stuff out," right?

His genre-meshing isn't the only break with more traditional urban fantasies, however. Indeed, his character choices show he tries to stay away from the obvious archetypes-become-stereotypes whenever he can.

Matt also manipulates many urban fantasy tropes to come up with unique ideas as Deena tames the dark magic which lives inside her and manifests itself as deadly, magical art upon her skin. Throughout time, cultures have viewed the tattoo as mystical and reverent, and Matt expands upon this anthropological rite of passage in a macabre, but sensational way. It is a perfect example of how he plays to genre expectations one moment only to catch the reader off-guard when he makes the unexpected choice later on—like a de-aging protagonist who finds it difficult to be a tough-as-nails enforcer when she looks and feels like a fourteen-year-old.

His twists through this speculative labyrinth keep the characters moving and the plot morphing just like Deena's "Dark Energy." And, it seems he saved one of those twists and salvaged an extra villain for the next book. Remember when I said he loves what he writes? Well, so do I and I look forward to seeing dear Deena and her magical tattoos again in book two, *Invisible Ink*.

-Heidi Ruby Miller
Uniontown, PA, February 2015

1

Deena Riordan's plane would be landing in Seattle within the hour, and she was ready to put this business to rest. She slouched down, pulled a magazine out of her bag and flipped through it. She didn't feel like reading, but the pictures calmed her mind and gave her something to focus on.

Deena had watched Frank Harris discreetly through three flights and eight hours of layovers, waiting. The more time the man had to think he'd made a clean getaway, the greater the shock when she told him otherwise.

He hadn't been terribly cautious or observant in his crazy zig-zag course across the country and he let a little more of his guard down as the trip went on. Harris seemed to think a fake name and doctored ID made him invisible. Even if it did, Deena was sure she could find him by his stench; he smelled like a combination of body odor and airport gift-shop cologne, which made her blink uncontrollably. She mourned for what the smell did to the expensive new suit that he'd been wearing for going on two days.

On previous flights, her tickets put her far enough from him that the smell wasn't a problem, but now she found herself sitting next to him on the short hop from Milwaukee. Her eyes watered a little.

Deena ached with exhaustion, but could feel the familiar buzz building up inside. She bit her lip hard enough to make it bleed in an effort to chill out. It didn't work and she struggled to keep a grin from appearing.

This should be fun.

"Can I get you anything?" asked the attendant with the fake tan and the tight smile. "Pillow, blanket?"

"How about a drink or three?" Frank said.

"We'll come back around with beverage service soon."

"Maybe a blanket?" Deena asked

"Sure thing." The attendant drifted off down the aisle with a look of vague purpose. There weren't many other passengers in their section, but the woman stopped at each of them.

"Cold?" Frank asked.

She looked up at him from her magazine. "Yeah." Immediately, she looked back at the page and turned it.

"Always freezing on these flights." He pulled his jacket closer about him. "Why do they need to keep it so cold?" He gave her a questioning look that lingered. Deena just shook her head and shrugged.

When the attendant leaned over with a thin blanket, Deena took it and wrapped it tightly about her legs. She knew Frank was still looking at her. She turned slightly and held her magazine up closer to her face, as if trying to get better light so she could read. She didn't like his stare.

"I thought you were a bit older when I first sat down," he said. "You seem kind of young to be flying all alone." He sounded suspicious.

"I get that a lot."

"Where are you headed?"

She didn't want to have to play twenty questions with Frank. "Are you a cop? Air Marshall?" She gave a mocking look of shock. "Truant officer? That's it. You've come to take me back to school. Oh, what shall I do? You've found me out."

"Take it easy."

"Fuck you."

"What?" Frank looked around to see if anyone else heard her, but no one seemed to notice.

"You heard me," Deena said. She was enjoying winding him up.

"Jesus, kid." Frank's face got red. "Look. Maybe one of us should see if we can sit somewhere else? I don't want to put up with this the whole flight."

"Give me fifty bucks and I won't tell the stewardess you put your hand on my thigh," Deena said. She wanted him off balance when the real trouble began.

"What the hell? I did no such thing. What are you trying to pull? Think you can get a little money out of me? Go ahead, call her. Let's get the stewardess over here and see who she believes. Maybe you can talk to airport security when we land? See how fast I have you busted. See how funny your shit is then."

I guess now is as good a time to do this as any. Deena thought. *Excellent.* She smiled and held up a placating hand. "Easy there, Frank. We both know you're not going to talk to anyone in law enforcement. Not with your recent history."

He narrowed his eyes. "I never told you my name."

She smiled and started rolling up her sleeve. "Oh, didn't you? Hmmm. Are you sure? When you were making a pass at me, I swear you mentioned it." She said it loud enough so that others could hear, if they cared.

"What? I never did any such thing." Frank looked alarmed and scanned the cabin again for anyone who might give a shit.

"Easy. Easy. It's true, you didn't." As the material of her shirt came up to her shoulder, a mass of ink revealed itself near her pale bicep.

"What is wrong with you? What're you doing?"

She nodded toward the black stain.

"Great, the little psycho has a tattoo," he said. "So what?"

Deena closed her eyes for just a moment and concentrated. She envisioned a radio glowing in a car dash. She could see it clearly in her mind, including the hand that came down and turned the knob to get the station she needed. When it was done, she opened her eyes. The mass on her arm went from an indistinguishable blob to another, more definable shape. Frank squinted, and then recognition came across his face. Deena knew he doubted what he saw; he had to wonder if his eyes were playing tricks on him. She never looked at what was happening on her arm; she didn't need to. She knew there were blotches moving around slowly, separating and coming together; they were doing it at her command. They pooled and stretched, leaving skin exposed and then covering it up again. When it was all over, she exhaled and waited for his reaction. He blinked rapidly and she knew he was trying to place exactly what was on her arm.

He leaned in to get a closer look. "Is that supposed to be me?" The likeness was better than could be expected from black ink on pale white skin; it was nearly photo quality. Deena had been working hard to expand what she could do with this power inside her and she'd gotten pretty good at silly little parlor tricks.

"What's going on here? How do you know me?" The tattooed image of Frank's meaty face began to twist and contort again, the dark wavy hair melting into the wide nose, the chin sliding over into the ear. It swirled and formed itself into a fist. Knuckles defined themselves, hairs came into view. Once the image of the hand had settled and rested a moment, the middle finger extended itself.

"Hey, what the—"

"Shut up, you greasy fuck and pay attention." Deena's mouth curled into a smile. She called the power her Shadow Energy. Every time she used it, it seemed like a shadow fell across her arm or across the ground, sometimes even her victims. She'd found that no one else saw the phenomenon, just her. "I'm not here to answer your questions. Just sit there, with your mouth closed and listen. 'Kay?" Before Frank could respond, she gritted her teeth and retuned her radio image to conjure up the new picture she wanted.

The ink started to swirl again. It didn't take long for the image of another face to appear on Deena's arm. This time it was a thin man with small glasses; he was a bit older than Frank, maybe in his late fifties, early sixties. Deena watched Frank's face. This was the part she loved: seeing the instant when the stupid actually realize they're stupid.

Once the image was as clear as it was going to get, it began to move. Frank gasped and tried to back away from it.

"Hello there, Frank," the tattoo said, mouth moving. "Good to see you again."

Frank shook his head and looked around to see where the voice was coming from. Not finding any other source, he looked back at the image. It was a fully animated likeness of a man he knew very well. "Mr. Marsh?"

"Oh, good. I was afraid you'd perhaps forgotten my name, seeing as you left town so quickly. Worried maybe you'd forgotten it and therefore weren't sure where to leave the giant pile of money you owe me."

Deena laughed at the image of her boss, even though she was beginning to feel lightheaded. The initial playing-around had drained her more than she'd expected and faking a moving image of Marsh was adding to the strain. She also hadn't fully recovered from her last job before her handler hustled her off to this one and it was taking its toll. This one was a rush deal, and she didn't have time to regenerate and rest as much as she needed. To top it off, this radio thing was the toughest spell she'd ever tried. Still. If she hurried, it shouldn't deplete her too much. A good nap would work wonders. Some crackers. A tall cup of something with a metric ton of caffeine in it wouldn't hurt either. She was sure she had enough in reserve if she stopped playing, though. If not, she could be screwed.

"You see," Mr. Marsh continued, "when you incorrectly guess the outcome of several games of chance, that's called 'losing.'" He paused to let the lesson set in. "And when there is money involved, the loser has to pay the winner. Make sense?"

A line of sweat ran down the side of Frank's face. It was obvious he still wasn't sure where he was supposed to direct his voice and he looked from the tattoo's face up to Deena's and back. "I did pay you. I signed over everything I had.

In fact, it should have been worth ten percent more than I owed." He looked earnest, if not panicked.

The image nodded. "True. Quite true. Except when we began to process these assets, we found they didn't actually belong to you. Excellent forgeries." Mr. Marsh face was stern. "Good work, but the real owners found you out already and the court froze those properties and assets days ago. We're lucky someone didn't catch us snooping and think we were the ones that stole them. That would have been terrible." He sighed. "You didn't want that to happen did you, Frank?"

Another trickle of perspiration joined the first on Frank's head. "Oh, no. Of course not. This must be a mix-up. You'll see, it'll straighten itself out."

The Mr. Marsh image was silent, as if thinking. "Perhaps. But in the meantime, I think it best for us to make other monetary arrangements. A wire transfer or cash would be preferable. No checks. No collateral. Gold would be nice if you have it on you."

A look of defiance came across Frank's face and a charge of excitement went up Deena's spine. *Stupid people being stupider.* "You know, once we land, you'll never be able to touch me," Frank said. "You're right, I dabble in identity theft and once I hit the ground, I'm gone."

Deena laughed to herself. "*I dabble in identity theft.*" Idiot.

"I understand that possibility," Mr. Marsh said. "Though the presence of this lovely young lady should indicate that I can find you anywhere."

"With the state of security these days, I doubt your little messenger here smuggled a weapon onboard, and I don't think there is one waiting for her in the airport. Speaking of which, this little girl doesn't look too tough; I think I can handle a sixteen-year-old." He looked at her, and his eyes narrowed. Deena smiled. "You looked sixteen a minute ago. Now…"

"Think I could pass for twelve? Maybe I could get a discount at one of the terminal restaurants?"

Mr. Marsh spoke up. "I'll leave it up to you to decide what course of action is best for you, Frank."

"If you kill me, you'll never get your money," Frank said.

The little tattoo head nodded in agreement. "Yes. That's true, but the next man that thinks maybe he'll put one over on me might take notice and decide it's best to pay."

Frank stared at the tattoo as it dissolved back to an indistinct black blob. Deena reached over toward Frank and he jumped.

"Easy there, fat boy." She reached to the back of the seat in front of him and took down the airphone's handset. "I'm just the messenger, pal. I'm not here to kill you. I do, however, suggest you start moving money around."

He took the phone and stared at it.

As she pulled her sleeve down, she saw the attendant approach, pulling a cart.

"Sorry for the delay." The attendant smiled and looked from Deena to Frank. "We're going to have to rush drink service. What can I get you?"

"Scotch and soda." Frank put the airphone down. "As much as you can give me."

"Drinks are seven dollars each and I can only give you two at a time."

"Fine."

The attendant turned and smiled. "Can I get you something, young lady? A cola or juice?"

Deena shook her head.

"I know!" The woman dug into her pocket and pulled something out. "Here." She handed Deena a small plastic pin with the airline's logo with shiny wings outstretched on either side of it. "I'll let you clip it on, but be careful not to stick yourself." The tiny grey feathers gleamed in the light of the sun streaming through the windows. The attendant took Frank's money and left him his drinks, which sloshed around in the clear plastic cups as the plane hit turbulence momentarily.

Frank finished the first glass with one swig. "You going to stab me with that pin now?"

"Please. I'm not going to lay a hand on you. Besides…" she held up the wings. "The tip isn't even that pointy. See?" She jabbed him in the arm with it.

Frank jumped, spilling ice into the aisle and dropping his cup. "Christ, kid." He looked at his arm and noticed the pin hadn't even made it through the fabric of his jacket.

Deena thought it was funny that he called her kid, like she was some kind of child on a school outing. She was feeling a little addled and could barely keep from giggling at the thought of a killer on a class trip. She needed rest. *Just a few more minutes and this will be over.* She reached over and grabbed the airphone once more. "Make the call, Frank. They won't let you use the phone when we start our approach to land." She shook the receiver in front of him. "Then it will be too late."

Frank took a sip of his remaining drink. "Look, I don't know what you think you're going to do, but come on. Wise up, before you get hurt."

"I don't think I'm going to get any wiser at this point. Maybe you should take your own advice.

"Pffftt." It seemed the alcohol was going to Frank's head rather quickly.

"Well put. You're obviously an educated man, but let me lay some knowledge on you. Mr. Marsh is not a charity that just gives shit away for free. Neither is he a bank that lends money to dumbasses and then writes it off when they don't return it. He's a businessman."

Frank swirled the ice in his cup and shook his head, smiling. "Look, little girl, you had a nice trick with the thing on your arm, but unless you've got something a little more persuasive, I'm going to walk off this plane and disappear."

Deena nodded and closed her eyes. An acidic taste was permeating her mouth, churning up from her stomach. She was nauseous, but she knew it would be done soon. It would be done, she would finish up on the plane and then go home and sleep. She might not leave the bed for days. She swallowed hard—her throat was dry, and started to whisper the new words she'd practiced. New images flooded her mind and she chose the newest one in the repertoire: a spear. She wasn't concerned whether it was going to fail or not, she just had to go with it. If it didn't work, she'd go with plan B. Actually, she'd think of a plan B and then go with it. She could feel a little sweat on her own brow.

Several low tones sounded over the aircraft's speakers, followed by the attendant's voice. "Ladies and gentlemen, we'll be starting our approach to Seattle-Tacoma International Airport momentarily. I'll come back around to pick up your beverage cups and trash immediately. If you'll please set your tray tables to their upright position, and make sure your lap belts are securely fastened, we'll be on the ground shortly. Thank you."

In the midst of the speech there came a new sound, like someone chewing Jell-O with their mouth open. If anyone other than Deena heard it they didn't seem to react. She looked over at Frank and saw what she expected; it looked like someone had drawn three short black lines on the man's face and neck. One behind the ear, one on the cheek and the other just below the jaw. They weren't large, but they were noticeable if you knew what you were looking for. Frank stared straight ahead, eyes wide, head bobbing slightly with the movement of the plane. A trickle of blood began to swell from each wound.

A black ribbon found its way back from the cuts and collapsed itself into the area where the tattoo's mass had been just moments before. It swelled and raced restlessly before settling into the image of a dagger through a broken heart.

"Shoulda made the call. I always have something up my sleeve, Frank," she said as she smoothed her sleeve back over her arm, revealing several strips cut wide in the fabric. Deena leaned forward, nauseous. Her eyes watered. She put her head against the seat in front of her and placed her hands on the armrests to steady herself.

She wondered what her sister was doing and hoped she was well. They hadn't had breakfast together in weeks. Fruity Pebbles and toast.

Deena closed her eyes for just a few moments.

She awoke to the sensation of the plane roughly hitting the ground upon landing. Her head was still against the seat in front of her but her arms dangled at her side. She started to push herself upright, but stopped cold. With her head in that position that, she had a clear view of the floor below her as well as her own legs. The blanket had fallen off her legs and she was startled to see her feet weren't touching the floor. She leaned back and examined herself. Her clothes were huge on her, to the point where the pants would probably fall if she stood. The t-shirt almost came down to her knees.

She tried to fight through the sudden adolescent fog and panic that gripped her mind. She'd never gone this far before. Her instinct pushed its way to the surface and she took the belt from her pants, wrapped it around her waist and forced a new notch in it. It wasn't exactly fashionable, but the shirt almost passed for a dress.

She pressed her way past Frank and tightened her backpack straps on her shoulder. It was heavier than she expected and she nearly fell backward as she stepped into the aisle. What people there were on the flight crowded together, forming a line to get out. Deena slipped easily in between them and nervously smiled at a crew member and the pilot who were saying goodbye to people as they left. The attendant at the door wasn't the same one that had brought her a blanket and given her wings, and Deena walked by without a second glance.

Once off the plane, Deena slowly made her way up the grey tunnel to the reception area. After a moment it occurred to her that she was barefoot and had actually stepped out of her shoes on the plane. She hoped no one would question a little girl walking shoeless through the airport, but decided none of them would care. They were all around her, hugging loved ones, greeting business partners and waiting for the plane to empty out. The airline employees were concerned solely with getting everyone off the plane, out of the tunnel and on their way, so the plane could be prepped for the next flight. There wasn't a footwear check or anything. Still, the carpet felt strange on her bare feet as she padded away from the plane as quickly and nonchalantly as she could.

She saw Avi Nolan, her handler, waiting on the edge of the crowd. He looked calmly, casually up and down the line of people that were disembarking. He chewed on a pretzel while he waited. Twice she noticed him glance directly past her without a glimmer of recognition. *I've never gone back this far; of course he doesn't recognize me. He's looking for someone much older.*

She had another fit then, a bout of nearly unstoppable laughter and she started to skip a little. Her hair tickled her neck with each step as she moved right past her handler and into the food court area. It was easy, and she didn't look back. She couldn't even remember why she'd need to talk to him. The dead man on the plane was becoming something that seemed like a long time ago—maybe when she was younger or lived somewhere else. He was a lost teddy bear or a broken bicycle.

Next to a pizza place, a shop sold sunglasses and she caught her reflection in a mirror. For a brief moment, she thought about how stupid people looked when they realized they were stupid. In her reflection, she noticed her hair was a mess and she fixed it as best she could. She knew she was supposed to be thinking about something very important, but her hair was the only issue she could pay attention to at the moment. The smell of fresh breadsticks turned her head and she dug into the backpack to find some money.

As she searched the pack, she found the airline wings the flight attendant gave her. She thought about the plastic feathers on the little badge, thought about flying away. She took a second to pin it onto her t-shirt before scooping up a handful of coins and dashing for the food court.

2

The toy monkey with the cymbals showed up sometime during the eighth hour of Morgan's vigil. It waddled toward the barrel of the sniper rifle, whirring and clanging as it went. Morgan kept his right eye against the scope, but could still see the monkey clearly with the other eye.

The monkey stopped near the tripod which held the barrel a few inches over the table, twirled and started beating its cymbals together.

Clang! Clang! Clang!

Morgan ignored it and focused on the window of the high-rise nearly a quarter of a mile away where his target was overdue. He'd strategically positioned himself on the dining room table of this apartment just after nine o'clock the previous night, pointed his gun out the open window and hadn't moved since.

The monkey spun itself in a circle and slapped the cymbals together again.

Clang! Clang! Clang!

It rolled toward the edge of the table and spun to face Morgan. The lips curled back. "You missed your chance. No killing tonight!" The monkey's lips pulled even further back in a wide smile as it screeched at him. "Too bad."

Clang! Clang! Clang!

"Too bad!"

Morgan stared through the scope and let the annoying little toy dance around. In the apartment he was watching, everything looked quiet. He could see the curtains moving slightly in the breeze, the light on the answering machine blinked red staccatos in the dark room. The target was due to return home after a late dinner with friends. That was hours ago.

"Somebody's getting sleepy."

Morgan shifted his gaze back to the room he was in. On the other side of the rifle barrel, a large brown teddy bear had appeared.

"I can see your eyelids getting droop, droop, droopy," it said to Morgan. "Come on. Cuddle up with your old buddy, Mr. Hector, and take a little nap."

The monkey's eyes blinked. "Couldn't hurt. Besides, you aren't going to shoot anyone tonight anyway."

Morgan planted his eye back on the lens.

The happy expression on Mr. Hector's face drooped. "Aw. Come on. Why so glum?"

"Don't take it personally, he hasn't talked to me either," the monkey said.

Morgan blinked his eyes a few times to lubricate them. They were drying out more and more as he stared through the scope. It had been ages since he'd had to wait out a target for so long. He kept eye drops in his upper left shirt pocket, but hadn't broken down and used them yet. That would require him to look away for longer than he was willing to allow at this point. That was the same reason he'd forsaken his spotting scope; he figured he'd only have one opportunity and needed to be ready quickly once the target appeared.

The little bear with the red bow around his neck climbed over the barrel of the gun and started walking closer to Morgan. "Remember how inseparable we were? Oh, you took me just everywhere with you," Mr. Hector stood a foot away from Morgan's face and smiled. "You used to keep me in that suitcase, even when you went off to college. Remember?" The bear's smile faded. "We didn't get to stay there very long, did we?"

Morgan drew a sharp breath at the thought of college. He flunked out before the end of his first year and ended up leaving town altogether just to avoid facing his failure. A swooping movement of the curtain brought his attention back to the apartment in his sights. He mistook it for his target arriving and his heart leapt with excitement before he realized he was wrong.

"He had all kinds of trouble back in college," an airy female voice came from behind him. "Funny that you use a gun now, 'cause you surely couldn't pull the trigger back then."

Morgan wanted to turn and see the person who was talking, though he already knew who it was.

"We talking relationship difficulties or a limp noodle?" the monkey sneered.

Mr. Hector put his paw to his face and giggled.

"Oh, he had all kinds of problems—in and out of the sack."

The sound seemed closer to Morgan and he almost broke his stance to turn and see her. The cigarette-raspy voice belonged to Nadine Anderson, briefly his girlfriend back at school. He could still close his eyes and remember her stark naked in front of him, every line and curve memorized, but her face wasn't coming to him today. Still, he could feel himself getting a little hard just at the thought of her. It was no wonder he never made it to many classes back in college.

"Oh, heavens. Don't get me started about the problems little Morgie had in bed." A new woman's voice emerged from the hallway to Morgan's right. This voice was also unmistakable. "Wet the bed every night until he was eight. Horrible mess. Had to buy those rubber sheets, I was constantly doing laundry. Terrible." Out of the corner of his eye, Morgan saw his mother emerge from the dark. He hadn't laid eyes on her since he walked out the door to join the army, and now she was standing next to him wearing the same dull green, flowered dress with white fringe, her hair up in her usual bun style, the Charlie perfume she wore wafting into the room. His erection left town in a hurry.

Clang! Clang! Clang!

"Morgie is a bed-wetter! Morgie is a bed-wetter!" The monkey danced in circles.

Morgan pursed his lips tighter together and stared into the scope. Still nothing.

"Why don't you just forget about it?" Mother said. "Go home. Nothing's going to happen tonight." She was standing next to him as she spoke. "You were always such a nice boy."

Though he couldn't see it, Morgan could hear something dripping nearby.

"Oh. Remember that time you almost drowned in the city pool?" Mother said.

Mr. Hector waved his arms. "I do! He came home and hugged me all night long!"

"Yes. He was such a nice boy for weeks and weeks after that. Did everything I asked, without me asking twice." Mother smiled. "It was wonderful."

The dripping sound became steadier.

Nadine's voice came from behind him. "Is that why you never wanted to shower with me? Afraid of the water?"

The monkey clanged in circles again.

"And who saved you from drowning?" Mother asked.

The monkey stopped spinning and looked at Morgan, Mr. Hector joined him.

"Son, it's not polite to ignore someone when they're talking to you."

Morgan squinted down the scope again and moved it to see in the windows of the apartment. He could vaguely see the outline of a bed through the white lace curtains of one window, he could see a couch and the answering machine on a table through the sliding glass door and the other window had a heavy shade drawn. His scope was sighted in perfectly, but he reached up and fiddled with the adjustor just to give himself something to do. Everything got blurry, then focused again, then blurry.

"He's probably not talking because of that horrible Foghorn Leghorn accent of his," Nadine said. "Sometimes I couldn't understand a word he was saying."

"I say, I say, I DO buh-leeve ah wet my-uh beyud." The monkey bared his teeth, then laughed. The others joined in.

The trickle of water Morgan heard became a steady stream and he leaned away from the gun to try to find the source.

"Give it up Morgie. You're done. The target ain't showing and your boss is going to be peeved at you," the monkey said.

Morgan didn't want to think about what his contractor, Mr. Marsh, was going to say if this job didn't happen as scheduled. He wasn't known for his understanding, though he was extremely generous with people who followed through on their commitments.

"Come on, son. Let's go home."

"Morgan's got ish-shoes!"

The voices all joined in at once, taunting him as he looked around, moving as little from his stance as he could. The water sounded like it was coming down in buckets. From his new vantage point he could see it pouring in over the sill of the open window. Morgan decided it must be some flood, if it had risen high enough to flow through a fifteenth floor window.

Clang! Clang! Clang! "Morgie fucked up! Morgie fucked up!"

"Go home Morgan, it's over," Nadine said.

"Shut up," Morgan said a little louder than he had intended. "Shut up, she'll be here." His body ached from being in that position for so long. His lips were dry and cracked.

"She?" Mr. Hector asked. "You're going to shoot a woman?"

The others got quiet and turned to look at Morgan. There was only the sound of the water. He looked away from them, back toward the gun. He took a deep breath and leaned his eye close to the scope. Everything was blurry from when he was playing with the scope before and he started adjusting again.

"I knew he had issues with women, but wow," Nadine said.

Mother just shook her head.

Morgan never understood the added weight everyone put on killing a woman. Why were they more important than men? Was it the idea that they were less likely to be bad people than men? Maybe everyone assumed that the men must have done something to deserve it, where ladies must be completely innocent. Morgan didn't care one way or another; a job was a job. Marsh gave him the information on a target and that was it. Morgan didn't ask questions and he didn't want to know more than he had to. The woman he was waiting for now could be a former business partner, an employee who stole from him, a pro who cheated at one of his casinos or a witness going to court in the morning, it didn't change what he did or how he did it.

"Whooo!" Mr. Hector said. He trundled to the edge of the table and looked over. "That water is getting pretty high."

"Hope you've learned to swim since that time you almost drowned." The monkey laughed his shrill cackle. "The lifeguard ain't here to pull you out this time."

"Sure I am," Mother said.

The monkey's mouth opened wide and its eyes bulged. "Mommy saved you? Your mommy pulled you out of the pool?" He laughed again.

Out of the corner of his eye, Morgan could see a thin layer of water forming on the floor. He heard splashing footsteps approach him from behind.

"You can shoot all the people you want, but it won't make a difference. No matter what you do, no matter how hard you try, you'll never be good enough for me," Nadine said. "You'll never be good enough for any of us."

He turned then, wanting to see her and say none of it had anything to do with her, that she was less than a footnote. There was a splash as he turned. The room behind him was empty; just the dining room chairs that he'd moved aside to get on the table, the plates in the hutch, the artwork on the walls. The water on the floor was new though, it was getting higher, ankle deep from the looks of it.

Morgan turned back to the window. The monkey was leaning against the barrel on one side of the rifle, Mr. Hector was doing the same on the other side, and Mother was standing at the end of the table, between the business end of the gun and the window. Morgan looked at each of them suspiciously and got back into his prone firing stance, eye to the scope. He had to concentrate for a moment, had to try to imagine what the space in front of him was like without his mother standing there.

"Let's just go home, Morgie," Mother said.

Morgan wavered and might have pulled back if he hadn't seen a light start glowing within her stomach. It was a soft yellow light that made him feel at ease for a moment until he remembered why he was really there. He squinted then blinked a bit to clear his vision. When he refocused he found the glow was a light that had come on in the apartment he was watching.

The target was home.

He moved the rifle minutely, searching the windows for movement, any sign of where the target might be. His mother's image faded until he saw a silhouette in the curtains of the bedroom for a second, not long enough to get a bead on the woman.

He moved the crosshairs to the balcony, looking into the living room beyond the sliding glass door. In a moment, the form appeared there and moved around. Morgan made sure to keep his eyes trained on the torso and the heart, afraid that if he looked at the head he might see his mother's or Nadine's face and falter in his task.

"Don't do this, Morgan." The voice was indistinguishable; it could have been any one of them - Mom, teddy bear, monkey or ex-lover."

The woman stopped at the table that held her answering machine and he could see her press the button to retrieve her messages, just as he'd planned. She was standing still to listen to them.

Mr. Hector stepped toward him. "Look, let's just forget…" His words were cut off by a sharp report from the gun. Even with a top-of-the-line silencer like the one Morgan used, a gun still made a wicked noise. It bounced a little on the table as the recoil kicked the gun back. Though it startled everyone, the shock was gone in a couple of seconds. The monkey and Mr. Hector ran to the end of the table and looked out. Both leaned as close to the window as they could and narrowed their eyes.

Morgan sat up and started taking his gun apart. As he did, he watched the water on the floor below him start to recede. By the time he was ready to get down off the table and put his gun in the briefcase, the water was gone completely.

From the table, the monkey screeched, "Hey. Hey! You shot the wrong woman!" He danced in a circle.

Clang! Clang!

"You shot the wrong woman!" Mr. Hector joined in.

Morgan carefully put the pieces of the gun into place in the case and closed it. He looked over at Mother and watched her face. She wasn't joining in with the others in doubting what Morgan had done. Even though he hadn't looked at the target's face, he knew he got who he came for. "No I didn't." He walked to the foyer as the clanging stopped.

"She's getting up!" Mr. Hector said.

The monkey just shook his head. "It's over."

Morgan opened the door slowly and peered out, looking cautiously from side to side. Seeing nothing, he closed it again, leaned down to the bone-dry carpet and picked up the emerald case with his rifle in it. Across the room his mother, the monkey and Mr. Hector stood staring at him.

The monkey's lip curled at one side. "See you next time?"

Morgan smiled then, knowing himself the way he did. "I suppose you will." He opened the door again and this time, even though the hallway was windowless, sunshine streamed in like a hot summer's day. Two small cartoon bluebirds fluttered in and he watched them circle his head twice before they flew back into the hall. One of them tweeted something in his ear. He nodded and followed them toward the stairs.

3

The activity in the airport died down a little the later it got. Fewer people came through the restroom and it got quiet. Deena hovered somewhere between asleep and awake, in a fog. At some point, she'd made her way into the ladies room, sat down, locked a stall door and gotten comfortable. She was sure she'd managed to get some rest, but she truly felt like she'd been awake the entire time. When she finally got the inclination to move, her muscles ached, every one of them. Her face was especially sore as it contracted and expanded. In the last couple of hours, her body had shrunk to the size of a fourteen-year-old and then started snapping back to her twenty-seven-year-old self. She felt like Silly Putty.

Her stomach ached for similar reasons, coupled with the fact that she'd eaten poorly. She struggled to remember whether she had actually spent close to ten dollars in change on chocolates, garlic bread and sour candies. The rumble in her stomach suggested she had.

The battered and threadbare backpack sat on her lap—she'd been using it as a pillow—and she decided it might hold an idea of what she should do next. Manipulating the zipper caused a spasm in her shoulder that sent pain throughout her system. Inside, she quickly located an envelope with cash in an inner pocket that was zipped shut. She'd dug out all the change for snacks earlier, and hadn't thought to look for cash. It would get her just about anywhere she wanted to go in the immediate future.

She pulled out a cell phone from another zipped pocket. She remembered enough to know it had three numbers programmed into it: The first belonged to her handler, the second to her sister. The third was a text-only number where she could leave messages in an emergency. She turned it on and texted "call me" to the man on the other end.

There were still magazines inside the bag and she took them out and set them on top of the toilet paper dispenser. She placed the tickets and various papers with flight information there as well. There were tissues and scraps of airport bar napkins and a broken pencil. Beyond those scant few items, the bag was empty and falling to tatters. She took the money out and started to shove it in her waistband when she realized she still had just the t-shirt on and not much else. She'd need to keep the backpack and maybe buy some shorts or pants in one of the airport shops, if she could find one that sold more than just Seattle Mariners shirts.

And *shoes*. She felt gross putting her bare feet down on the nasty bathroom floor.

She gathered up the junk and threw it in the trash after she left the stall, leaving only the money, phone and the snapped pencil to put back in the bag. As she did, she noticed the faded words written in marker on the inside of the old backpack.

If found return to 4486 Southmoore Ln. Talmadge, Calif.

Deena thought about the address. It was where she and Harper had grown up. She wondered if her dad still lived there, if the old fort was still hanging in the tree. She wondered if everyone still remembered what happened, what she did there.

She stared at herself in the bathroom mirrors and tried to figure out a way to make it look like the "nude except for a t-shirt" look was what she was going for, but it wasn't working. She stretched the shirt as far down as she could and managed to get it to cover up the important parts. She wished she had a fanny pack instead of a backpack. There was no way to strategically tie a backpack around her waist without looking completely crazy; as opposed to an exhibitionist teen.

She took one last look in the mirror as she prepared to walk out. *God, I hope teenage girls are still dressing slutty this year.*

Deena's phone rang. She pressed the button to answer, put it to her ear and said "I don't want to do this anymore. I'm out." She said it on impulse, though the idea had come to her earlier. She was a kid again. She could pick an entirely new path for herself. Even if her second childhood might only last a day or so, at least it would be different. "Goodbye."

4

Morgan watched Mr. Marsh hang up the phone. They'd talked about the call Marsh had received from Deena and this next conversation only seemed to confirm she'd gone off her nut. He was slightly uneasy when the older man turned his attention to him. "That was Deena's handler, Avi. He says he never saw her get off the plane and she hasn't contacted him yet. He's looking for her, but no success yet."

"So, you think she's serious about leaving?" Morgan asked.

"Hard to say. We knew it would happen sooner or later," Marsh said. "I was beginning to hope for later."

Morgan tilted his head slightly and furrowed his brow. "She's done this before. It's no big deal. She'll be back."

"She's gone off on her own, but she's never actually told anyone she quit before."

It was true. In the many years Morgan had worked with Deena and her sister, Harper, he could remember Deena vanishing for days at a time, resurfacing as if nothing had happened. "First time for everything."

"You know the sisters, yes? You're aware of the younger one?"

Morgan almost laughed. "You know I know them. I was there when you brought them on. I remember that witch, Deena, or whatever she is. Everyone that works for you knows about her."

Marsh smiled. "We get things done here. When someone hires us for a job, they know it's going to get done in a manner that bespeaks professionalism and, when necessary, haste. That girl is a big part of that reputation, though she seems to be slipping in the former."

Morgan was pretty sure Deena hadn't cost them any work yet, and her slips involved getting a bit more creative than her orders allowed for, but Marsh generally spoke well of her and seemed pleased with Deena's work. Still, a girl like that could be a handful if she decided to stop listening to reason. Morgan knew that the older sister, Harper, was also a rapidly growing liability. She didn't have the power Deena did, and was a fuck-up of the highest magnitude. She didn't take to the training, didn't learn, didn't adapt as phenomenally as her sibling. And she certainly didn't have any unique abilities. But the witch defended her. And no one wanted to be on that girl's bad side.

"This could just be one of her episodes, a lapse in judgment or a similar problem and it will pass, you're right. But I want you to find Deena and bring her back. If it looks like that won't happen, if she seems to be trying to leave our organization, or if her behavior is too far out of sorts, you're to terminate her. No nonsense, no bargaining, no bullshit."

Morgan took a breath and waited for a moment. He'd seen up close what Deena could do. She was unpredictable on a good day, but she could be crazy and vicious when backed into a corner. "I'm not a big talker. I doubt I'll be able to convince her to come back if she doesn't want to. I certainly won't do a better job of it than her handler or her sister."

Morgan could see the wheels spinning in his boss's head.

"If Deena isn't coming back, I have no use for her sister either. In fact, after Harper's latest catastrophe, I believe we are done with her," Marsh said. "She's been nothing more than a carrot to keep Deena focused, but it isn't worth it anymore."

"Maybe killing Harper isn't the best way to go about it; could she be leveraged some way?" Morgan was wondering if his guns would be a match for the young woman's magic. Deena was a growing legend in the local world of professional killers, though very few of them knew the limits of her power.

Marsh shook his head. "Not worth the trouble."

"If I kill her sister, I don't see Deena coming back here. But if you utilized Harper, if you used her to get Deena to come back, it would make more sense. Bring her back to help her sister and we can take care of them both here."

Marsh grabbed a tennis ball and rolled it around on the table. "If she were confused enough, there's no telling what she would do. It seems the more she uses her powers, the more off kilter she becomes. Strange. Erratic."

"We knew that the first time we met her. She was always going to be a wild card."

Marsh nodded and his face went sour. "We knew that much, but it seemed like a winning proposition. Someone with her abilities, in our organization? It's too bad we couldn't keep her on task."

There was a chance for gain here. There was the real possibility for Morgan to come out ahead in the situation. He paused as he approached the door. "I'll go after her, if that's what you want, but what would be my compensation for this? Hunting down, how did you put it - erratic? Hunting down an erratic witch is more than a little dangerous."

"It always comes back to money in this world." Marsh sighed. "The monetary benefit would be great. But, in the long run if they don't come back, I'll need someone to do their jobs. That makes the future a bit brighter for you, doesn't it?"

Morgan nodded. "It does." He was already getting a good share of work just on his reputation, but Marsh had increasingly been handing Deena more of the prime jobs. And what was worse, Marsh was paying her much less than he should for such jobs and pocketing the additional money for the organization. The little witch didn't know any better. Or she didn't care. The joy of the hunt seemed to be payment enough sometimes for her.

"Pack a bag and head for the airport. The company jet will be waiting to take you to Seattle. You can be there in a matter of hours. Maybe her trail hasn't gone completely cold."

After Marsh dismissed him, Morgan made his way to his car and pulled out onto the street, making his way to the freeway and out of town. No matter how concerned Morgan was about magic spells and witches, money would make it all better. As he drove down the winding canyon road out of the city, Morgan added up the possibilities of taking over the business the girls would leave in their wake. It was tantalizing to say the least. Still, the witch scared him. She'd pulled off some amazing jobs using those weird powers of hers and no one really knew what she was truly capable of.

"You know you can come out of this ahead, or you can come out of this *way* ahead?" Morgan could hear the voice near his ear. "Get your head out of your ass."

"Shut up." Morgan stared at the road.

"Please. You know I'm right."

Morgan looked into rearview mirror and saw his old mentor, Brandt Stewart, sitting in the back seat. "You want me to cross Marsh? That's crazy. He finds out, he'll send someone to gut me."

"Who's he going to send? All his best people are busy. You kill the girl and who's left? Besides, you could go work for Marsh's rivals at the drop of a hat. Savannah Thorpe has been trying to bring you over to her gang for years. That lady is no small player herself."

"But I don't have the power that Riordan girl has."

"Not many do."

Morgan watched the trees as they appeared to zip by his window. He pushed the button and his window went slowly down. He pressed the accelerator a bit more and leaned his head into the breeze, cool air rushing into his face.

"We're not just talking about money here. This is a step up. Hell, if you kill these girls, you'll be the number one problem-solver on this coast." Brandt paused for a reaction but Morgan refused to give him one. "Maybe you can get paid twice before Marsh figures it out. Get a competitor to pay you for killing the witch and get Marsh's money in the process."

"I'm not switching teams." Morgan leaned further into the wind; let it blow his hair around, fill his ears.

"Are you even listening to me?" Brandt asked as he leaned forward.

Morgan thought he smelled the stench of a cheap brand of cigars that he hadn't smelled in years. After a moment, the only aroma was the salt of the sea air as he guided the car toward the airport.

5

After she left the restroom, Deena wandered through the concourse toward the baggage claim, where she could find a taxi or shuttle to get her out of the airport and into the clear. She was surprised to catch a glimpse of Avi out of the corner of her eye. He was hard to spot, because he blended so well with the rest of the crowd in the airport. He didn't appear panicked, but he was by no means relaxed. Deena had known him long enough to spot the difference. She'd passed him. She was in the clear and could walk off without a hitch. The automatic doors that led outside opened for her and she paused.

Unfortunately, they had a history and she felt she owed him an explanation for his kindness.

Deena pulled her bag up higher on her shoulder and approached him from an indirect angle, passing through the seating area of a boarding gate before sitting down near where he was standing. "Let's go," Avi said. "I have a car in the lot. We can get out of here and you can rest up for a while before your next job. I'll check in with Marsh on the way."

Deena was surprised that he'd recognized her and noticed her approach. "No."

Avi was already two steps toward the corridor that lead to the parking lots. "No, what? We need to get going before the police come looking for you to ask what happened on the plane."

"I'm not going back." Deena set her pack on her lap. "Something's changed. I'm…"

"You're tired. You'll feel different after you sleep for a few hours, you always do." His eyes were slowly taking in the escape route. He was doing a great job of hiding it and keeping his face neutral considering the situation. He continued walking, dismissing what she'd said.

Deena stayed in her seat. "Something has changed, Avi. Fucking listen to me. I'm not going back."

Avi looked around at the crowd in the airport and casually walked back to the seating area. "What're you going to do? Throw a tantrum? This isn't the way to stay under the radar of the authorities."

Deena knew that she couldn't explain it properly to Avi in a manner brief enough to make him listen in their immediate situation. His job was always to get her to safety with as little fanfare as possible. But it was also to get her back for the next job. Avi started walking away again. Quiet and quick and the whole thing would be over. It was the way it worked. Deena stood and followed Avi at a distance. He didn't turn around, though she knew he was checking her progress in store windows and other reflective surfaces. He moved quickly, but not more than anyone else around him that might be trying to catch a flight. Avi never looked up, never consulted a map or any other directions. As was the case with any job, he'd likely memorized multiple escape plans.

She wondered if this was still his Plan A, or if they'd already moved on to Plan B or C.

As they neared the people mover that would carry them closer to the parking garages, three Seattle police officers stepped out from a service door at the side of the hall. They looked side to side at the people nearby, and Avi turned into a gift shop without missing a beat.

The iced coffee in the cooler drew Deena's attention. She could use caffeine. Lots of it. As bad as her stomach felt right now, a nice vanilla cappuccino sounded awesome. As she pulled the handle to slide the door open, Avi grabbed her and whispered, "They're gone."

They moved quickly through the rest of the airport and out into the chill of the open-air parking garage. Avi's car was just a few steps away and he stepped in fluidly. "Get in, and let's go," he said.

Deena paused. As soon as they got in that car, he'd start trying to convince her again that they needed to get back. He'd stop listening. He'd call Marsh. These were all things that Deena didn't want. Standing there, the sounds of sirens were still easily heard, even over the traffic of the garage, the roar of flights taking off and the general mayhem of a giant airport like the Seattle–Tacoma International. She felt herself once again weighing bad and worse scenarios and thinking that if she could do just one more thing, she'd be in the position she wanted to be in. She opened the door and got in.

"Finally. Let's get on the road. I want to be a couple of hours away from here before we stop for the night. I'd love to just drive all night and not rest until tomorrow, but I don't think you're in any shape for that. And I certainly don't think you're in any condition to do some of the driving for me." A hint of panic had slipped into Avi's voice now that they were away from the public.

There was no way she could do that much driving and she knew it. She could barely keep her eyes open and even that gift shop coffee wouldn't have helped. "I have to explain this. You need to know."

"Rest and then tell me when you're coherent. I'll wake you up when we get to the hotel." Avi pulled out his cell phone.

"Wait. You're not calling Marsh, are you?"

"He needs to know I have you and that we'll make it for your next job," Avi said. "He's not happy that you didn't contact me straightaway when you disembarked."

She put her hand on his arm. "Just... just wait." She couldn't find the right words to explain to Avi about the buzzing in her head that went silent on the plane and how she hoped it would never return. "I'm not going to do that man's bidding anymore. I'm not killing anyone again." She felt tears well up in her eyes as she thought of all the people that were dead because of her. It quickly seemed like a movie, like she was watching someone else do it. At the time it was no big deal; her brain filed it away and let it go. Now, they were all catching back up with her. She stared at the dashboard as faces and names came back to her. "Oh God, what did I do?"

"Deena," Avi reached out to touch her arm and calm her but she pulled away.

She closed her eyes to try to block out the memories. "No. No. I'm not going back there. Something about that last hit strained my power and it crumbled. I feel like a rope around my neck snapped and I'm not suffocating anymore. I don't feel right about anything I used to do. It's a change in my—I don't know—in my brain."

"You need rest, that's all."

"In all the jobs we've worked together, no matter how exhausted I've been, have you ever heard me say I wanted to quit?" She hadn't. Up until an hour ago, using her powers to chase down, maim, injure or kill Marsh's targets was a thing of joy to her; a job that she was uniquely suited to and that she excelled at. "I called him. I called Marsh and told him I was done."

"So you decided all of this? Just decided all of this since you killed that mark on the plane? You went from contract killer to pacifist in a matter of minutes?" Avi took his eyes off the road for moment to look at her. "You've thought about the implications? You've considered how Marsh would react? He's not just going to let you go."

"I'll just run. He can send whoever he wants. They won't find me."

"They will."

"Let them. I can handle myself."

Avi sighed. "You said you had a change in your brain because you stressed your powers. Do you even know if your powers still work? Maybe they're gone. What then? You can't handle yourself against his killers if that's the case."

The possibility that she was now powerless never occurred to Deena. She'd lived with the Shadow Energy since she was a teen and assumed she'd always have them. But if she was changing her entire life, it seemed fitting the thing that had made her life hell would be gone. "And if I don't have powers, I'm no use to him anyway. If I went back and he found that out, he'd kill me. I have to run."

Deena could see Avi's lips press together tightly as he checked his rearview mirror. He flipped the left blinker and passed another car on the highway. To stay inconspicuous he set cruise control to just above the legal limit, as usual.

"I haven't heard you mention your sister once. What about Harper? Hmmm? Where does that leave her?"

6

Stanley Yuko watched as four men led Harper Riordan off the elevator. He'd known it was only a matter of time before something like this happened. Harper's latest disaster with the bus was certain to draw unwanted attention from law enforcement, and in turn, from Marsh.

Stanley pressed the intercom button. "Harper is here."

"Harper is here? You make it sound like I had an appointment or something," Harper said. The girl sneered down at Stanley in his chair and he felt himself shrink back. He looked away and stared at the tape dispenser on his desk, not wanting to meet Harper's eyes. He straightened the pens and the staple remover on his already immaculate desk. Stanley waited until his boss's voice came from the speaker. "Send them in."

Stanley nodded to the men. "Go ahead." He tried to sound cordial as he pressed the buzzer to unlock the door to Marsh's office. He pulled his finger off the button as they went in. Once the door shut, he pulled out his cell phone and hit the speed dial.

"Hello?"

"It's Stanley. They have her. They have Harper Riordan," Stanley said. His heart was beating hard enough that he could feel it as he talked. He stood up and walked over to the elevators, hoping not to be heard. It was dumb to have dialed the phone in the first place, he could be easily overheard. He just hoped that everyone was too busy in Marsh's office to notice.

"Slow down. What do you mean? She works there. What do you mean they have her?"

"She screwed up a job last night. And Marsh was upset after a call with her sister. I think they're going to kill Harper," Stanley said. "Oh, they're going to kill her." Stanley hated how dramatic he sounded, but he couldn't help himself. He needed the federal agents to do something quickly.

"Kill her? When?"

"Now," Stanley said. If he pressed his ear against the door, maybe he could hear what was happening in Marsh's office. That simply wouldn't look good if someone caught him. Still, he stared at the door. "They might be going to kill her now. I don't know. I don't know."

There was silence on the other end of the phone. "Agent Rivers? What should I do?"

The silence lasted a few more seconds. "Just stay put. If you feel like *your* life is in danger, leave as soon as you can. I'll see what I can do on this end." He hung up.

"What? What should I do?" Stanley said as loud as he could without getting too loud. He knew there was no one there anymore, but he couldn't believe he'd been hung up on. After another moment with the phone to his ear, he quietly slipped it back in his pocket. He'd never felt like his life was in danger at the office. Not in all the years he'd worked for Marsh directly. He took a breath and analyzed the situation. It wouldn't make sense to kill Harper in the office. Too much of a chance to be caught, to leave evidence to connect Marsh with her death. He was far smarter than that.

The elevator bell rang and the man from tech support stepped out when the doors opened. Stanley hated having to call the tech people in. They always sent James, the weird guy that smelled strongly of body spray and took far too long to get around to fixing problems. The tech liked to make small talk and chat about things that Stanley had no interest in. Sports. Video games. Beyonce and Kanye West.

"Hey. What's the problem today?" James set an extremely large drink with a straw sticking out of it on Stanley's desk. Stanley watched beads of sweat immediately begin dripping down the side of cup.

"I can't connect to the server," Stanley said.

"Can you get to the internet?" James sounded bored already.

"Yes. I can get everywhere but the server."

James took a long drink of his soda and looked over Stanley's shoulder at the monitor. It didn't seem like he was in a hurry to get started.

"Have you played the new Grand Theft game?"

"No. I really don't have time for games," Stanley said. He went into his shell and began ignoring James and waiting for the problem to be solved. He took an antiseptic wipe from his desk and wiped down his office phone, his stapler and each of his pens. He finished by scrubbing the arms of his chair and then throwing the wipe in the trash bin. The whole while, he ignored James.

He thought about Harper and convinced himself she was safe for the moment. Just the moment, though. But how long would that last?

7

Deena felt sick. Really sick. Her hands were trembling and she was sweating just a little. Her stomach was doing noisy flip-flops and she had a hard time standing still. The water in the sink felt cool on her face, but it did nothing to calm her nerves.

The doorknob rattled and she yelled louder than she meant to; "Occupied!"

Deena cursed the lady on the other side of the door under her breath. She flipped open her backpack and found enough cash there to buy one more tall frozen mocha mint coffee before they had to go and catch the train. She'd had four coffees in the last three hours and they were playing havoc with her already messed up body, but one more wouldn't kill her. Deena didn't know where the coffee jitters stopped and the effects of her powers began. They were wrestling with her psyche and her brain, making every thought painful and forcing her to question each decision. Was she a twenty-something or a teen? It was hard to separate the two. She stuffed the rest of her things—notebook, makeup, brush, extra socks and gum she'd bought at the airport—back into the bag and unlocked the door.

As she stepped out, a woman waiting nearby rushed in.

"Grow a bladder, lady," Deena said. She stepped to the end of the hall and peeked around the corner. Though there were four people standing in line at the counter, she all but ignored them. She also looked past the pudgy, dark-haired girl pouring milk into a mixer near the display case of muffins and bagels. Her gaze landed on the young man at the cash register. She'd been mesmerized by him from the moment she stumbled in off the street looking for someplace warm. His hair was gelled all crazy, every which way and he had a hint of stubble on his cheeks and chin. She thought he looked a little like a popular singer whose name she couldn't quite place. He had to be eighteen, twenty, tops.

He'd upsized her regular to a large for free when he saw how flustered she was when she first walked in and that was all it took. Deena knew how fragile she was as she was rebuilding herself, her power, but she didn't care. She nursed that first coffee as long as she could, staring out the window and checking her watch, waiting for Avi to return from his errands. She was wearing the Mariners shirt and matching sweats she'd bought at the airport. At the time, over-the-top team apparel seemed like a good idea to help her to blend in. Now, she felt like an idiot.

Kevin, she knew from his nametag, gave her an incredulous smile this time. "Back for more? You're out of control, girl." He wiped his hands on his earth-toned apron and prepared to tap her order into the computer. "Same thing or can I get you something a little… calmer? Less caffeinated."

Deena giggled, caught herself laughing a little too much and forced it to stop. "Oh no. You find something that works, you gotta stick with it. Can you make this one a bit mintier? Put a little more mint in? I like the mint." She felt giddy and out of control and tried to remember when the train was leaving.

"Sure. That's not a problem," Kevin said. He turned and grabbed a metal cup and started pouring ingredients.

The crunch of a blender startled Deena and she felt her arm throb reflexively. She looked down and saw the black ink creeping out from under her sleeve toward her wrist. She took a deep breath and pulled the arm of her sweatshirt down a bit lower. Once her pulse slowed, Deena scowled at the heavy girl mixing another customer's drink.

Deena retreated to her table, spread out the maps and brochures in front of her, and eyed them. They were announcements and flyers for all the touristy things to do in the area. Deena had pulled them out of a display at the last rest stop to distract herself. They meant nothing, but she still read them over and over to keep from screaming about the things they'd done and the things to come.

She and Avi would take a taxi to the train station, get tickets and go. They could hop a train to anywhere and then start sorting out Deena's life. That was the only plan she had for now and she clung to it tightly. She'd left a message for her sister to call her. Deena would explain the whole thing and tell her where they could meet up.

The only thing she didn't have a lock on was Avi. For now he seemed to be going along with the plan. He agreed to put her on the train, but she wasn't sure he'd follow through. Would he buckle to his fear of Marsh, or stay loyal to the past that he and Deena had together? It could mean the difference between making a clean getaway and being delivered back to her old life. She thought about Harper and wondered how she would feel about running away and leaving her life behind. Images of the things she'd done began to flood back to her, but she pushed them down and swallowed them like the heavily minted beverage in front of her. She stared at a trifold brochure about rafting down a nearby river. With the next sip, she got instant brain freeze. It was a nice distraction from trying not to remember what it was like to actually be fourteen years old back in the day.

8

Deena at 15 the first time around

The tree fort that Deena made in the woods near the highway wasn't the most spectacular thing ever, but it was stable. Stable enough. She'd borrowed a few old busted up pallets from behind the Kroger, pocketed a handful of nails from the nearby hardware store and used a rock to pound them all into a decent flat surface to sit on.

She used to come to sit and watch the traffic zip by on the four-lane and wonder where they all were going in such a hurry. Life in Talmadge didn't lend itself much to rushing for anything, so it was always a novelty. Deena couldn't remember being anxious to do anything except get away from this place. She figured everyone was on their way to San Diego or Los Angeles or some other city on the California coast. She hadn't even made it to those places, close as they were. She and Harper begged on a regular basis to make any one of those places a vacation destination, but no luck.

Lately though, she'd been coming to the little sanctuary to stare at the black and blue blemish on her arm that had appeared, seemingly overnight. It was prominent one day when she went to wash her face before bed and it puzzled her as to whether it had been there before. It was halfway between her elbow and wrist, about as big as the head of a screw.

She licked her thumb and rubbed at it, but it didn't come off. She'd tried it all before; scrubbed it with a washcloth and soap, rubbed it with an emery board and a pot scrubber, but no luck. It was an ugly little blemish and she was stuck with it.

"Deena? You up there?"

It was her wet-blanket sister, Harper.

"Yeah," Deena answered and leaned over the side of her dumpster-salvaged platform, careful not to put her weight on the cracked plank that she feared might snap if she wasn't careful.

"Dad just left for work and we have to wash the breakfast dishes and vacuum the living room before we can leave for the pool," Harper said. "So let's go. I'm not doing it all on my own and I want to go swimming today."

"Ehh," Deena said.

"Dammit Deena. Don't screw around. Mike is going to be there at noon and I want to get there early to claim a lounge chair that he has to walk by to get to the diving board."

"Meh." Deena liked torturing her sister. It was becoming something of a pastime. She was an easy mark.

Harper practically growled up at Deena. "I will climb up there and drag your bratty ass down and shove the dishes down your throat if I have to."

"Bullshit." If Harper wanted to go so bad, she would cave in and do all of the housework herself. Deena knew that and was prepared to wait it out. She sat up and leaned her back against the tree and watched the traffic quietly. After a moment, she heard her sister stalk off, stomping her feet on the leaves and twigs as she went. The sound dissipated in the distance and Deena could feel a smirk come across her face.

She raised her arm and stared at the dot. It was just over her wrist and had swollen to the size of a penny. In the time she'd briefly interacted with her sister, it had become twice as large, and it seemed to have moved several inches. Deena was fascinated... and worried.

9

Morgan sat in the comfortable seat of Marsh's private jet and stared at Wallace. "Marsh didn't say anything about bringing you along. Shouldn't you be babysitting Harper? Surely the sisters will be in contact."

"I dropped her off with Marsh. They have a bunch of his thugs guarding her. She isn't going anywhere."

Morgan nodded. He'd figured Marsh would take his advice and make her the carrot that brought Deena in. He hadn't, however, counted on being saddled with Wallace while he hunted the witch. "Well, at least that's one of them off the street."

"We have people at the train stations and airport already watching for Deena. If they see anything, we'll know. We're watching whatever public cameras we can get access to. If she shows up, we'll have someone on it." Wallace was drinking a can of soda through a straw. The slurping sound annoyed Morgan.

The clouds were thin outside the plane and Morgan looked out the window to watch them go by. He'd have to ditch Wallace one way or another once they got to Seattle. While he could be helpful to an extent, for the most part he'd just be a hindrance. He knew things and didn't mind doing leg work, but Morgan worked alone. Mostly. Just him and his demons.

"Look. I've done tons of field stuff for Marsh. We get after Deena, catch her, drag her home, and we both come out ahead," Wallace said. "No big deal. We do what we do, and then we go back to our jobs. I'm not here to cramp your style or get in your way. I don't want to be stuck looking after Harper for the rest of my life. Once she and her sister are out of the way, I can move on to bigger and better things."

"This is your captain speaking. If you look out over the left side of the plane, you'll discover that Wallace is going to kill you." It was Mr. Hector's voice and it seemed to be coming from the plane's speakers, though Wallace didn't notice it. "Why is he here? He's going to kill you, that's why. First chance he gets. Why else would he be here? He shouldn't *be* here."

Morgan pursed his lips tighter, struggling not to answer the voice, and struggling to keep more from showing up.

"Beat him to death with a tray table and throw him out the cabin door." The voice was scratchy through the speakers. "Problem solved."

"Avi had a room at a hotel near the airport. Hopefully, he stayed put, but he hasn't been in contact with anyone since he reported Deena didn't get off the plane. Who knows what he's up to? I just want to get on with it."

"I hope he's useful in some way." Morgan tried not to panic at the words. He was looking for hidden meaning in everything.

"Get on with it? What do you think he means by that?" Mr. Hector whispered ominously from the speakers. "It means he wants to kill you, I bet."

10

Special Agent Garrett Walters stood within the police-tape perimeter and took in the whole scene. It was easy to focus on the small bits and pieces and miss what the whole area was telling him. The debris field also had spread so far from the blast that it was hard not to step back just to see what exactly had happened.

One of the young officers working the crowd stepped up to him. "Sir, you wanted to see me?"

Garrett nodded. "You were first on the scene?"

"Yes, sir. My partner and I were just around the corner at the light. Another second or two and we would have seen the explosion with our own eyes." The patrolman pointed toward his cruiser, where another officer was interviewing a witness.

"So as it is, you only heard it?" Garret asked.

"Yep. And kind of saw the flash."

Garrett sighed. "But not the actual blast?" It would've been nice to have a cop's eye view of the explosion. He lifted his arm and pointed to the crowd, following their faces down the line with his finger. "How 'bout them? How many of them saw it? And I mean *saw* it, not sort of saw it, not looking at the clock in the bank building and turned around when they heard it, not driving in front of the bus and looked in their rearview mirror when it happened. How many had eyes on that bus when it went up?"

The officer held up his notebook and flipped through the pages, checking a couple of notes twice. "Well, so far forty-six claim to have seen the whole thing. But we've got a ways to go yet."

"How many of them have mentioned this in their statements?" He nodded to the dark green ambulance on the opposite side from the crowd where they'd found the shooting victim. Evidence techs were swarming over it like ants looking for a crumb.

The patrolman shook his head. "None that I've interviewed. I can check with the others," he said.

"Do that. Thanks." Garrett watched the patrolman walk away.

"Want some good news?" Beth Pelligrino, one of Garrett's team, walked up from the side. "Well, potentially good news?"

Garrett admitted to himself that he needed a little cheering up. The case was only a few hours old and it was already giving him a headache; a blown up bus with nine dead passengers, three hanging on in intensive care; a man shot dead in a nearby ambulance—an ambulance whose registration didn't exist; and dozens of city officials who already wanted answers. "Sure, Pel, that'd be great."

Pel pointed upward to the roof of the bodega behind Garrett.

Garrett looked at it and shrugged. It wasn't pointed at the bus or the ambulance. Maybe it caught someone in passing, but certainly nothing regarding the explosion. "So?"

"I got a quick look at the footage before I grabbed it. The thing was trained on that alleyway over there, right?"

"Get on with it," Garrett said. He wasn't in the mood to play guessing games.

"Nothing during the explosion, obviously. But some time later, this huge guy with a nice suit comes wondering out of the darkness. No big deal, I guess. A minute or two later he comes back with a woman and they disappear back the way he came." Pel smiled.

Garrett looked at her for a moment. True, it could be something, but no reason to get as excited as Pel was. "Is there more? Or do you think my requirements for good news have dropped considerably in the last few hours?"

"Oh. Did I not mention that the woman was pulling off what appeared to be a jumpsuit as she hit the alleyway? Possibly the type of coveralls worn by paramedics?" Pel smiled as she held up a baggie with a video tape in it. "My bad."

Garrett was tempted to take it from the woman, run back to the office and watch it, but he knew it would be a long while before he'd be able to leave the scene. It was tempting, though. "Log it into evidence, and start watching it as soon as you can. Don't hang around here to do anything else, just go. Print out pictures of the two in the alley, start trying to match them in the database and bring me a print-out when you get a chance."

"I could email a copy to you on your phone," Pel smiled. "Be a lot easier than bringing a physical copy."

Garrett shook his head emphatically. "Stupid thing is broken. Won't turn on."

"Did you remember to charge it today? When's the last time you plugged it in?" Pel's smile grew wider.

"Fuck you, I charged it." He hadn't. "Just go back to the office and get to work." His hatred for electronics and handheld devices was legendary, which was probably why they teamed Garrett with the tech-savvy junior agent.

Pel started off, but paused. "Oh. On my way over, one of the officers said they think that our ambulance was the first on the scene," she said.

"That's something." Garrett looked at the ambulance again and discovered Pel was staring at it as well. "Are you waiting for a fist bump or something?"

Pel shook her head and disappeared into the crowd of police and fire officials.

At least that's something, two somethings really. Garrett thought. *And those are my only somethings at this point.* He turned just in time to see several men in ridiculously expensive suits cross under the yellow crime scene tape. Garrett knew two of them from the mayor's office. The others were new, but he figured them for one of the other government agencies that would be interested in this madness. In his job with the FBI's special teams, he'd come to know everyone else there, but the new guys could easily be CIA or DEA or any number of letter collections in the alphabet soup. He straightened his tie and started walking toward them, all the while wondering how much time his interaction would take away from the investigation.

11

"Aren't you going to answer your phone?" Kevin asked.

Deena had been half asleep with her head propped on her hand. "Huh?" She thought maybe she was dreaming, the haze of sleep in her eyes made the young man look angelic in the light from the window. It was nearly dark and Deena had drifted off while waiting on Avi to come back and trying to come up with a better plan.

"Your phone. It's ringing."

The sounds of a generic bleating ringtone emanated from somewhere inside the pockets of Deena's backpack. "Wow. Uh, thanks. I really spaced out there," she said. She unzipped the bag and dug through the junk inside. The phone was familiar in her hands, but she couldn't remember her number or anyone else's for that matter. Luckily, the caller ID showed the incoming call as "SIS", saving Deena from wondering who it was for too long. She flipped it open. "Hello, Harper? I've been trying to call you all day."

She was not greeted by the voice she expected. "Not Harper."

"Marsh."

"You remember me. Good. I was thinking you forgot," Marsh said on the other end of the phone. It was what he typically said when she was late checking in with him. "Seeing how our call went earlier today, I was sure that you'd forgotten how to talk to me politely."

"Why do you have Harper's phone?"

Marsh laughed. "Did you not think there would be consequences to walking away from me? What sort of childish notion did you get in your head that made you believe that would be all right with me?"

"Where's Harper?" Deena believed her sister would have had time to get out before Marsh decided to do anything drastic, but Marsh was right—it was a dumb move. Since the break from her former self, everything seemed urgent. Like if she didn't do the things she wanted to do, right away, they wouldn't happen and she would slip back to what she was without taking advantage of her window of time.

"Your sister is right here. She's fine. For now. Say hello."

Harper's voice came through the speaker. "Deena? What the hell is going on? They have my hands tied."

"Everything will be fine. Just don't worry," Deena said. "I'm sorry. This will all work out."

Harper's voice abruptly stopped, replaced by Marsh's. "Yes. It will be just fine. *If you do what I tell you.*"

"What do you want?"

"Your sister has messed up yet again. She'd made a spectacle of my business and I'm afraid it will cause me undue attention. I have no use for her," Marsh said. "If you want her to continue living, you'll come back here. You'll do another job for me and I'll let her go free to live her life. And you'll continue working for me without incident. If you don't agree, I'll kill her now. And then I'll kill you. Simple. You want your sister to continue to be in good health, yes?"

"Yes."

"Good. I'll see you soon." Marsh ended the call.

As she tossed the phone into the backpack, Deena watched Avi walk into the coffee shop and calmly order something. After a minute, he returned to the table, stirring coffee in a pale ceramic mug. He didn't look surprised as she relayed the contents of the call. "He'll kill you both. You know that."

Of course Deena realized that, but for whatever reason, she hadn't considered it would come down to that. She really believed she could walk away and start anew. "But it keeps my sister alive until I get there."

"Maybe."

"You should go back in. Call them and say you lost me. He'll leave you alone, then." Deena took another long drink of the minty concoction in front of her. "I don't want your life to get fucked up as well."

Avi stood up and pushed his seat back in behind him. "I dropped my car at a movie theater parking lot down the street. It had a tracer in it that Marsh's people could have used to track the car."

"What was showing?"

Avi paused. "What? At the movies? Why do you want to know?"

Deena shrugged. "Just curious."

"I don't know. Some stupid shit romantic comedy. Can we get back to the plan?"

"They could have found us right away in your car?"

"They're actually probably on their way. Marsh has local muscle he could call in to pick you up."

"So where are they?"

"I'm hoping at the movies, watching some stupid shit romcom. But I doubt it," Avi said. "I also ditched my phone and grabbed one in a superstore nearby," Avi took out his phone and grabbed Deena's. "I'm programming this new number into your phone."

"Shouldn't I ditch mine? Can't they follow me with it?"

"Not if we leave it turned off until we need to use it." Avi slid it across the table towards her.

She stared at it for a minute, realizing it was her only link to her sister now.

Avi grabbed her arm and tugged her to her feet. "Train station is just across town. Let's go. Pick it up."

12

Deena at 15 the first time around

"Pick up the controller."

"No."

Deena grinned. "Quitting again?"

Harper leaned back on the couch and folded her arms.

"Baby." Deena pressed reset and the game started again. She guided her Samurai Super Warrior up the stairs and through the door, breaking everything in the little animated fighter's path on the television. She loved the game. It was all so delicious, the swords and the knives the blood. It was all fake, but she loved it. She had strategy, when she needed it, but mostly, it was brute force, not finesse that got her through.

She was getting tired of whupping on her sister all the time, but no one else would play with her anymore. The neighbors weren't her age and didn't want to come around to play with the little weird neighbor girl. Her parents sucked at all the games, but they never wanted to play anyway.

"Come on, one more game. You can even use cheat codes. And you can have the good controller." Deena held up the illuminated blue game controller.

"No." Harper grabbed a magazine from the pile next to the couch and started leafing through it. Deena turned back to her game.

The clicking of Deena's fingers on the controllers became a rhythm that got faster and faster. The images she saw on the screen became more and more indistinct and she began to react to shapes and colors, sounds and eventually to instincts and feelings. She didn't think about it, much. She usually just let whatever was happening happen. All she knew was that when the game was over, she was sad. She felt an unbearable weight descend upon her chest and she wanted to play again. She wanted to run, jump, fight and slash with a sword of her own.

"Christ. You need to get a life," Harper said. She tossed her magazine on the table and walked out of the room. Deena could hear the back door swing shut as her sister walked out of the house.

Deena didn't look away from the screen. "What the hell are you doing with yours?"

Whenever Deena found herself alone with nothing else to do, she would look at the dot on her arm and try to decide whether it had changed, or if she was just imagining it. It seemed bigger some days and others it appeared to have moved a little to the right or left. She could never be positive, and she hated talking to her sister about it. Harper had gone to their dad and told him about it. He suggested they needed to make an appointment with a dermatologist to have it looked at, but he never pursued it.

When she finally put the controller down, Deena noticed the little blemish sort of looked like the yellow button on the game controller that she pressed to shoot at things in some games and swing her sword in others. It was still round and black, but it seemed to have a raised 'X' in the middle.

It faded quickly, and Deena decided to keep that to herself.

13

Two men in ill-fitting suits intercepted Pel and Garrett as they got closer to the mayor's people. "We need two minutes," the larger of the two said.

Pel started to point to the group they were headed to talk to.

"Just two minutes," the other man said. He nodded his head toward the mayor. "Those guys aren't going anywhere."

"We've got…" Garrett began.

"We could be done talking by now." The men were adamant about Garrett coming with them for a talk and confident that everyone else could wait.

"What can I do for you?" Garrett looked around the men to make sure the mayor wasn't, in fact, going anywhere.

"Step over here," the large one pointed to a nearby car and walked over to it. He opened a door and waited for Pel and Garrett to get in.

"Seriously? Is this necessary?" Pel asked.

"Two minutes," the shorter one said as he opened a back door for them.

In the comfort of their incredibly non-descript sedan, the tall one behind the driver's seat spoke first. "I'm Agent Rice, this is Agent Rivers. We just want to talk to you about the crime scene."

"Agents of which agency?" Garrett asked.

"One of the less flashy subdivisions of the Bureau," Rivers said without missing a beat. "Reports put this event as beginning at 6:13 p.m. That's about four hours ago."

"Give or take." Garrett didn't look at his watch.

Rice shifted uncomfortably in his seat to get a better look at Garrett who was sitting directly behind him in the back seat of the car. "So, what do we know so far?"

Garrett didn't like the sound of that. The way the 'we' just snuck into the sentence was subtle and was, in Garrett's experience, a prelude to someone horning in where they didn't belong. "Unfortunately, not a lot. The explosion took out quite a bit of the evidence. As I'm sure you know, it'll take quite a while to reconstruct the device for any clues it might give us." He gave them the general overview that could have been easily gleaned from looking at the scene. Garrett wasn't about to spill anything to some guys that wouldn't fully identify themselves.

"*Right.* Tell us about the ambulance." Rivers looked tired to Garrett, but then he supposed that could be the agent's normal expression.

"Not much to talk about there yet. We're running the plates and numbers on the ambulance to see where it came from. The company name on the side isn't from around here, we know that much already. No ID on the victim, but we're looking into him." Again, nothing but surface-level stuff.

Rice shifted again, awkwardly pulling a file folder from between the seats. He opened it and handed a picture back to him. "That your guy?"

Garrett saw the man in the photo and cringed a little. It was a picture of the victim, minus the bullet holes. "Yes, that's *our* guy."

"Federal witness in an organized crime case. Tom Jessup. We'll give you his stats and whatnot."

"You think he was supposed to be on the bus?"

"That's a possibility," Rice said.

"What was he doing roaming around free if he was in danger?" Pel asked.

"How the hell should I know? Wasn't our case," Rivers said.

It all fell into place for Garrett. The hit man went to the extreme of bombing an entire bus to make sure the witness didn't get off. It was overkill, but hits like this often were, just to make a point. Unfortunately, the mark never got on the bus to begin with. "So, this was a mob hit? Great. Are you guys going to take it off my hands?"

"I'm sure someone will come along and help you with that aspect," Rivers said. "What else you got?"

Garrett wondered again how much they knew and wanted him to tell them. "Nothing." He waited to see their reaction. "Seriously nothing."

Rivers handed Pel a small laptop. "How 'bout we both take a look at what's on the tape?"

Pel looked at Garrett for guidance and the senior agent nodded affirmative.

"Wow. This is a great little piece of hardware," Pel said as she attached the drive to the USB port. "Hendica? They're not even distributing in America yet. Nice."

Everyone in the car tried to shift to get a view of the screen. The men in the front leaned over the seats, hanging halfway into the back. Pel tried to turn the laptop around and work the video controls from behind until she discovered the screen itself swiveled, enabling her to work the keys while the others got a decent view of the screen. It would've been comical, if not for the fact they were at a crime scene.

They all watched exactly what Pel had described to Garrett earlier, culminating with the woman walking off into the alley next to the large black man.

"Can you freeze it on a good view of the woman?" Rice asked.

Pel paused the video, and then toggled it backward a bit until she settled on a relatively clear view of the side of the face. She zoomed in a little and copied a grainy close-up of the woman's face and left it up in the corner of the larger picture. "Best I can do. Dark alley, poor quality video. Give me some time back in the lab and I can do much better."

The men looked at each other and then back at Garrett and Pel. "OK. Thanks." They both turned and faced forward, Rice's hands moved to the steering wheel. They all sat in silence for a moment and Garrett couldn't believe that was the end of the conversation.

Rice revved the engine.

"All right. What the hell?" Garrett asked. "You pump us for information then you don't reciprocate? Not going to happen. Let's go, make with the story."

"Yeah," Pel said. "Squid pro quo."

Garrett never knew when Pel was being purposely funny or blissfully ignorant. He wasn't going to ask.

"Guys, I'm sorry. This isn't something you need to know. We've told you what's pertinent." Rivers threw his hands up. "You have the victim's name, a good motive. I'd say we've been more than helpful."

Garrett leaned forward. "How about a little more on the motive? Who was he going to testify against? Why weren't your people protecting him if he was such an important witness?"

"He wasn't scheduled to testify against anyone, therefore, he wasn't under anyone's protection. It was who he *could've* testified against." To Garrett, Rice didn't seem all that focused on the story.

"Who are we talking about?" Garrett asked.

Rivers and Rice looked at each other again and their expressions didn't change. "We need some good people on our team for this investigation, maybe even on a permanent basis," Rice said. "You've got as much info as anyone. Maybe we could ask you to be assigned to a detail with us."

Garrett was astounded. They dragged him into a car, gave him bullshit info and now wanted to offer him a job.

"What exactly are you looking for?"

Rivers continued: "Specifically a new field tech person and a lead investigator who can follow instructions and get results for us."

Garrett turned to Pel and saw the woman looked as incredulous as he felt. "Are you guys seriously offering us jobs? Here?"

No one answered him.

"Tell you what," Garrett started fumbling through his pockets. He had a crime scene to get back to that wasn't getting any fresher. He'd wasted his time just long enough with these clowns to ensure everyone at the scene had tromped over evidence and then promptly put their thumbs up their asses. "I'll give you my card, when you're ready to talk about this thing seriously, give me a…"

He was interrupted as Rivers leaned back and handed him a different business card. Garrett looked at it carefully, and found his own name on it. Garrett Walters, Lead Field Agent—it said. The phone number wasn't his. The office address wasn't from his building on Hudson, rather on the west side, a Newell address on the 3rd floor. Below it were the initials FEI Garrett looked at it closely, wondering if the letter E was just a faded B.

The doors unlocked unexpectedly. Garrett wasn't even aware they'd been locked. Garrett opened the door immediately and Pel followed suit.

As they both slammed the doors simultaneously, one of the men inside the car called out, "Be seeing you."

Pel joined Garrett and they walked toward the scene together. "What the hell? I told you to go straight to the office and check that tape out."

"An agent stopped me and said you were looking for me."

"I would have called you.

"Sorry. It's a fucked up night."

Garrett sighed. "True. You got me there."

The mayor's people were standing around talking to Garrett's bosses, Division Chief Harris among them. They didn't look happy at all. Several more unfamiliar faces had joined the group.

Harris waved Garrett over. "Walters, this is Marty Tan, he's with the anti-terrorism taskforce." He pointed to the man next to him in jeans and a windbreaker. "And this is Kara Lanford, she's with the ATF. Marty and his people will be taking the lead on this one, Kara will be helping out. I need you to fill them in on anything you've got so far and hand over any notes that might be helpful."

Garrett looked closely at his boss's face to see what he could read there. He wondered if Harris had any say in the decision to take the case away or if it was something forced on him. He couldn't discern anything by looking, but he guessed the latter. "Are you kidding? I've been on this scene since the beginning. I've watched them carry the bodies, and bits of bodies out of the wreckage." He moved closer to Harris until his face was a foot away. "And you're going to just let them take me off this?"

Harris pulled Garrett away from the group and talked to him low. "Jesus, Walters. What do you want me to do? This falls into their jurisdiction. It's not like it's a quiet little crime where we can stand and argue about who gets what. This is big, you know that." He nodded around to all the camera crews that were set up around the scene. "I'm sorry, but let it go. This is obviously something we need the terrorism team in on."

Garrett pulled his arm away from Harris. He didn't lower his voice like his boss. "Terrorism. Shit, this has nothing to do with terrorism. This is a mob hit, a plain old everyday mob hit."

The group of people they'd walked away from looked over, very interested in what was being discussed. Garrett nodded at them.

"What the fuck are you talking about?" Harris asked in his low tone. "Where did you get that idea from? Jesus, look around you. Where's that coming from? Did you find something that might point to a hit?"

Garrett tried to identify the car they'd sat in, but it was obscured by a crowd of onlookers and an emergency vehicle. "Some agents gave me a heads up."

"What fucking agents? WHOSE fucking agents?"

Garrett wanted to kick himself for not following up with their claims of where they were from. "The FEI?"

"What the hell are you talking about? Did they show you any evidence, or are you just going on the say so of some guys you've never met?"

"Pretty much just their word, sir."

"So you're shouting crazy, unsupported theories for everyone to hear based on nothing whatsoever? That right?"

"Yeah."

Harris stared at Garrett hard for a minute. "I think maybe you need to get back to the office and help coordinate things there. And you'll cover anything else that comes in. The next case is yours and you're out the door, your involvement in this ends at that moment. Got it?"

Garrett thought hard about what to say. This was a new side of his supervisor that he'd never seen. They worked well together because they could bounce ideas off each other and collaborate in helpful ways. "Yeah." He turned and started toward the yellow police-tape perimeter. His route took him past Marty Tan.

"Don't forget to leave your notes," Harris called.

Garrett took his notebook out of his coat pocket and handed it to Tan as he passed. "Good luck reading this, my handwriting sucks." He didn't wait for a reply.

"You don't use your tablet for notes?"

Pel laughed and fell in step behind him.

"They didn't banish *you*," Garrett said. "Just me."

"I'm not hanging around to work with those assholes," Pel said.

"You don't even know them, I'm sure they're lovely people."

"Right."

They ducked under the tape and pressed through the crowd. As they rounded a police van, they came to where Rivers and Rice had been sitting in their car. The two agents and the car were gone.

"Great. I had a question or two for them." Garrett felt tired. The weight of the day caught up with him quickly.

"Well, at least now we'll have time to polish up our resumes before we see them again," Pel said. "Let's just go back and look at that video and see what else we can see, maybe copy it before we give it to the terrorism guys."

Garrett walked a few feet before he discovered the woman wasn't following anymore. He turned and saw Pel just standing there with her face scrunched up. "You didn't take the disk out of the laptop when we left the car, did you?" Pel asked.

Garrett had to shake his head no. "It crossed my mind, it really did, but… I had no idea how to do it."

"You're the most technologically challenged federal agent I know."

"I'm taking classes," Garrett said.

"They're not helping."

14

In the cab, Avi spoke in low tones. "Why did you run away from me at the airport? If you were having so much trouble, you should have told me," Avi said. He reached out and she moved away from him as best she could.

"Avi, I don't know what…"

"And why are you suddenly acting all Amish?"

"Amish? That's a good one. Were you expecting me to jump you? Were you hoping that the little teenager would grab you hard and stick her tongue down your throat? That what you were looking for?" They'd had a pretty tumultuous relationship, punctuated by periods of deciding it was a bad idea for people in their line of work to be together in any sort of emotional entanglement. The times in between were not really much of a relationship. They had to keep things hidden from everyone in the organization, her sister included. It boiled down to brief periods of intense sex. "Pedophile much?" The cab driver looked at them in his rearview mirror, but Deena couldn't be sure he heard her. She frowned at him and he turned away.

"What the hell? What do want from me? You leave on a job, we're all handsy and fucktacular, you come back like a Catholic schoolgirl on a fieldtrip and announce you're joining a convent." Avi looked understandably confused. "And you expect me to shift gears without missing a beat? Fuck you."

"Oh, poor you. Poor Avi. You're not getting laid today. That's much worse than what's going on with me. Take a good look at me. I lost ten years of my life here. My mind constantly fights with itself as to whether I'm going to have a coherent thought, or if I'm going to repeat lyrics from boy band songs over and over for an hour," Deena said. It was frustrating to explain such a profound change to someone who didn't seem to want to know.

"You already look older than when we met up in the airport. You'll snap back. You always do."

"Maybe my body will, maybe even my mind, but I've never questioned my life this way. It can't go on the way things were. And you have to admit it's a horrible time to become addlebrained, no matter what I decide to do."

Avi took a deep breath and Deena was sure he still didn't believe her. "Just get some rest when we get on the train. We'll decide what you want to be when you grow up later." He turned and looked out at the city.

"Jesus. Stop saying that. I don't understand it, and I keep hoping it will get sorted out by the time we hit Los Angeles, but I don't think it's going to." Deena looked at the little spot on her right arm. It looked innocent enough; small, lighter than normal. She knew it could turn on a dime if it were any other day. "I feel like I have the ability to make choices for the first time here. It's always felt like I had to do what this inner voice has told me to for so long, for as long as I remember." Deena didn't look at him. She couldn't come right out and say there was no way for them to be together again. She faked looking at traffic, but knew he could see through her. "All I'm asking is that we take our time getting back to the city. Give me time to heal. Maybe I can get myself figured out so I handle this change."

"I understand changes, I get it. But that doesn't mean you stop being the person you were." Avi sounded bored with the conversation already.

"In this case it does, I know it does. I can't feel the same things the same way."

"You said it yourself, you aren't completely back to normal yet, you're still healing and you will be for some time. Remember that job in Omaha? It took you most of a week to recover from that."

"Avi. I had a migraine. This seems like a little more than a bad headache."

"So maybe by the time we get back, you'll see things more clearly and you'll know what's what." Avi fell silent for a few miles.

She wondered what ideas were forming in his head, how he was going to move forward with the new information. His loyalty to Marsh went back further than his affiliation with Deena. "What's going to happen when we get to L.A.?" Deena asked. "Are you going to let me do this? Or are you siding with Marsh to try to get me to stay?"

"We'll be at the train station in a few minutes. What say we pass that time in silence or play that game? I Spy?" Avi folded his arms and fidgeted in his seat. "I spy something that begins with the letter 'D'," he said.

Deena looked around at the quiet streets. "Is it a dumbass? A douchebag, maybe?"

The driver chuckled a little. Deena leaned back in her seat and took Avi's first suggestion—passing the rest of the short ride in silence. The area of town was quickly fading from busy office buildings to smaller shops and storage units. She'd grown used to the same type of scenery for the past several years. She hadn't been back to the country much since she left home. She missed it really: the trees, the open air. It was a part of her that she'd shoved down deep since she left.

15

Deena at 15 the first time around

"It moved," Deena said.

Harper threw her dirty jeans in the basket and chuckled. "Didn't."

Deena pulled her sleeve up to reveal the tiny blemish. "Look. It was closer to my elbow last night. Swear."

Harper barely glanced. "Same place it's always been."

Deena sighed. She'd been sure of it this time. The blemish had jumped from place to place a number of times, but always ended up back where it started when she went to show someone. "It is now, but yesterday..."

"Yesterday, whatever." Harper looked around their bedroom and spotted more rumpled clothes and stuffed them in with the rest.

"Come on," Deena said. Her sister was always dismissing Deena. It wasn't just this little pimple or mole, or whatever the hell it was, she never listened to anything Deena had to say. They were separated by just a few years, but they never seemed to see eye to eye on anything.

Harper tossed the laundry basket on the bed and pulled open the drawer of their dresser. "Fine. Come here."

"Huh?" Deena was afraid of what her sister was up to. The sudden interest felt like a trap.

Harper grabbed Deena's arm roughly and found the spot with her finger. "This is it, right?"

Deena nodded.

Harper popped the cap on a permanent black marker and drew a wide circle around the dark thing on Deena's arm. "There." She tossed the marker onto the top of the dresser. "Now we'll see if it moves. Now we'll know for sure and you can shut the fuck up about it. Sound good?" Harper went back to gathering clothes for the laundry.

Deena stepped back. Her big sister rarely cussed. "Geez. Take it easy. Don't let Mom hear you talk like that."

"Whatever." Harper grabbed the laundry and walked out the door.

Deena looked at the mark on her arm. The circle drawn there had the blemish nearly dead center in the middle. Her sister was ever the perfectionist. At first it seemed a little stupid, but she realized it might be the only way to convince Harper what was going on.

She licked her finger and scrubbed at the black circle. "Crap, that looks really stupid."

In study hall the next day, Deena caught herself staring at it. There was nothing else of interest to do, really, other than homework. She gauged how close it was to the edge of the circle her sister had drawn. It certainly seemed to have moved closer to the edge, or maybe the round spot itself had just gotten bigger. With a little spit on her fingers, Deena rubbed at the marker, trying to get it off.

At the front of the study hall, three students came in late and handed the monitor a note. One of the tardy students was Mike Fischer, the boy Harper had been dating for a few weeks. He was kind of a dick and Deena didn't really care for him. He played soccer, told rude jokes and didn't seem to care that his grades were in free fall. There were rumors that he was cheating on Harper, but no one could really prove it. Deena grumbled to herself about Mike being late yet again to study hall and went back to trying to remove the mark from her arm.

She was surprised to see that the little dark point on her arm no longer seemed to be circular. As she'd been watching Mike, the dot had flattened itself out and appeared to be more of a curved line. In fact, from her vantage point, it almost looked like a frown. She nearly jumped up from her desk to run and show her sister. Deena wanted to do it immediately, before the blotch had time to change again. As soon as she stood, the study hall monitor gave Deena a dirty look. Deena had pressed her luck with the monitor before and there was no way the frowny face spot on Deena's arm would be a viable excuse to get out of the room. Study hall was her last period of the day and she could easily catch her sister at home afterward.

Deena sat back down and stared at the spot some more. It still showed as a frown. For the rest of the study hall, she looked at nothing but the curved black line on her arm. She wondered if she could change it even further. Deena had sworn it had moved around, but she'd never seen it as anything but round. Yet here it was: a curved line, a frown, like the circle had detached and moved to the new shape.

After school she ran home to show her sister. By the time she got there, the line had once again become a circle.

16

Stanley walked with the men to the empty suite two floors up from their own. It was originally owned by an insurance company that suddenly went out of business after the owner was killed in a tragic car accident. Stanley stopped being surprised by tragic accidents that occurred around his line of work. It was tough figuring out whose heart attacks were natural and whose were brought on by nefarious means. No death ever seemed perfectly innocent to him anymore. Natural deaths felt like a thing of the past.

One of the men, Frank, pushed Harper to make her move faster. "Let's get this over with." He waved to the room filled with office furniture covered in plastic. "We're going to hang out here and wait. Nothing stupid, please. Mr. Marsh asked us not to make a mess, but made it clear that he didn't give a shit if you lived long enough to see your sister."

Stanley was still having trouble looking Harper in the eyes. Each look could be the last time he saw Harper alive and maybe, by diverting his eyes, he'd keep the girl from dying. There was no way they would kill her if Stanley didn't get a last glimpse. Statistically, that held no water, he realized. "I've checked to make sure the bathroom in the suite is stocked with the necessities, so you should be comfortable in that respect. There's a break room with some cups and a water cooler. If anyone gets… you know…thirsty or anything." There really wasn't much to say, but Stanley felt an obligation to play host and make sure everyone was comfortable. It was an odd thought to have at the potential scene of a murder.

"Oh, thanks. The fact that I can pee freely really does put me at ease," Harper said.

"Shut up," Frank said. "Is there any food? No telling how long we'll be here."

Stanley turned to the door. "I'll bring up what I can from downstairs." He got closer to Harper. "Are you sure there isn't anything I can get you?"

"A gun," Harper said.

Frank chuckled. "Not like you'd be able to hit anything with it."

Stanley walked out of the office, followed by two of the men, who rolled chairs out into the hall and sat down to guard the door. Stanley got on the elevator and pressed the button for the ground floor. He felt helpless and his fingers curled into fists, he wanted to yell and punch the walls but held back. If anyone saw him freaking out, they'd know something was wrong. He couldn't have that. He had to remain as he'd always been, with a stony exterior. The FBI agents told him it wouldn't be long now and they'd be able to get him out and shut down Marsh for good.

They'd been saying that for months, though.

Stanley kept the books nice and neat. All of Datura Industries' honest businesses kept in perfect detail, while the rest of the money was hidden, kept in other coded ledgers that no one except Stanley could fully decipher. He hadn't handed any of that over to the FBI yet. Samples. Cookies that kept the authorities interested in helping Stanley, without busting him straight away. There was no chance he was going to jail. Not if they wanted Stanley to testify against Marsh. And if a sudden "accident" were to befall Stanley, Marsh himself wouldn't know the extent of his own empire. Money was scattered across the globe in secret accounts and other holdings. Most were there at Marsh's behest. *Most.*

Back at his desk, Stanley stirred his coffee in tight little circles with a flimsy red straw. He stared at the elevator, wanting hordes of heavily-armed federal agents to come pouring out with bulletproof vests and heavy machine guns. Flash grenades and riot helmets. Brass knuckles and broken beer bottles. Whatever. Stanley loved the magic of spreadsheets and numbers; violence wasn't his thing. He was fine with marking down the money Marsh brought in from murder and mayhem. He didn't have to look the victims in the face - they were numbers with commas and zeroes. They were an abstract, a placeholder, a bar graph and he generally never knew their names or faces.

He'd looked Harper in the eyes time after time before today and no amount of looking away could make him forget what was going to happen to her.

Stanley redialed Agent Rivers' number again and it went to voicemail. He hung up without leaving a message.

17

Deena and Avi got on the train at the last second. She watched the people board with their luggage and briefcases and she tried to scan for anyone that might be pursuing them. There were men in suits, families in flip-flops and women with flowery cheap mu-mus. Well, there weren't that many in mu-mus. She supposed each of those people could be a killer with a pistol concealed under their clothes. None of them did anything unusual. She watched Avi. He was much better at being discreet in his observations. She tilted her head, tried to use her sunglasses to hide her eyes as she scanned, but she was sure she gave herself away.

"Ma'am, please find your seat," a man in a navy blue uniform said.

She nodded and stumbled toward the seating. She saw Avi already at the other end of the car and she moved to join him. On the way, she passed person after person and imagined each of them staring at her—some actually were—and believed they might all be working to keep her disoriented and alone. There was a man in his early thirties with headphones lodged in his ears sitting near Avi. He gave her a glance and then looked away. He might be here to kill me, Deena thought. She wasn't sure if she was being paranoid or crazy, but she looked him over and decided she could take him out, no matter who he was. She wondered for a moment where that thought had come from. Was there a time in her recent past when that was a logical thought? Had she always been that alert, that paranoid before? Was that what made her good at what she did? And would that instinct ever come back in full force? She kind of hoped it wouldn't.

She sat down next to Avi as the train began moving. She plopped down and locked her seat belt, pulling the strap tight and then hugged the bag from the coffee shop that held all her possessions. She'd most likely never get back to her own apartment. All of her clothes were there, all the souvenirs that she'd acquired from her travels, her wide-screen TV, stereo. It was all gone as of a few short hours ago. She would be an entirely new person with all new crap. And right now, it was all in a cheap plastic bag from a coffee shop where Kevin had made her heavenly, minty cups of awesome.

"I want to turn my phone back on," she said.

"No."

"What if Harper is trying to call me? Or Marsh?"

"They aren't. He wouldn't alter the conditions. He wants you back. And you know he doesn't like screwing around during a job. He wants what he wants and he wants it on his terms," Avi said. "Any calls at this point would be to mess with you and try to get you off your game."

I'm already way off my game, thanks. No need to help me there. Deena looked down at the mark on her arm. It wasn't in the form of a fancy design or the familiar smiley face. It was just a dark blob, dormant on her arm, just as it had been since the airplane. There was magic in there somewhere, or there had been, but was it still swimming in her blood, ready for a fight? It wouldn't be so bad if she were just a normal girl without the Shadow Energy flowing through her. It would suck if she were a teenager all over again, though. *That* wouldn't be good at all. Deena threw herself back on the seat and wiggled around in an effort to get comfortable, but she couldn't do it.

"You want to settle down a bit and not draw attention to yourself? Jesus," Avi said. "You wanted to ride the train back, we're riding the train back. Just stop acting like an idiot, please." He shook his head and pulled out a crossword book he'd picked up at the train station. "I swear, it's like traveling with Rain Man."

"Nice, current reference there."

Avi looked her up and down. "You'll think it's funny when you're older."

"Doubt it."

18

Deena at 16 the first time around

"Are you giving my sister shit?" Deena asked as she pushed Mike Fischer. "You think you're cool or something, treating her like that?" Even Deena had trouble remembering what had set her off, just that she'd run up and started shoving Mike at the bus stop outside the school.

"Jesus Dot, leave him alone." Deena didn't react, so Harper grabbed her. "Knock it off."

A small crowd had already gathered around, and Deena knew they wanted to see a fight. The bus stop was always a popular place for settling scores after school. Deena had actually been in the center of that crowd more than once, getting into it with another girl for one reason or another. But never with a boy.

"Not until he tells you he's sorry," Deena said.

Harper pulled on Deena's arm harder. "Sorry for what?"

"Your little sister is nuts," Mike said as he turned to leave with some of his football buddies. "You better get her on the bus before I mess her up."

Deena broke free from Harper's grasp and yelled at Mike as she started toward him. "Where you goin', you wuss?"

Harper ran after her sister as Mike turned. "What? You don't want to fight for real, do you?" His friends backed away to give him room.

Deena wasn't afraid of what Mike would do. Mike had a temper, and, as a football player, worked out every day with the team. Plus he had nearly a hundred pounds on her. Still, nothing in Deena made her at all concerned about the stupid jock's fighting skills. She could, however, see fear in her sister's eyes. It was obvious Harper was worried Deena would make her look stupid in front of the whole school.

Deena stopped just a couple of feet from Mike. "Sure. A real fight sounds like fun."

Mike laughed at her, as did the crowd behind him. As he turned to look at his friends, Deena hit him hard in the stomach. He grimaced and bent at the waist, clutching his midsection. She hit him again, quickly, this time square in the jaw. He fell to the ground with an astonished look on his face. Harper reached out and grabbed Deena's arm. "Jesus, what the hell?" They both watched a dot of blood roll down Mike's chin. "Let's go," Harper said.

"Not yet," Deena replied. Somewhere deep inside, she enjoyed the fight and didn't want to walk away. There was a buzz in her brain that was feeding off the confrontation. "Tell her what you did, asshole." She looked at Mike.

Mike stared up and Harper watched the expression on his face change to determination. "Fuck you." He stood up and took off his jacket, handing it to one of his football buddies. "I was going to let your mouthing off go, since you're Harper's sister, but fuck that." He raised his arms, hands turning to fists. "I'll hit a chick when I..."

His words were interrupted as Deena closed the gap between them and hit his jaw with unexpected ferocity. He gave a startled yelp and stumbled backward. Deena stayed with him landing another punch on his arm, one in his gut. She could feel something guiding her punches and making her continue.

Mike flailed, half punching, half grabbing. None of his blows landed, but he managed to catch Deena's shirt and held on. As she attempted to hit him again, Mike stumbled back, taking her with him. He used his momentary advantage and strength to whip the girl away from him.

"Fuck, what the hell is going on here?" Harper asked. She stepped to Mike's side looking at the blood on his chin. It was obvious that she wasn't quite sure Mike was going to come out on top. "Let's just go," she told him. "Let's stop this."

Mike shoved Harper away, knocking her to the ground. "Get away," he said.

Deena looked at Harper, sitting on the ground. Her whole body suddenly felt like concrete was flowing through her bloodstream. "Bad idea, jackass. Bad idea," she said. She stepped toward Mike, both hands flexing to make them feel less stiff.

"Fuck you." Mike's voice sounded unstable and wobbly. Deena wondered if he might be on the verge of crying.

Mike stepped quickly toward Deena, his first punch going just past her head. Deena let his momentum carry him past her and planted her elbow in his back. He cried out again and turned to face her, just in time for Deena to punch him directly on the nose. He stumbled back and fell, blood started to drip from his nostrils and then the drip became a flood. His legs went limp and Deena was thrilled that everyone in the crowd got to watch him fall on his butt.

"What the fu..." Again he didn't get to finish his sentence before Deena was on him, knocking him on his back. He put his hands up to block the blows, but it didn't help, Deena punched around them. She landed punch after punch on his face, ears and throat.

"Just tell her the truth you fucking dickbag," Deena yelled over Mike's screams.

It was like a dream to Deena; something that she was watching without the ability to control.

Harper grabbed Deena's right forearm as she prepared for the next blow. "Deena. Look," she said quietly between clenched teeth.

Deena didn't turn immediately. She struggled a little to free her arm then followed her sister's gaze. Deena's knuckles and right hand had turned dark, it was obvious even through the rusty hue of Mike's blood.

When Harper looked to Mike, he was moaning. His face was cut to ribbons, part of his earlobe was lying on the ground next to him. "Christ Deena…" Harper said. "What the fuck? What did you do?"

Deena shrugged off Harper's grip, stepped up to Mike and kicked him in the ribs. "Tell her now." Her voice was strained with anger.

Mike's only response was a wet gurgle. Deena wondered how badly she had hurt him. She kept looking at her arm. It looked like someone had painted it black with a Sharpie.

Harper grabbed Deena again, this time forcing Deena to look her in the eye. "Whatever it is, we can talk about it later. We really should just go."

Deena's eyes narrowed. "He fucked Heidi Connors after the game on Friday." The contempt in her voice was unmistakable. "Right in the parking lot. Then he came and picked you up from work and took you out bowling or some shit, didn't he?" Deena thought she might kick Mike again.

The color drained from Harper's face, but it was hard to tell if it was because of the news or the sight of Mike's beaten and battered form on the ground. "Let's just go. Let's just go home," Harper said. She turned and pushed her way through the stunned crowd.

Deena looked at Mike again. "Asshole." She followed her sister through the crowd and wiped her hands on her pants. No one said a word and no one tried to stop her. The darkness on her arm faded slowly.

Two days later, Mike died in the hospital and Deena convinced Harper to run away with her.

19

Garrett stood as still as he could make himself and glared at Rivers and Rice. "Seriously? That's the story you're sticking to? You're interested in this girl mainly because her sister is a witch? Like a real, pointy-hat-wearing, black-cat-having, broom-riding witch?" Garrett was already regretting letting Pel talk him into meeting with the mysterious agents again. They'd called Rivers and Rice the next morning, followed their directions and eventually ended up waiting in a walkway that crossed over Eastern Avenue to the mall. Eventually, Rice showed up and led them to an SUV driven by Rivers. When everyone was in, the vehicle took off. It was all too cloak and dagger for Garrett's tastes, but he let it go, hoping things would make more sense soon. No such luck. "Are you shitting me?"

"You weren't really listening were you? We don't think she's a witch, we just think she has an unusual power." Rivers held up a tablet, which Pel quickly took and started tinkering with.

"I'm no scientist but it looks like your only conclusion to these crimes *involves* magic. Locked doors, heavily guarded cells, armored cars. All of these things seem foolproof but people still got killed, money stolen, whatever," Pel said.

"No, that's not our conclusion. Those stats are from various police departments and agencies around the country. They list the crimes as unsolved and/or open," Rice said. "We know exactly what happened."

"Rogue tooth fairy?" Garrett asked.

Pel laughed.

The conversation went nowhere, until they pulled into an old parking garage on the west side. It was crumbling, with graffiti on the walls and a number of cars in disrepair on the first floor. As they drove around in a circle that led them to the next floor down, there were more dark SUVs, unmarked cars and plain white vans.

"Follow me," Rivers stepped out when the vehicle came to a halt and motioned everyone to the nearby elevator. Pel and Garrett fell in behind with Rice in the very back. As soon as Rivers stepped in front of the elevator, the doors opened and they entered. The doors closed and the elevator started descending on its own, no buttons pushed.

"This is getting a little too 'Mission Impossible' for me," Garrett said. "What in the hell is going on?" He said it more to himself, rather than as a question to the agents who'd brought them there. Truth be told, he was now more intrigued than annoyed. The secret underground base put him over the top. The FBI, as a rule, was pretty mundane. There was an office, or field office, desks, security guards and so on. There was nothing cool about it. Nothing intriguing or mysterious. Agents showed up. They did their jobs. Kind of ho hum. Whatever happened with Rivers and Rice, at least it wasn't boring.

The elevator stopped abruptly a few seconds later and the doors slid open again. A small, bare room awaited them with just a single uniformed guard with an assault rifle. The man nodded to Rivers and a new door opened onto a long, narrow, hall. After another door, they all stepped out onto an elevated metal walkway that went all around a huge circular room. Below, in the middle, was an expanse full of desks, computer monitors, and uniformed personnel.

"This way," Rivers said and opened a door by sliding a badge across a lighted panel. In the next room, Garrett saw several men standing around a table in lab coats and goggles. Along the walls, more men sat at computers and microscopes, none looked up. Garrett noticed a bank of monitors on the far wall. Two had maps; another had what seemed to be a close up of a drop of oil.

"What's going on here? Seriously, it's just one thing after another with you guys. If you've got something that will help us understand what's going on, great. If you don't, we'll just take our tape that you snaked and be on our way." Garrett said.

Rice ignored the question. "See the map on the right? The red dots represent crimes that we're pretty sure one of these subjects is responsible for."

Garrett looked up and squinted. He guessed there were close to one hundred of them. "So it's not just this girl you think we're dealing with." He found himself biting on the premise that this girl was a killer, but not that she was supernatural.

Rivers pointed to the other map. It had far fewer dots on it. "We believe these nineteen are all the work of this one girl. We can't be sure but they seem to fit the pattern and we have some inside information on things this girl has been assigned to do."

"If you have someone on the inside, why not drop the hammer and arrest the girl, why all the cloak and dagger X-Files bullshit?" Pel sounded just as confused as Garrett felt.

"We're working on it. We've only just established the informant. We can't spook him." Rice absently added to the conversation while he scanned the map.

"And this informant tells you the girl is a magical fairy?" Every time he started to feel comfortable with the agents, the same nagging concerns came back to Garrett; he had no idea who these guys were and they had some fairly messed up ideas. "I think your informant is already spooked. Spooked in the head."

"No. The girl has some of the same traits as others we've come into contact with and captured," Rice said. He pointed up to the blob on the screen.

"What's that?" Pel asked.

Rivers leaned over to one of the men at the computers. "Can you pull back on screen two?'

The image got further away a little at a time until it was obvious that the blob was on someone's arm.

"Is that a birthmark?" Garrett asked.

"Bad tattoo?" Pel suggested.

"Good guesses." Rivers stepped to an open terminal and typed for a moment. The map of all the crimes disappeared and showed a picture of a large black blob writhing on a table. "Near as we can guess it's some kind of parasite."

"Wait. That blob is what you got when you removed the tattoo?" Pel put her hand to her mouth. "There's one of these inside the girl you're looking for? Ewww."

"We think so. Her and others," Rice said. "We call these people Incubators, or Inks for short."

"Better than calling them 'Bators, I suppose," Pel cracked. She still managed to look disgusted at the images.

Garrett stepped up. "But, if you have this one, that means you can remove these…"

"Parasites," Rice said.

"Leech thingies," Pel corrected.

Garrett didn't care what they were called, really. He was more interested in the end result. If the agency knew about these things, there must be something they could do about them. "If you can remove them, then the people they infected can go back to normal, right?"

Rice and Rivers looked at each other for a moment.

Garrett pointed up at the screen with the blob on it. "How many people have you removed these things from?"

"Total? Twelve," Rivers said. "We've studied twelve subjects that were good candidates and we went ahead with surgeries to remove the parasites."

"How many survived the process?" Garrett asked.

"None," Rice and Rivers said in unison.

"As soon as they're removed, the Ink, or host dies," Rice continued. "Every time."

Garrett walked around looking at screens and charts, but his mind glazed over quickly at the technology and gizmos. His phone gave him a headache; this stuff was a thousand times worse. He walked over to the image of the blob that the agents had pointed out. It was one thing to arrest criminals and punish them for crimes, but this… catching people with things growing inside them. It wasn't something he was trained for. "What's it made of? It was analyzed right?"

"Nothing came up. We have no idea what it is. The organic material doesn't match up to anything we know. We keep thinking it might be an actual parasite, an animal or insect of some kind, but once it's removed, it turns to goo. Mostly water actually."

"Really? You've taken these people apart and all you know is that if you remove the mass, the people die?" Garrett thought the mass looked like a pile of raspberry yogurt.

"We can't say much about the material, but we know a little about the Inks themselves. The most useful thing we've gleaned from incarcerating these people is that they seem to be able to detect each other within a certain proximity." Rice shrugged. "They go a little nuts when one of their own kind is around. Learned that the hard way when we captured two Inks at once."

"That's helpful." Garrett looked at each of the people in the files. He didn't recognize any of them. Never busted them for petty crimes or anything larger. "I suppose the question that remains is where did these things come from and how did they get there?"

"Yes. That is the question," Rice said.

Pel was right at home with all of the computers and tech that gave Garrett the willies. She'd quietly asked if she could sit at a terminal and nudged a technician out of the way. She tapped away madly at the keyboard. A beep and a warning screen stopped her progress. "Password?"

Rivers and Rice looked at each other. "You don't have clearance yet."

"So give it to her," Garrett said.

"You're onboard?"

"I think we are," Pel said. She looked to Garrett for confirmation.

"So let me get this straight, you want me come help you track down this freaky powerful girl and her friends? You guys are like the Men in Black and I'm Will Smith?"

The other three agents all chuckled at once.

"What?" Garrett asked.

71

Pel spoke up. "I wouldn't say Will Smith. Wow. Vain much?"

"Samuel L. Jackson in the Avengers?" Rivers asked.

"Not even," Rice laughed.

"Fine. I'm in. But if you don't get a little more forthcoming, I'm out quickly." Garrett looked back up at the screens and hoped he wasn't making an incredibly stupid decision. If it led to getting criminals off the street, he was all for it. If he started chasing aliens and chupacabras, he was going to feel like an idiot.

"Great, but did it sound like I was giving you a choice? My fault. We talked to your higher ups already and had you transferred. Your stuff is being brought over right now. It's a done deal." Rivers said. "Welcome to the FEI."

Pel and Garrett gave each other a glance.

"Done deal? Then why were you jerking us around about joining up? Just say you're borrowing us and move on." Garrett didn't like the start to this new employment relationship. If they were giant bastards about things from the beginning, what was in store down the road?

"And did you just say FBI?" Pel asked. "It sounded like..."

"FEI. Federal Entity Index. We investigate the validity of aberrant people and other creatures." Rice corrected.

"Like little green men?" Garrett asked.

Pel shrugged. "And witches?"

"Something like that," Rice said. He pulled two small boxes from his suit jacket and handed one each to Pel and Garrett. Inside were business cards with their names and phone numbers. "You'd still be working for your government. Same pay. Same health insurance. All that crap doesn't change. Let's go get you set up at your desks."

"What about vacation? Sick days?" It seemed to be all Pel could think to ask.

Rice pointed down the hall. "Human resources is right down that hall. They'll have all the answers."

Garrett looked up from his cards and watched the others leave the room. He and Pel already had cards and desks. The FEI seemed pretty sure he and Pel were going to be OK with moving to a new organization. He made a mental note as to where Rice said the HR office was as he put the cards in his pocket. With a sigh, he followed the others.

20

Morgan entered The Ground Up through the back entrance, staying as casual as he could. He felt naked walking around without his rifle, and found himself patting his denim jacket to make sure the pistol was still in the holster underneath it. He was also cognizant of the buck knife in his right boot, the small dagger strapped to his forearm and brass knuckles in his back pocket.

Harper's handler, Wallace, assured him the tracking device in Deena's backpack was working perfectly. Wallace had hidden it there at Marsh's behest when Deena started going missing and they began to worry the girls would run away. Across the street from the coffee house, Wallace was waiting in the SUV and Morgan was thrilled he didn't suggest coming in to help.

The place was pretty much empty, just a lone laptop guy at a booth and a young woman standing at the counter waiting for her order. Morgan casually stared at the menu for a moment, then the travel mugs and other crap on the back wall. Out of the corner of his eye he looked around to make sure he hadn't missed anyone in a dark corner.

He followed the arrow on a restroom sign to see the door to the women's room wide open. He felt the muscles in his back relax and he sighed in relief. As the woman walked off with her coffee, Morgan smiled and stepped forward. "Hi—" he paused to look at the kid-behind-the-counter's nametag. "Hi, Kevin. How's it going? Can I get a…" he looked back at the menu. "A large mega mocha?"

"You mean a vendi Mocha Mega?" Kevin said with a half-smile.

Morgan's eyes narrowed and he patted his jacket. "Right."

"Anything else?"

Morgan looked at the large glass case next to the cash register. "How about one of those blueberry scones? Those look good."

"It's actually raspberry, do you still want it?"

Morgan looked around and fixed his eyes on the guy with the laptop. He could be a witness. Morgan decided to play it cool since he needed the kid. Needed the information he might have. "Yes. That's fine."

Morgan heard footsteps behind him and assumed someone had come in through the back door just as he had. He casually started to turn to get a look at them.

"You're going to order a girly drink like that?" It was his mentor's voice. "Nice skirt, Sally. Want him to put an umbrella and a little slice of fruit in it, too?"

The kid fired up the blender to make Morgan's drink, creating a ruckus.

"Fuck off," Morgan mumbled.

Kevin stopped the blender and looked over at Morgan. "Did you say something?"

Morgan looked around innocently and then shook his head no. Kevin fired up the blender again.

"This is your chance, Morgan. You find this girl and you can write your own ticket. You want to be Marsh's number one again? *Kill both of the girls.*" Morgan could feel the breath on his neck, see Brandt leaning over his shoulder. "You want to get in good with one of the competitors like Thorpe and go to work for her as her right hand man? Hey! Kill the girl. It's a win-win." He stepped out in front of Morgan and looked him in the eyes. "Who do you help out by letting her live? Certainly not yourself. The plan has to be to kill Deena and Harper, and while you're at it, put some holes in that weirdo in the car." He pointed over his shoulder.

"Marsh wants me to try to talk to her first for some reason."

The blender stopped and Kevin smiled at Morgan a bit nervously.

"Marsh is a dumb-ass. Deena needs to be out of the picture, he just doesn't want to come right out and say it. It's a deniability thing."

Morgan leaned against the counter. "Hey. You seen a girl in here lately?"

Kevin looked at him blankly. "There are girls in here all the time. Constantly. I mean, like a stream of them. Anyone in particular?"

Morgan looked around again, fixing on the lone guy working at his laptop. "Long dark hair? Late twenties?"

"Not ringing a bell. Better description, maybe?"

"What a dufus. I think he needs some help with his memory," Brandt said.

Morgan shook his head a bit at the thought. "I don't know…"

"Does this help?" A photograph was thrust past Morgan to the clerk.

Morgan turned and found Wallace holding the picture. "You left this in the car," Wallace mumbled.

Morgan looked from Wallace to Brandt, who was standing behind him. He wondered where Wallace had come from and if he was really there holding a photo of Deena. When Kevin took it, Morgan was able to relax a little.

"Hmmm. You guys cops or something?"

"No. We're her mom and dad," Morgan said.

Brandt moved around the men. "This idiot's trying to horn in on your work. He was going to stay in the car, right? Now he's here? He's blowing the whole thing. What the hell?" He nodded at Morgan. "Watch your back, friend. Watch your back."

Kevin looked Wallace over and continued. "Looks like the older sister of the girl who was in all day yesterday." He stuck a straw in a drink and handed it to Morgan.

"Older sister?" Morgan took the drink and sucked some coffee through the straw before deciding it really didn't look at all manly. The coffee was good, though.

"The girl who was here had to be, I don't know, sixteen or seventeen."

"But they looked alike, right?" Wallace asked.

Kevin looked the big man up and down. "Yeah. The one in here yesterday had a birthmark where this one has a tattoo." Kevin pointed to the smiley face tattoo showing on Deena's shoulder in the picture.

"Not a tattoo, though?"

"Not unless whoever did it wasn't much of an artist."

"All day, huh?"

"A few hours. Then her friend came, she got a call and ran out." Kevin looked behind himself and then under the counter. "Left so fast she forgot her bag. It's around here somewhere." He opened a cabinet door on his right under the counter, then another on his left and pulled out the backpack.

Morgan's eyes narrowed. That explained why Wallace's tracker was off. She must've known about the device and dumped the bag to throw them off.

Morgan started to take the bag, but the kid stopped him.

"Mom and dad, huh?"

Morgan pulled out a fifty-dollar bill and stuffed it in the little plastic tip jar. "We miss our little girl so desperately."

Kevin took his hand off the bag.

As they walked out of The Ground Up, Brandt followed. "Are you stupid? You're giving that kid a fifty? That's nuts. You should'a clocked him or worse," he said. "In my day, this place would've been in flames by now. You're a moron. Since when do you leave witnesses? That kid will sing to every person with a badge that comes around. How many cameras did that place have?"

Crossing the street to their vehicle, Morgan wondered if the man was right. Who would really come looking out here for evidence, though? Who would think to stop at that particular coffee joint?

Morgan stopped as they reached the SUV. He yelled across the hood to Wallace. "Hey. I just remembered something. Be right back."

21

The rumble and sway of the train calmed Deena's nerves for a bit. Avi had deliberately picked a seat near the middle of the car, just in case someone came at them from either direction. He had left to find the bathroom and do whatever his morning routine was. He'd dozed a few times in the night, and so had she, but Deena couldn't imagine either of them had managed to get more than a couple of hours of sleep total.

Out the window, the vast countryside of the West Coast sailed by as the sun rose, with the ocean poking into her line of sight occasionally. The crumbling buildings of small communities and former one-horse towns filled her view every ten or fifteen minutes, with few larger cities to gain her interest. It was mostly cow towns and grain silos followed by the rocky greeting that northern California presented. They'd stopped twice so far at small stations. Even after the stops, no one had come into the car. She couldn't imagine many people had boarded.

She stared at wheat fields for as long as she could before digging in her bag for a magazine. It was a long trip back from Seattle to L.A. She flipped through the pictures, never resting her eyes on one for more than a couple of seconds before flipping again. She turned her attention back to the window and watched the scenery whiz by.

It was going to be a long trip back.

The men that came in from the next car appeared abruptly. They pushed aside the metal door and slammed it shut behind them. She recognized them from Marsh's organization. She'd worked with them in some manner or another on a job once. The lead man was very familiar. His name was Ramirez and he had a broad scar across his face that Deena had given him years ago. They were not friends. Another of them was a thug whose name escaped Deena, but she was sure it rhymed with tree or maybe limb. She only vaguely recognized the other two men. They all focused on her and approached without a word passing between them. She took a deep breath and waited for them to sit across from her.

"Hello, Deena," Ramirez said. He didn't sit. "We're here to make sure you make it back to the city. Boss wants to talk. He's kinda worried about you."

"That's sweet, but I'm not interested in going anywhere with you." Deena looked around the car to see only a couple of other people now scattered throughout her section of the train.

"What's going on? We're all on the same team here, right? You work for Marsh, we work for Marsh. Let's just go have a talk with him. Together." Ramirez said.

"I'm on my way. I certainly don't need an escort." She was sure of it.

Ramirez nodded. "They said you might be a little foggy. Said maybe that voodoo you do might have clouded your head, and that's fine. You'll get better." His tone was soothing. Like a TV doctor giving a patient a pep talk. He sat down across from Deena and smoothed out his khaki pants. "Just let us help."

"I don't need help."

"Your sister seems to think you do."

Deena was sure her sister did think she needed help. She always had. "I find it hard to believe you've talked to Harper. And I remember what happened the last time you touched her." Deena stared at the scar that went from his forehead down to his chin. "Didn't go so well."

Limb sat down across the aisle from Deena. He seemed to be a little more business-like than Ramirez. "At the next stop, in about five minutes, we're all going to get off this train. Some more of our coworkers will be waiting there, and we'll get in the car and go." Limb was posing, acting cool, but Deena could feel the tension. He'd been sent to bring back a very scary individual and he knew he wasn't up for it. "It can be that easy." He slid his windbreaker aside to reveal a pistol concealed there. "But we don't mind making it hard."

Deena laughed at him. "You *do* know who I am and what I can do, right? You think a gun is really going to throw a scare into me? I don't scare easily."

22

Deena at 16 the first time around

Deena loved it from the moment they stole the pickup truck and headed out on the interstate. It was a release from the confinement she'd felt from the day they ended up in the crappy little town their foster family called home. The breeze through the open windows made her hair wave in and out of the window like a majestic flag of her own tiny country.

They ended up camping at a state park for nearly a month. They'd driven for two straight days, taking turns every few hours. They hadn't had much time to pack before they left, but among other things, they had sleeping bags, bread, peanut butter and enough feminine hygiene products to last them into the next year.

The first night, they started a fire and made s'mores without graham crackers and stared at the flames from opposite sides.

"What're we going to do?" Harper said. "We can't keep driving for the rest of our lives."

"Why not?" Deena hadn't seen much of the world, and this seemed like the perfect opportunity. They could drive from town to town and eat peanut butter for the rest of their lives and that would be just fine with her.

"We've been lucky so far. No one's spotted the stolen truck, or speculated what two underage girls are doing driving it - first of all." Harper flung a burnt marshmallow into the fire. "Second; we didn't have that much money to start with and gas has already taken a chunk out of that."

Money wasn't a big factor in Deena's thinking. Only freedom and staying on the road made the list. "We could head to Augustine, the Thompsons moved there when we were in high school. You got along with Jenny Thompson. I bet they'd loan us some money."

"Did you have an aneurism that I didn't notice?" Harper asked. "They threatened to kill you the last time we saw them. You nearly burned down their garage."

Deena honestly felt the Thompsons would be willing to let that go. It was years ago, when she was six, and it was an accident. "You don't think they'd be over that?"

Harper's face was unreadable in the flickering light, but Deena was sure she was scowling.

"Fine," Deena said and stretched herself out on the sleeping bag. "We'll think of something." She rolled away from Harper. In the faint light dancing on the trees nearby, she thought about the fight with Mike and how easy it had been. How she moved so fluidly and how the blob on her arm had been itching ever since. And it had gotten larger.

"Dot?" Harper sounded farther away. "What do you think will happen when they catch up with us? Mike..."

"What're you complaining about? I'm the one who did it. All you did was try to protect me—least that's how I'll tell it."

Harper was sniffling. "Whatdya mean, that's how you'll tell it?"

"I'll tell them I panicked and tried to run away, but you wouldn't let me go alone. They'll let you off, no problem." Deena thought about how easily it had been to get Harper to leave. She laid it on thick about how the police would come after her too as an accomplice or an accessory or something. Harper was the one who panicked and went along with it. "I mean, they might ask you about who stole the car, you can just blame that on me. They'll never know you did it."

Deena thought again about the fight. She remembered the dark crust of her knuckles; the blood. She remembered the rush of adrenaline.

She remembered how much she liked it.

23

The room was quiet except for the occasional typing on keyboards. Garrett looked over at Pel, who he assumed was doing some high-level analysis of the data regarding Deena's whereabouts, or using the city's camera system for surveillance of ATMs or traffic lights. Or updating her Facebook status to read "Available". It was hard to tell.

Rivers and Rice were off doing God knows what - they'd left in a hurry. They'd talked about a breakthrough with something but refused to elaborate as apparently Pel and Garrett didn't need to know about whatever it was yet.

"Lot of government double talk," Garrett said.

The furious typing slowed long enough for Pel to mumble her agreement and then the tapping ramped up again.

"If they don't want us to know shit, why did they ask us to be here? Why did they even bother to find out if we wanted to come aboard?"

Pel looked up and her hands went still. She looked flustered and confused for the moment. "*Did* they ask us? Were we invited?"

"Sure we were."

"They said 'Would you like to come and work for our division?' at some point?" Pel asked.

"I…" Garrett stopped to think about it. Somewhere. The first conversation in the car, maybe? "Sure they did." Only the more he said sure, the less he was of it.

"Huh," Pel said and went back to focusing her attention to the screen.

There was a folder in front of Garrett with a map of possible sightings of Deena and her crew, which now apparently included one of their star witnesses in the eventual trial against Marsh, Stanley Yuko. The map was available on the server, but Garrett made Pel print him out a hard copy, even though the data online was updated in real time.

"You think we're doing the right thing, joining them?" Pel whispered.

Garrett looked up from his maps. He'd been contemplating that as well, mostly when he saw what had happened to the others like Deena. "I think everyone here certainly has the best interest of the public at heart."

"That doesn't really answer the question, does it?"

"I understand your concerns, I think. I have them too," Garrett said. "I'm worried about what's going to happen once we get Deena behind bars, if we ever catch up with her. Truth be told, I don't know if we can affect a change here and I don't know if I like being that out of control. And I'm not sure I like the way they treat these Incubators. They say 'Ink' with such, distain." It was the best answer he could give. His head hurt from thinking about it. So far, they were hunting criminals that happened to have a very special ability. What would happen when they just started rounding them up, no matter what their rap sheet looked like?

"We can always go back to our old jobs at the Bureau," Pel already looked a little defeated.

"And forget this is going on? No." Garrett said. "Besides, we just got here. With your tech skills and my good looks, we'll be running this place in a week."

"I think we—" Pel shut up when Rivers walked through the door.

"You both should come have a look at this," Rivers said. Rice followed him into the office.

"What is it?" Pel asked.

Rice looked extremely happy with something. Garrett guessed the man was pleased with himself more than anything, but Rice was hard to read.

"The Department of Justice has released a prisoner to us. It's an Ink we've been trying to get for a while." Rivers led the way through the hall into areas that Pel and Garrett hadn't been before. They passed offices with nameplates but no titles, bare white walls and smooth grey floors. In this section of the office, there were more people, most of them in white lab coats and shiny black shoes. It smelled more and more like a hospital, with a chemical stench that made him flinch at first.

Garrett looked at Pel and stood. "Is this guy beneficial to the investigation?"

"Beneficial to the whole department."

They walked further, twisting and turning, so that Garrett was eventually sure he couldn't find his way back. Twice, Rice took out his identification badge and placed it by the door before it would open. "What? No retinal scans? No fingerprint ID? I was starting to think this was a high-tech operation." Garrett said.

"You've seen way too many movies," Rivers said.

Going through the last door, they came to a hallway where one wall was all glass. Rivers and Rice stepped up and Pel and Garrett followed. The wall looked down on what appeared to be a hospital surgery room with a single bed in the center and equipment surrounding it. A large, muscular man was restrained on the table, straps holding him down at the waist, wrists and forehead. "This is Leonard Franco. Arrested a year ago in a murder-for-hire racket in Trenton, New Jersey. The feds have been holding him since his capture. He'd been making grocery money by killing scumbag husbands for harried wives and breaking kneecaps for a loan shark."

Garrett looked at Leonard. With the man's size and implied strength, it wasn't hard to see why he got into that line of work. Anyone saw him coming, they'd likely cough up what they owed. "How's he going to help us, exactly?"

"He has the same thing inside him the rest of our subjects do. Same thing Deena Riordan has," Rice said. "It's a good opportunity. He's the first Ink we've grabbed in a long time."

The man on the table hadn't moved since Garrett started watching. "Is he still all right?"

"What kind of question is that? Of course he's all right," Rivers snapped.

"With the track record of keeping these people alive, I thought it might be smart to ask," Garrett said.

"He's fine." Rice pulled out his phone and started tapping away on it.

"What's going to happen to him?" Garrett asked.

The clean white room was cold, quiet and smelled of antiseptic. None of the noises from the other room bled through, though there was a speaker on the wall that allowed everything to be heard if the switch was flipped into the on position.

"Same thing that's happened to the rest, I suppose. They'll study him to figure out what makes him tick, where his power comes from," Rivers said. He was staring into the other room with his arms folded. Rice stood next to him, doing the same.

"They'll dissect him like the ones you showed us?" Pel asked.

Rice looked annoyed. "I doubt it. That didn't work the last several times. Highly unlikely they'll do it again. We need Inks to use as long-term study subjects."

"Gets hard to explain to the superiors," Rivers said.

It was difficult for Garrett to believe that the only thing holding them back from cutting a man open and doing something that would surely end his life was the fact that someone would ask questions. Garrett knew the letter of the law as an agent of the federal government and was well versed in the rules of how prisoners needed to be treated. It made him wonder again what exactly he had stumbled into with Rivers' group. "Ain't that a bitch?"

"Look," Rivers added. "We've learned from our mistakes. The doctors will try any number of things before going to the extreme of removing that thing. Nope. Leonard here will be with us for a long time to come, if all goes well."

"And the girl? What about Deena? What if we get our hands on her?" Pel asked.

Rice put his phone back in his suit jacket. "We'll use what we learned from this guy and try to apply it to her."

"So you'll *try* not to kill her as well?" Garrett looked at the huge man on the table again. He could see a dark band around the man's arm and assumed it was the same thing Deena had on her.

Rivers turned and walked back toward the door.

"We always try," Rice said.

Men and women wearing alabaster clean-suits began to surround Leonard in the room below, checking the machines that surrounded him, and taping tubes to him that jutted out at all angles. More men came in with tablets and notebooks, collecting data and checking readings.

Rivers grunted and turned for the door. "We've got some time; let's check in with Stanley to see where we stand. I really hate to leave this guy, though. I think we could learn a lot from an Ink as active as this one."

"Yeah. Hate to take a break long enough to possibly save Harper's life."

"Marsh isn't going to do anything to Harper before Deena gets there. He wouldn't want to lose his bargaining chip." Rice said.

"You've got this guy to play with, why are you still so hot to get her? Maybe you should study him first." Garrett couldn't help but wonder aloud. After all, he didn't want two of these people hanging around. It sounded like more trouble than they needed. He was all for bringing criminals to justice, but why not go after her when they were better equipped with information from the man they already had?

"We're prepared to get these things off the street. *All* of these things. Would you rather have them roaming free?" Rivers asked. "If you have a gang that robs a bank, do you stop once you catch one? Is the job done? This is what we do here; we track these... creatures down. If getting a few Inks off the street helps us understand what makes them tick, maybe we can find a cure or a means of making them normal again."

"What if they don't want to be normal?" Pel whispered quietly, as if she were concerned the man in the next room could hear her.

"It's obvious some of them don't want to be normal. If they can use this power to create the kind of mayhem we've seen, why would they? They can do whatever they want and most of what they seem to want isn't good," Rice opened the door and held it for the others.

"We don't know if all of them want to use it for criminal purposes," Garrett said.

Rice nodded as Garrett walked past. "You're not talking about the girl, right? You took a look at that file on her and her sister, right? You saw what they've done."

"I didn't say anything about her. I'm just saying that we're lumping all of these people in based on just a few…"

"Just a few? How many do we know that aren't criminals? How many good Inks have we met so far? Exactly none." Rivers pushed the button for the elevator and sighed.

Rice handed Garrett a folded piece of paper.

"Go shake Marsh up a bit, just to let him know we're keeping him in our sights," Rivers said.

"Is that a warrant?" Pel asked.

"No. We haven't been able to obtain a warrant with the evidence we have right now. We know how your partner hates technology, so we wrote down Marsh's address for him on that piece of paper," Rivers said.

Pel laughed, though it was obvious she didn't want to give Rivers' joke any credit.

"Why do you want me to work here?" Garrett asked as he crumbled the paper and shoved it in his pocket. "We don't exactly mesh."

"I like you," Rivers smiled and stepped into the elevator.

"That's news. You're not exactly my favorite person right now."

Rice laughed. "He'll grow on you. He grew on me."

"Like a fungus, I'm sure," Garrett stepped to the back of the elevator with Pel.

24

Deena was keenly aware of the other passengers in the train car who had absolutely nothing to do with her life and the wrong turns it had taken. "Look. Let's stop this. Walk away."

"Or what?"

Deena knew they weren't giving up that easily, but wanted to stall them until she could find a way to move their conflict to a new location. That most likely meant waiting for the train to stop. Her arm was beginning to hurt—the skin felt like it was melting off her wrist and forearm. "I don't know what's going to happen here, guys. But it's been a pleasure working with you."

"What?"

Deena stood. "Well, I'm not getting off this train willingly. And I'm not waiting for us to get to the station where more thugs can gang up on me." She stepped into the aisle and walked toward the door. "I'm just asking that we take this somewhere farther away from these people." She nodded to the next train car.

The men looked at each other for a moment, clearly uncomfortable with engaging Deena or moving to another area. She felt a little better about the situation then. They were only there to stall her. For all their bravado, they were the delaying tactic. "Are you coming?" Deena put her hand on the handle to the door that led to the next car. She could see through the little window that the next car was more crowded. She wondered if the pain in her arm meant that she still could use the power she'd come to rely on so much. If she did, would it consume her again?

"Look, let's just sit down and talk about this," Ramirez said. "We don't have to get physical or anything. Just talk." His partner nodded in agreement.

"Afraid I'll make the good side of your face look like the other half? Nah. I think we should get it over with. I mean, we're not far from the next station, it's apt to get crowded in here." She moved herself back toward the men, feigning shock that they didn't want to follow her. She stepped closer, but her body was still angled towards the door. Ever since the plane, she'd felt clouded and hazy, but here, as the adrenaline built within her, she felt the veil lift.

The men were standing then, Limb held his hands out in a placating posture. "You should know Marsh has been clear that he doesn't much care if you come back alive or not."

"I figured as much."

"Just so we know where this is going," Ramirez said. He raised his hands and took a fighting stance in the aisle. The other men looked at him with widened eyes. Deena had been correct, none of the men really wanted to fight her except Ramirez.

He came on quickly, swinging a left hook and a follow-up right that she avoided easily. She responded by stepping closer and landing a punch to his ribs that left him gasping for air. A shout alerted Deena that one of the other men was coming up behind her. The scream had come from one of the other passengers. They were all on their feet now and moving toward the exits to change cars. She was happy that they were getting out of harm's way–a little dismayed that not one of them wanted to stay and help the girl being attacked by a bunch of large men, but oh well. She had no idea how the fight was going to go and would rather not see a Good Samaritan get hurt for no good reason.

The confines of the aisle limited what Deena could do in response to the thug that approached her from behind, so she swung back and kicked him in the jaw, then the chest, sending him sprawling into his companion. Ramirez attacked again, this time plowing into her like a tackling dummy. Much like the first time they'd fought, he had no style, just brute force. Fists over finesse. He got her in the shoulder with a solid punch then he was on top of her, forcing her to the ground with his weight. He continued to push her, though he was hampered from hitting her due to the seats on either side of them. She could see his crew was becoming bolder with the success he was having, and they moved in to help.

Her arm felt heavy, like it was tied to a cinderblock. Since she couldn't punch, Deena reached up and grabbed Ramirez's neck and noticed her hand was slowly turning black. She began to mumble words to control the Shadow Energy as it welled up within her. She didn't know what would happen this time if she let it loose.

"That crazy voodoo shit ain't going to help you this time," Ramirez said, and he swung his arm over his head to punch her just above the temple. He managed a second in the same manner. Deena could feel a trickle of blood start on her forehead.

"All right. That's enough." Deena could hear Avi's voice from behind Ramirez. "Let her up," he said.

Ramirez looked over his shoulder. "What are *you* doing? You're supposed to be driving this bitch back to the office right now."

"Let her up."

"What? Did she sweet-talk you or something? All you had to do was get her in the car and get back to the L.A." He looked down at Deena. "And yet, here you are."

Deena heard the hammer being pulled back on a gun.

"You gonna shoot me?" Ramirez asked.

Deena took the opportunity while Ramirez was distracted to bring her knee up into his groin, forcing him to crumple and giving her the chance to slide out from under him. One of the other men took out a gun and Avi shot him quickly. Everyone else ducked for cover behind seats and Deena was sure she heard more guns being drawn and wished she'd been carrying one of her own.

Ramirez and one of the other men she didn't know were closer to Avi, so Deena moved to the other end of the car, where Limb and the man Avi shot were. She moved quickly from row to row, using the seats as cover. The men fired a few shots as she got closer. She heard Avi and Ramirez fighting behind her. After she heard another barrage of shots, Deena ran toward Limb and leapt over the last row of seats to land on him, knocking the gun out of his hand in the process. She landed blow after blow quickly, not giving him a chance to recover. Limb tried to get up, but she got on top of his chest and planted one knee on his throat, choking off his air supply. He flailed with his arms, trying to knock her off, but he'd already begun to panic. His attacks were weak and she parried them easily. Limb's eyes were getting wide as he realized he was close to losing consciousness.

There was a shot then and Deena felt like someone had hit her with a hammer. She turned and saw the man Avi shot earlier was lying on the ground, but had a gun pointed at her. A wisp of smoke hung in the air in front of his face. She looked down to see a hole torn in her shirt near the center of her chest. Her lungs suddenly burned with each breath and she could see blood begin to seep out from between her fingers. Limb began coughing, as Deena's pressure on his windpipe eased, and he pushed her off. She sank against the side of the car, not sure what to do next or if there was anything she actually could do.

At the other end of the car, she could see Ramirez and Avi still fighting. The punches landed in slow motion until she saw the knife in Ramirez's hand. It swung in a wide arc, slashing across Avi's chest once, then twice. As Avi reeled backward into the train's doorframe, he lost his balance, and Ramirez took the opportunity to plunge the blade into Avi's stomach.

Deena couldn't scream. Her chest hurt when she tried. She looked down at the wound, and found that the blood that had been pouring from the hole had turned to black, like the tentacles that she'd hoped were gone from her life. It poured from the hole until the blackness caught up with, and enveloped, the blood.

She thought she might pass out as her chest became hot.

25

Deena at 16 the first time around

One day Deena and Harper pushed their stolen truck into the lake and proceeded to take two bicycles they'd found unattended in the park. They planned to ride into the nearest town. If they were lucky, they could eventually make their way to Los Angeles and get work. The city wasn't far. Another day or so by bike. They were filthy and starving. They'd been living like raccoons; breaking into coolers and stealing snacks from campers and hikers to get by. Deena was actually getting good at catching fish in the lake, sometimes grabbing them out of the water with her bare hands. Of course, Harper wasn't fond of fish. They'd avoided even little towns for fear of being recognized, but they were just desperate enough to brave the big city.

They took a back trail around the lake and through the pines, with the intention of taking an old service road into town. A good deal of the trail was uphill and, as undernourished as they were, they tired quickly and rested by walking the bikes for a bit.

"We really need to steal something good. Steaks, maybe," Deena said. "I'm sick of peanut butter and if we steal one more picnic basket full of baloney sandwiches, I'm going to scream." The lack of food was driving Deena crazy, but she knew it had to be killing her sister. Harper liked things just so. She liked particular brands of cereal in the morning, with fresh bananas and strawberries—usually organically grown. She drank her special morning blend of tea that she made Dad buy from the local market, thin sliced bagels with cream cheese and fresh squeezed orange juice. She was a pain in the ass. "Want to knock over a deli or something?" She said it as a joke, but the sudden burst of adrenaline that followed made her feel amazing. Catching the fish even gave her a rush that she hadn't expected. It reminded her of the day they'd left home.

Harper said nothing. She looked exhausted from the ride, and for the last few days seemed like she was seriously considering calling someone to come get her and save her from this nonsense.

"Roast beef! Goddamn I miss roast beef." Deena said. "Swiss cheese? Mmmm."

"Easy there Gilligan, we've been hiding in the woods for a month, not lost on a desert island for a year," Harper said.

"You have absolutely no imagination and no soul."

"What does roast beef have to do with having a soul?" Harper asked.

Deena was about to needle her sister, just for something to do, when she heard voices ahead. "Shhh. Harper, wait." The two stopped and Deena guided her sister closer to a nearby tree. In the distance, a shiny black car was idling on the service road. A white cloud streamed from the tailpipe and they could see the outline of someone sitting in the driver's seat.

"Maybe we could go kick this guy's ass and take his car," Deena said. She was desperate enough to try, and she felt her arm ache again when she suggested the violent act. She'd done nothing illegal in her life. Never stolen anything. Barely jaywalked. Never got into a real fight, other than the one with Mike, of course. But she was sure she could do it and she was itching to give it a shot. Something told her in the back of her mind that she could do anything she wanted. And it made her want to try. For the first week after they ran, Mike's death was all she could focus on. She shook violently as she cried some nights thinking what she'd done. Her conscience managed to break through the fog in her head in tiny random moments. The guilt had nearly made Deena cave to Harper's pleas to return home. But the next week, the dot on her arm began to grow larger, and the death moved to the back of her line of thinking. By the next week, the whole incident seemed like something that had happened to someone else. Maybe she'd seen it on television or a video game. It got so she had trouble remembering his name.

Harper winced at the idea. "The car looks pretty fancy, I think someone would be more apt to come looking for it than they would the crappy pickup we sent swimming this morning."

They soon found the source of the voices; three men were standing in the ditch by the tree line. The girls were startled that they were so close to them without noticing. The two men in back were shoving another man in a torn trench coat; moving him along with no allowance for him to walk on his own. The man was cussing and screaming at the other two, who gave no response.

"Let's get the fuck out of here before they notice us," Harper whispered.

"Why?"

Harper gently pushed her sister. "Just go."

The girls jumped when a loud crack cut through the relative silence of the woods. They turned to see one of the men had pulled out a gun and shot the one they'd been shoving. He kept the gun trained on the man in the trench coat as he fell face first to the ground. A wisp of smoke trailed out of the barrel.

"Christ." Harper's eyes got wide.

Deena instinctively reached up and covered her sister's mouth before Harper could make another sound. "We're not leaving. We're going to hold perfectly still right here until they leave. If they see us, we're dead," she whispered. "Nod if you understand?"

Harper's panicked expression told Deena everything. She was completely freaked out. She wanted to run. She wanted to get their bikes and pedal back to the campsite, hell, back home, but if the men hadn't seen them yet, moving would probably change that.

Harper nodded slowly and Deena took her hand away. Deena could feel a tear run down her own face, and didn't realize she'd begun crying until then. She didn't think it was out of fear. It felt more like happiness. Like she'd found something she'd been looking for.

They watched the men half-heartedly kick leaves over the body before brushing their clothes off.

"Mitchel!" Neither of the men had spoken and Deena turned to see a trio of men standing by the still-running car. The oldest of them was pointing at the girls. "Over there." The men closest to the girls looked around the woods for a moment before picking the sisters out. Both stepped toward them quickly and pulled their guns from their pockets as they did.

"Let's go, let's go, back to the bikes and take the trail down to the campsites," Deena said.

Harper leapt over tree roots and ran the way they'd come. Her footfalls crunched leaves and twigs as she stomped unsteadily down the incline.

The crack of a shot rang out as they ran, and the bark of a nearby tree splintered. "Oh God," Harper said.

"Keep moving, stay as close to the trees as you can." Deena was breathing heavy from the excitement and the exertion. Her head ached the moment that shot narrowly missed them, but it wasn't because she'd been hit by the bullet or anything else, it was like a compass in her head was pushing her to move in a different direction than she believed was wise. It was like the ache was moving her towards danger rather than away. Her limbs tingled and her head felt like water.

More shots filled the silence as they went. Deena watched Harper move on ahead, until she was behind some trees, and then Deena stopped following. She listened to the guidance her mind was giving her and moved in another direction.

Unfortunately, Harper chose a poor time to look around and tripped over some branches in her path. Her momentum carried her a few more feet in the air before dropping her on her face in the dirt. Deena heard the heavy footfalls of the men and watched her sister struggle to get up. Deena moved to conceal herself from the approaching danger, all the while following the pull in her head. She climbed the tree by bounding up it and grabbing a high branch to pull herself up. She'd never moved that quickly, that fluidly before and she had no idea she could climb a tree like that.

The men came around the tree from opposite sides. "That's enough," the tallest one said. They both immediately moved to Harper and towered over her. "Do you see the other one?"

Harper managed to scramble onto her butt, though the killers weren't going to let her do much more. "Look, just let us…"

"Shut up." The tall one again. "Find her." The chubby one started back toward the car.

Deena heard the tall man say, "Sorry chick, nothing personal," just as she dropped out of the tree onto the fat guy. That one shouted then, a deep roar of pain as she punched him. She withdrew her hand to hit him again and found the skin on her right hand had turned black. She let go of the man and he stumbled, clutching at his neck. She had no idea how hard she'd hit him.

The man menacing Harper turned his head to see what was happening, so Deena pressed her advantage. She grabbed the fat man's coat and pulled him closer. There was a flurry of suggestions in her mind and Deena opened herself to all of it. She slashed at the man's face with her hands, sending blood flying off into the woods. They fell to the ground together and rolled in the leaves and twigs on the forest floor before stopping perfectly still and silent.

Deena could see Harper and her would-be assassin both lean forward, both puzzled and both expecting either Deena or her opponent to stand up. Deena stayed still as she watched the tall man approach slowly. He stepped toward the tangle of people and clothing. "Mitch?" he asked to no response. He moved forward a few more steps, leaving Harper behind.

Deena waited until she heard her sister scrambling to her feet and running away. It would be the smart thing for Harper to do in the situation. Go get help. Run away. She heard her sister cautiously take a few steps before turning to run.

Harper got exactly ten steps before the gunfire began.

26

"We're looking for Deena and Harper Riordan," Garrett said. He showed Mr. Marsh his badge. Pel half-heartedly showed hers as well. She was looking around the room at all the tennis balls scattered around on the floor.

Marsh shrugged. "Look. I'm sorry. I run a large business here. Those names don't ring a bell with me."

"Sisters? You don't remember employing sisters in your office?"

"I don't get out in the field much, I'm more management. What do these girls do for my company?"

Garrett shrugged his shoulders. "We hear they kill people for your company."

"Heavens," Marsh said, almost laughing. "That's absurd."

"Is it?"

"Of course."

"What does Datura Industries do, then? If you don't mind us asking," Pel said.

"We have a number of divisions. We have an all-inclusive shipping and transportation wing, a construction arm, several Internet ventures. We're thrilled to see our research and development business is blossoming. I can't imagine listing them all for you."

Garrett turned and looked out at the gorgeous view Marsh had. He could see all the way up Figueroa and into the city. It was most likely a very expensive way to see L.A. "All completely legal and above-board, I'm sure."

"I'm sure," Marsh echoed. "I'd be happy to have my assistant, Stanley Yuko, give you a brochure or something detailing the vast Datura Industries empire. Stanley would be glad to put you in touch with our human resources department. They can tell you whether those girls you mentioned work for me."

"Deena and Harper Riordan," Pel said.

"Whatever." Marsh began to roll a ball around with his palm on his desk.

Garrett turned back. "Are we boring you?"

"I have to get back to work here. The 'vast empire' isn't going to run itself, you know."

Garrett winced at Marsh's huge fake smile. The overly white teeth seemed unnatural. "Take a look at these for me and we'll get out of your way." He pulled pictures from his jacket pocket of the sisters and put them in front of the man.

After just a second, Marsh pushed them back across his desk. "Sorry. I honestly have nothing to do with human resource decisions."

Garrett was flustered. He knew at least one of the girls was here. Stanley had told Rivers exactly where to find Harper, but they hadn't been able to get a warrant. At least that's what Rivers had told them. Garrett was only to ask questions, not explore the building and look for either of the girls. The hope was that Marsh wouldn't be stupid enough to kill the girl with the authorities sniffing around him. The fear was that the visit might spur him on to take her out of the building and have her killed somewhere else.

Of course, the wild card in any plan was what the other sister, Deena, would do. If the girl was as powerful and unpredictable as they said, there was no telling what she would do, and maybe that would keep Harper alive a little longer. Maybe long enough to actually get a warrant.

"I'm surprised you don't know Deena. I heard she was a big part of your organization," Garrett said. "I heard she was a pretty important part of the team."

"I know all the most powerful people here. I think I'd remember her."

Garrett nodded to Pel and they walked towards the door. "I'm sure if she gets here, she'll remind you."

If Marsh was afraid of Deena, his face didn't show it. "Well. If that's all you have for me, and if you don't have a warrant, I'll have my security personnel escort you out. I'd hate for you to get lost on your way back to your vehicle." Marsh waved to two tall men in matching navy blazers with the Datura Industries logo on them who had suddenly appeared in the doorway.

"That's kind. I'd hate to get lost too. Freaks me out," Pel said. "I'm shaking just thinking about it." She looked completely unaffected to Garrett, but he was still getting used to his new partner.

Garrett gave Marsh a wink and left the room. "See you soon." Without a warrant, things would be difficult.

27

Deena at 16 the first time around

Deena did a mental check of her condition, she didn't feel anything too wrong, other than a couple of dings in her arm and thigh that would probably become bruises later, but she couldn't be sure how bad it was until she moved. The problem with that, she found, was that her right arm was trapped under the heavy body. The tall man had moved out of her field of vision, but she could hear crunching leaves nearby where the man was approaching.

She was thankful the trench coat was over her, to provide some cover, but she couldn't see anything or anyone around her. She slowly moved her left hand over to attempt to free her other arm, but it was blocked by an object attached to the man's belt. She felt around and discovered it felt like another gun. She carefully removed it from the holster. She oriented it correctly in her hand and let it rest there. She'd never fired a gun before, though it felt right in her hand. It felt like another part of her body a part that had been kept in check for far too long. It was quite a bit heavier than she'd expected, and the fact that this man had been carrying two of them amazed her. It would have been a lot of weight to carry. The fact that she couldn't move her right hand reminded her that the man was used to carrying a few extra pounds. She was right-handed, but the gun felt just fine in her left.

She pressed the gun against the coat and pointed it in the direction she thought the footsteps were coming from. She heard Harper begin running in the opposite direction.

The first shot tore a hole in the coat and Deena choked at the acrid smoke that was trapped under the coat with her. She waved the gun hand wildly, pushing the jacket away so she could see and fired another shot at the same time which went wild. She spotted the tall man on the other side of Mitch. He looked surprised, like he'd just turned to shoot Harper when he was interrupted. As he turned, Deena shot him twice and forced herself to stop in case she needed the ammunition later. The whole thing took seconds, and Deena shuddered as the tall man fell. She turned and placed her foot on the fat man's side for leverage to free her trapped arm. The nudges her mind gave her made it all so easy.

Her arm ached and throbbed as she pulled it loose—she guessed it was from lack of circulation. But the more she examined it; she discovered it looked just fine. The blemish had migrated to her wrist and it seemed to be the source of the pain.

She knew Harper was talking to her, but she couldn't tell what she was saying. There was a sudden buzz in Deena's mind that seemed to make the rest of her body vibrate as well. The buzz sounded like a whispering voice telling her to do something in a foreign language. Nearby, a twig cracked. She pointed the weapon toward the noise.

There stood the men from the car. The older man had his hands in his pants pockets, but the other two had guns pointed at Deena. "Look little girl," the man said. "You won't kill us. You did what you had to do in the heat of the moment with Alex and Mitch there, and I'm impressed. But it's over now. You're not going to look me in the eye and shoot. Not when you have to think about it."

The joke's on you, Deena thought. I can't think. I'm reacting; I'm listening to the buzz of whatever is building its nest in my head.

Near Deena's feet, the fat man started groaning and writhing on the ground. As he rolled over, she saw he was bleeding heavily and his hand moved to the wound trying to stem the tide. It was a losing battle, but he struggled to his feet and took a swing at Deena. She twitched, like a jolt of electricity had coursed through her. She blocked his arm, preventing him from hitting her and then punched him with her free hand. A shadow passed over them and Deena looked for a bird flying in the trees, but found none. As she hit him again, a feeling like a dozen needles seized her arm. Her fist had not only turned black, but thin, jagged ridges were pushing their way up through her skin on each knuckle. She stepped back and screamed as the points pushed through.

She closed her eyes from the pain and lashed out at Mitch, hitting him again and again until he fell from her reach. Deena took deep, sucking breaths as she attempted to get a hold of herself. When she opened her eyes, she saw her hand was still black, but the strange protrusions had disappeared. Her knuckles weren't just black; they were crimson from all the punches she'd landed on Mitch. He was lying at her feet, his face an unrecognizable mess of slices and cuts.

"Impressive," the old man said. "That's something new."

Deena took a few breaths to analyze what had just happened. The now-constant rumble in her head told her it was perfectly natural. She struggled to argue with it because something about the fight seemed… less than natural. She kept the gun pointed down and decided that diplomacy of some kind might be good. The armed men kept coming out of the woodwork and who knew how many more were out there? "These two were pretty good at shooting an unarmed man in the back of the head, but they seemed to have a world of trouble with two small girls." She was just talking now; fully prepared to babble on and on until something felt right.

"Fuck! Deena, what are you doing?" Deena had all but tuned Harper out since the buzzing had started and as it reached a crescendo, Deena noticed her sister was standing by the big tree; looking from Deena, to the two dead men, to the newest men with guns. The look on Harper's face was slowly dissolving from horror to something else.

The men hadn't lowered their guns as Deena had. "Seems like the bulk of the trouble came from just one of the young ladies," the old man said. "Be that as it may, I assure you that Rousch and Morgan here—" He nodded to the man next to him. "Can more than handle little girls."

"They can handle little girls? Hope you don't ever have any full-grown adults come after you. That could get messy." Deena's body was still humming with anticipation of more violence. Anticipation, rather than dread.

The man smiled and shook his head. "You have a mouth that could get you in trouble. But from the look on your sister's face, she's used to it. Are you a troublemaker, young lady?"

She tapped the pistol against her leg involuntarily. It was as natural as someone else drumming their fingers on a desk when they were bored with a phone call or a business meeting. "So where does all this leave us? We gonna shoot it out? Or is there a middle ground here somewhere?"

The man's weak smile turned genuine. Deena could see he was amused by the tough-talking girl with the shaky hands. "Middle ground? What sort of middle ground?"

"You seem to be short a few goons. Maybe you want to upgrade to someone who can do some real damage." Deena felt a certain satisfaction at the look of shock on her sister's face. They had no prospects other than going home and that wasn't an option. Neither of them had been in contact with their foster parents and they hadn't heard any news on what sort of fate awaited them, but with Mike dead, it couldn't be good.

Harper moved only enough to sit herself down fully under the tree, the crisp crackle of the leaves the only sound. While her eyes still brimmed with tears, it appeared the rest of her had shut down. It was similar to the look she'd shown when Deena had first convinced her to leave after Mike's death.

28

Deena watched as Avi slid to the floor, his eyes staring blankly upward. Ramirez turned with his blade dripping blood and smiled at Deena. He'd seen she was still conscious and he began to advance.

The black ooze that was coming out of her gunshot wound had stopped flowing, and as she watched, it seemed to pull itself back in. The pain turned to numbness flanked by a tingling sensation. It was becoming easier to breathe with every inhalation. Her right arm still seemed heavy, and a glance told her it had turned completely black.

She looked over at the men next to her. The one who'd shot her, the one with a bullet in him, was hanging on. He was leaning on his elbow with his gun still in his hand. The man that she'd fought with and almost beaten was catching his breath and looking from her face to the rapidly closing wound on her belly.

With the wall of the train car to help her, Deena pushed her way to her feet, letting her body make some final adjustments. She reached deep within herself and thought of the words and images she'd used to control the Energy when she was doing work for Marsh. The images of power and the images of strings and ribbons. She thought of the words 'Sharp' and 'Cut'. She pictured a boiling pot bubbling over. Her body, the energy within, felt sluggish, but it was responding.

She let go of the wall as the man with the gun fired. He was five feet away, but she reached for him anyway, commanding the darkness within her to grab him. Long strips of blackness pulled themselves from her arm and wrapped around him. She pulled the man off the ground and slammed him against the wall, breaking the windows and sending spider web lines of cracks in the glass around him. His terrified cry was cut off after a second. Deena could feel the power building in her quickly, faster than she'd ever experienced it.

She heard a shot from the other end of the car; the man next to Ramirez had pulled his weapon and was shooting at her. She could feel the bullets hit her and exit the other side, but it didn't hurt, it was more of an annoyance. She looked down at the wounds in her body, where the bullets had entered, and saw the holes closing up with black liquid. Deena pulled the first man's limp body from the windows and threw it at the other end of the car, hitting the newest gunman and pinning him to the floor beneath what was left of his cohort. Ramirez managed to dodge and hide himself between the rows.

Behind Deena, Limb reached out and grabbed her right leg. She looked down at the man as he wrapped both hands around her knee. She thought of thorns and suddenly, thin, black spikes popped out of her jeans, forcing themselves through Limb's palms and fingers. As he shouted in pain, she extended the points further, until they pierced his face and further into his head. She withdrew the thorns and Limb's body fell to the floor.

"So I guess you didn't forget who you are after all," Ramirez said. He was still advancing on her with his knife, though more slowly. "I thought it was awfully easy for us to beat you."

No words came to Deena's mind, she just lashed out. She swung her hand in front of her and a whip's length of darkness issued from her left hand. She swung it in front of her and it sliced along the windows, leaving a cut in the glass and filling the air with a smell like burning wire.

"I've seen your tricks before. I'm not impressed."

Deena swung her arm again and the black line sliced the tops off the row of seats in front of Ramirez. It had sliced through the metal frames with ease.

Ramirez's face didn't register the fear that Deena knew he had to be feeling. Even she was surprised by what she could do. When she'd given him that scar on his face years ago, she'd been unfamiliar with her powers and still learning. But now she was more practiced, more deadly.

Deena reached out with both hands and grabbed Ramirez with the half a dozen tentacles that reached from her of their own volition and threw him into a row of seats behind her. She ran to Avi and dropped to her knees, scooping him up with her dark arms. Her body strength was amazingly increased and she lifted him with little effort. She stared down at him. "Avi? Avi? Talk to me." The darkness receded from her hand as she put her fingers to his neck to feel for a pulse. She couldn't find one. "Damn it." She felt his chest for movement, but all she found there was blood. "No." She wouldn't cry. Her body wouldn't let her. Instead, it covered up her hand in darkness again. She turned to see the man who'd been trapped by the body she threw. He was staring at her in shock. Not moving, his eyes wide.

As she advanced on him, he began shaking his head.

"Let's go, bitch," Ramirez had gotten himself out of the seats and was again standing in the aisle. A bloody cut had formed on his chin from his impact. He had his knife in his hand. Deena turned to face him and offhandedly a long jagged tendril shot out from her back and stabbed Ramirez's other goon. She heard a gurgle and then nothing.

"This is how it's going to be? Just us?"

When Deena spoke, her voice was almost a sigh. "There won't be two for long."

Ramirez began running at her and she did nothing to stop him or slow his progress. He was there in just four steps and she brought her arm up to block his slashing knife hand. She wrapped a tendril around that hand and tied it to her own and soon the blackness was reaching out from all over her body to grab his and bond it to hers. Their faces were just inches apart when she closed her eyes and thought of a buzz saw that would reach out to cut Ramirez to bits.

There was a screech that echoed in Deena's ears and a thud that shook the whole train car. When Deena opened her eyes, she was flat on her back, looking up at the ceiling of the car. She could see open air through a wide slice in the car above her. There were lines on either side of it where ragged swaths were also cut. She could hear the whistle of air coming in as the train continued on. Deena stood and found a wide cut had been gouged in the car below her. There was blood on the floor, but no sign of Ramirez. She walked toward Avi again, and noticed there were broad slices in the sides of the car as well. Apparently, whatever she'd done, whatever her power had done, had nearly cut the car in half. She got within a few feet of Avi and the car lurched. She heard the high-pitched squeal of metal on metal as someone applied the brakes to stop the train.

Deena put her hands on Avi's chest and kissed his forehead. She knew her powers still worked and that she was more or less in charge of them. She stared at Avi and considered how she would use those powers to get revenge for Avi and freedom for Harper. She'd done a lot of messy jobs for Marsh, but fighting her way through whatever he threw at her would likely top them all.

She looked at her torn clothing and saw that the Shadow Energy had withdrawn. The wound where she'd been shot was completely gone. It was healed over without a scar or a scratch. Expending that kind of power should have torn her apart. It should have regressed her back into diapers, but she felt fine. No, not fine. Just not like she was slipping back into the abyss of darkness she'd lived in for too long.

29

Deena at 16 the first time around

Deena could hear the words coming out of her mouth, feel her tongue forming the words. The more she looked at this man, the surer she was that she wanted to be a part of his world. She felt like a hand puppet with someone else calling the shots. The idea that Deena was actually angling for a job with this killer was unbelievable, and yet there was some desperate logic in it. They had nowhere to go, and instead of trying to find some menial job and slide by in the ugly world of fast food prep, to Deena working for a killer was the next step. And considering she'd just killed at least one of the criminal's men, Deena wasn't sure that was far from wrong. She had turned an accidental meeting into an all-or-nothing prospect. Guided the whole time by pushes and pulls from inside her head. Even if they had managed to get away, Deena feared the man would find them and kill them as witnesses.

"What are you doing?" Harper whispered to Deena. "These guys aren't fucking around."

Deena made a show of looking at the blood on her own shirt and the pistol at her side. "Duh."

Harper still looked vacant and spoke in a low monotone as she turned to the men. "We can do all kinds of things." She took a moment, and Deena hoped her sister could think of something worthwhile. "I'm a good driver."

There was still that odd smile on the old man's face; it looked a little pained as he responded. "My dear, I already have a driver," he nodded at the other man. "And he's rather good."

The other man nodded, a confident smirk on his lips.

"Surely you have other…" Harper jumped as a gunshot cut through the quiet forest.

The big man next to the boss took a step, as his head jerked back. The gun in his hand dropped slowly, and two reports issued from it, the muzzle flashes almost blinding to Harper. Bits of the earth and leaves between the two groups flew up as the shots landed harmlessly on the ground.

Deena's gun was smoking, pointed level again. "Looks like you're going to need a lift home," she said as the driver's knees gave out beneath him. He fell hard and didn't get up. Deena turned to her sister and winked. "Good thinking. Great idea." Deena

101

could feel a difference in herself, like her body was filling with a new sense of purpose and accomplishment. Harper's face sank.

The old man and his last man standing didn't change their expressions one bit in light of the new circumstances. None of the carnage seemed to faze them in the least.

"You think this prepares you to come work for me? You think this qualifies you?" The old man gestured around the forest. "You think killing a few poorly-compensated thugs is some sort of initiation? My name is Mr. Marsh. I control a very sizable portion of criminal activities in Los Angeles."

As the man spoke, Deena had trouble concentrating on what he was saying. She felt compelled to be with him and see to anything he wanted done. She looked at the ground, searching for a weapon one of the nearby men might have dropped in the scuffle, just in case someone else got antsy. She tried to keep her eyes on Mr. Marsh as she did. "I think you've got other problems than reading over my resume." Deena gestured with her own gun.

"What's to say I don't let you take me home and then have my doorman take you out into the alley behind my building and shoot you in the back of the head? And your sister, of course."

Harper looked like she was going to throw up. "All right. Let's just calm down here and decide how we're going to end this."

"I'm calm," Marsh said. And Deena felt it was true. He wasn't emotional, didn't raise his voice.

"Same here," Deena agreed. Her face was tense and her voice was tight, but her hand didn't shake and she seemed perfectly in control. There was just one of the man's goons left; the one he'd called Morgan. He stood with his arms crossed, looking just as passive as his boss.

"I run a number of businesses. Somewhat legitimate businesses. You can work for me in one of those," Marsh said.

Deena stared at him and thought about the gun in her hand. "I think we can do something more for you."

Marsh sighed. "What you've done here is quite impressive, but puts me in a tight spot as to what to do with the mess. I think girls of your age should take the time to grow up a bit before you so rashly start wishing for things you can't undo."

Deena looked around her and knew he was right. "There are already a number of things I can't undo."

Marsh nodded and pointed to the car. "I'm offering you a chance. We can each go our separate ways right now, or you can get in this car and come with me. You're obviously scared and confused and looking for something that will bring you some sort of stability. How long have you been living out here in these God-forsaken woods? The bugs, the animals. Ugh. You want a job? Get in the car and I'll find something for you to do. It may not be what you want, but it'll be a roof over your head and a little money until you figure out your life. I'll admit you have me intrigued."

"We're not signing up to be whores or anything. You understand that, right?" Deena said.

"I think we understand each other. That's an enterprise I've never found profitable to get involved with," Marsh said.

Deena started nodding and was ready to agree when Harper spoke up. "Wait a minute. You're making a deal for both of us? I get some say in this." Marsh turned to look at her and raised his eyebrows expectantly. "You say one of your legitimate businesses, what are you talking about?"

"We'll find something for you to do."

"For example, where?"

Deena watched them and couldn't help but be suddenly amused by the situation. It was an eighteen-year-old girl bargaining with a mobster over where he was going to let them work in his organization since they wouldn't be allowed to kill for him. They could leave. They could walk away right now, just as he said and find some life doing something else. Hiding somewhere else. But she didn't like living on the run. She couldn't imagine scrounging for food the way they had been. She'd told him they wouldn't be whores, but how long could they survive on the streets without turning to that?

And there was something about Marsh that made something within Deena complete. She'd stopped looking for another gun and found she couldn't take her eyes off of him. His voice had a quality that made her want to listen. Made her want to ingest all of his words, bit by bit.

"I have a restaurant in mid-town. They always need waitresses," Marsh said. "You can start there and we'll see where that takes you."

"Legitimate business?"

"Are you bargaining, now?" Morgan asked. "Take the damn jobs or hit the road."

Deena glared at him. Something made her want to fight—made her want to fight everyone. She felt like she could attack a whole army and win. Her heart felt like a stone rattling around in her chest and her arm was heavy. She looked at the little dot that had caused her so much concern as she was growing up. It had settled and almost resembled a smiley face.

"I don't know what you're doing," Harper said. "*You* don't know what you're doing."

"Then go home. Tell Dad I'm sorry for whatever shit I may have caused." For a moment, Harper looked like she might actually turn and go. But then, something sank in her and her shoulders dropped, arms unfolded and her hands fell to her side. "I can't let you go alone."

30

The doctors, scientists, men with clipboards, and women with needles cleared out of the large room, leaving only Pel, Garrett and Rivers with Leonard. Garrett looked around the room, taking in the equipment and stifling a sneeze from the smell of bleach. He settled himself onto a rolling chair that the doctors used to wheel themselves from station to station. Pel stood against the nearest wall, clearly still uncomfortable with the whole situation. Both she and Garrett were fine with interrogations, they'd questioned suspects before, but this would be something different. They were quickly entering a gray area, one clouded by the mix of drugs that had been fed to Leonard to keep his power from emerging. But how much was that cocktail affecting his judgment, were they essentially asking the man things he had no choice but to answer?

"Let's talk about how you became this thing," Rivers said.

"Thing? I think I'm pretty handsome. What'd'ya mean *thing*?" Leonard sounded tired, but defiant. "You don't find me hot?" His chest rose and fell with a little more labor than it should.

Rivers was unfazed. "We're talking about that power inside you. The power that landed you here in our company today. Where did it come from?"

Leonard's eyes drooped a little. "Who's the blonde? She's a little too hot to be a federal agent."

Pel rolled her eyes, but blushed in spite of herself. "They've changed the requirements at the academy."

"I have a thing for women with ponytails," Leonard said.

Garrett watched the exchange and understood it for what it was; suspect and interrogators feeling each other out to see their boundaries and how far they could go before they had to get down to business. The only difference was that Leonard had been through this already. He'd answered questions for the last year or so from dozens of different people. He'd spilled as much as he wanted and knew his story forward and back. Rivers was new to this particular party. He was asking the same questions everyone else had.

"We don't care about your criminal history. Don't want to know everyone you've robbed, smacked around, bludgeoned or looked at cross-eyed. We just want to understand what's going on inside your body," Garrett said.

Leonard laughed. "What's going on inside my body? Is this a high school Sex-Ed class? Are you going to tell me why I'm growing hair in my special place?"

"We were really hoping you could tell us all about those things," Rice entered the room with a tablet and crossed to hand it to Rivers. "How did this happen to you? How did you get this power?"

"Fuck you. I want special consideration." Leonard pulled at the straps holding his hands in place.

"Do you even know what you're saying? You have a decent list of pretty nasty crimes on your sheet and you want us to treat you with kid gloves? I don't think so," Rice said. "You'll get the same as everyone else."

"We hear how you normally treat our people."

"Our people?" Rivers asked.

"Inks. You don't think we know what you call us? Word gets around. People with shadows running through their veins don't do well in your hands." He tugged at the restraints harder. "They tend to disappear."

"Doesn't let you off for your crimes." Rivers looked indifferent.

"When you call us Inks, are you talking about the thing inside us? Or are you talking about us?" Leonard squirmed a little, getting comfortable.

Rivers' expression didn't change. He looked bored. "You just got here. Maybe we should talk in a few days, when you're less bitchy."

"I'm always this bitchy. A few more days of drugs and shock treatments aren't going to change that. You need me. You need me intact and cooperative if you want this whole thing to go well for you. How long did it take you to catch me? How long has this girl you're after been on the run?" Leonard was taking deep breaths. It was obvious that something, probably the drugs, was making him work harder just to talk. He wasn't pulling against his restraints like he had been. "I can help you. We find each other easily. Keep me happy and we can round the rest of them up."

"You're going to help us. Don't worry," Rivers said. "We're not making any deals though." He got up and walked towards the door.

Garrett had been taking it all in. He'd assumed that the FEI was a super-secret organization since he hadn't heard of it, but it was beginning to look like he was wrong. If the agency was already known by the very people it was tracking, they must not have a lid on it. He leaned close to Rice. "He's right, though, isn't he? I don't want to coddle a vicious criminal, but he has some sort of insight that we don't. He could be an asset."

"These people have never been straight with us. They say whatever they think will get them lenient treatment and never produce results. We've tried to be reasonable," Rice said. "We won't negotiate again."

It was quiet except for the hum of the machines pumping Leonard full of various liquids. "I volunteered."

Garrett turned to the prisoner. "What?"

"I volunteered to have this put into me. In the army. Back in 1975."

Garrett watched Pel finally step into the conversation. "That was forty years ago. You look about thirty years old to me. How's that possible?"

"How the hell would I know? I was thirty and I volunteered for an experiment. Every time I used this damn power, it took years off my life—not shortening it, no. It was like a rewind button. Making me temporarily younger when I used my powers. I steadily used them and managed to pretty much feel, think and look the same age for quite a long time. Others had different consequences, but I got to keep my boyish good looks."

Garrett looked the man up and down again. Leonard seemed like a fugitive from a bodybuilding contest where steroid use was encouraged. The veins in the man's arm were as thick as Garrett's thumbs. "What experiment?" Garrett asked. "Who did it?"

"It was some military thing. They wanted better soldiers."

"Military thing? What division? What branch? Name some doctors. We've heard this shit from a number of Inks now, but no one can give us specifics," Rivers said. "Give us something we don't already know."

Garrett was taken aback. There was nothing in the files or any of their conversations that mentioned a military experiment. "You already knew this stuff? Why didn't you say something? We are working on the same side, right?"

"We've heard this stuff before, but no one can prove it. There's no record of it in any of the research we've done. No other agencies have any info on it. It's hearsay," Rice said.

"Hearsay that you've heard from a number of your subjects now?" Pel was thinking along the same lines as Garrett. "Come on."

"If we're going to work together, we need to be able to trust you, and believe that you're being completely open with what's going on. I don't like surprises." Garrett understood the old "need to know" information dodge. He'd had superiors that withheld important details of an investigation on him before. But this was crazy.

"The federal government would never hide information on something like this," Rice said.

It was silent for a couple of beats before Leonard started laughing. "Whatever."

Garrett leaned close to Leonard. "So give us something new. Tell us something that makes you valuable to this investigation and not the smug crap everyone else has put out there. You're worried about not making it out of here? Hand us something."

"How the hell do I know what they've told you?"

"Start talking and we'll tell you when you hit new territory," Rivers said.

Leonard's lip curled as he stared at Rivers. "We know who you are. We *all* know who you are." He mumbled it, but Garrett was close enough to hear it.

"What's that?" Rivers said. "I didn't hear you."

"I was watching the Discovery Channel or some shit, and there was this show about parasites. Turns out there are all kinds of… bugs, I guess. They grab on to other insects and animals and kind of hijack them. And make them do things they normally wouldn't." Leonard took a second to think. "What the hell were those things called? Fuck, I don't know. But those parasites took over and made their hosts do whatever the parasites wanted."

"I saw an article on Reddit about those. They make their hosts do all kinds of crazy things that aren't in the host's best interest. It was pretty gross. Sometimes they lay eggs in the host to keep their offspring safe until they hatch. Nasty," Pel said.

"Something like that. Only here it messes with your mind and your better judgment. The first time that black shit bursts through your skin, you're done. You're not yourself anymore. The first person you see when it bursts out for the first time is suddenly your favorite person in the world. You'll do whatever that person says. Like those bugs? Those fucking bugs? You're totally in their power. You're basically at their whim. You'll do whatever they tell you to."

"They put an actual parasite inside you? It's a bug or something?" Garrett asked.

"I don't know, how would I know? I'm not a doctor. When the darkness burst out of my hands the first time? I was in the process of punching my commanding officer in the face. After this thing burst through my skin and it came out? I wanted to do everything the man said," Leonard's eyes narrowed. "Every little thing—no matter how much I didn't want to. It was like he had a remote control to my brain. Shoot someone? Yes, sir. Tear that guy's arm off and beat the ever-loving shit out of him with it? Yes, sir."

"And where is your C.O. now?" Rivers asked.

"Dead."

"You kill him?" Rivers followed up casually.

"Nope."

"You wanted to follow his orders so bad, what happened when he died?"

Leonard thought about it for a second and it looked like he might try to rip out his restraints again, but he didn't. "When that happened, I pretty much wanted to destroy everyone and everything. If someone wanted to pay me to get freaky, that was great, but no one ever had the same control over me again. No one." He took a couple of labored breaths. "And no one ever will."

"And what happened to this program you volunteered for?" Rivers asked.

"When they saw the terrible things that we were doing, they shut it down. Burned the program to the ground," Leonard swallowed hard and closed his eyes. "The higher-ups weren't too keen on the whole mind control, out-of-control aggression thing."

"But we have people running around right now with these things inside them. How did that happen?" Garrett was sure that Deena Riordan did not receive a super warrior injection from the army in the seventies.

Leonard didn't open his eyes. "No idea. Someone must've taken over the project."

Garrett motioned for Pel to join him outside the large interrogation room. "Well? What's your take on this?"

"We might be working for the wrong people," Pel said. She began leading the way down the hall, keeping her voice down.

"How so?"

"I'm worried about what might be happening to these people in our custody. I mean, I get what happened in the past. The military and the government didn't know what they had on their hands. But now they do." Pel stopped a good distance from the room. "These Incubators that we're tracking down? It's not really their fault someone tampered with their wiring."

"So we don't bring the girl in? We let her stay out there and kill whoever she wants?" Garrett said. "She's dangerous and unpredictable. It doesn't matter what's making her that way." Garrett considered the things Leonard had said about imprinting and focusing on the first person nearby when the power emerged and what that might mean for Deena. "Who do you suppose might have been the first person that Deena saw when these powers broke for her? Who do you think controlled her?"

They didn't have time to finish their conversation, as Rice interrupted. "We've got a possible sighting. We need you two to go check it out."

31

From a nearby hill, Morgan and Wallace stared down at the stopped train. They weren't alone. The hill was just off of a secondary highway and a dozen or so curious people had stopped to look down at the scene. What they saw was a common, everyday passenger train with several large rips across the roof and sides. Various law enforcement agencies surrounded the affected car; FBI, local police and sheriff's officers, and others were rapidly multiplying in number. Two deputies stood near the onlookers from the hilltop vantage point.

"Think they got her?" Wallace asked.

"You mean caught her? Nope."

"Killed her, then?"

Morgan squinted as the sun glanced off of another car pulling off the road. "Doubtful."

Brandt stepped through the crowd and approached Morgan. "Why are you just standing here?"

Morgan looked back at their SUV. "We should get going. We aren't going to learn anything standing up here. We might as well assume she's on the run and start looking for her."

"How far could she get on foot?" Wallace asked. "It's only been, what? An hour?"

"This jackass is slowing you down. You work best alone, and there's no reason to change that now," Brandt leaned in through the open window of the vehicle. Morgan sat down and slammed the door. "Get rid of him." Morgan looked over at Wallace.

From the back seat, Mr. Hector's voice chimed in. "No! The more the merrier. Let's all go look for the pretty girl."

Wallace pulled back onto the road as the monkey's cymbals began.

CLANG!

"Morgan? Hello? Where are we going? What's the plan?" Wallace asked.

Shutting his eyes and taking calming breaths, Morgan held his hand out the window to feel the wind blow across his fingers as they sped north into the mountains.

Wallace's baritone voice broke Morgan's calm. "Can we talk about what happened back at the coffee shop? Was that necessary? I mean seriously? We're trying to keep somewhat of a low profile here," Wallace asked. "That kid was cool with letting it go after you slipped him the cash."

Morgan had always been little intimidated by Harper's handler. Probably for the same reason many people made him nervous, the proximity. He loved to be miles away from people, loved the silence when it was allowed. Here, in the confines of the vehicle he could see the man's thick muscles straining against his tight jacket and in the dark skin of his hands gripping the wheel. He could picture the man getting angry and reaching over and strangling him easily.

"Exactly. He seemed a little too cool about things. It had to be done, he'd seen our faces and if anything went bad, he could've pointed us out to the police or whoever came looking into the whole thing with Deena." Morgan felt it was as good a reason as any and would stick long enough for him to get back out on his own.

"Look…" Wallace began.

"I don't want to talk about it anymore. It's done. We move on." He folded his arms in what he hoped looked like a gesture of finality, but he was actually calming himself by feeling the guns strapped under his arms. It was relaxing, assuring. *Let him try to strangle me with those fat hands,* he said to himself.

"Marsh is going to shit monkeys when he hears about it."

Morgan looked over at the man behind the wheel and stared at him hard. "You gonna tell him?"

"Even if I don't, do you think he won't find out? You don't think two dead people in a burning coffee shop won't make the news?" Wallace shook his head.

"Local news, maybe. We're pretty far away from home. No reason he should care about it, unless someone makes him care about it." His fingers tensed on the guns under his jacket.

"Anything in the bag?" It was obvious to Morgan that Wallace was uncomfortable with the conversation.

Morgan took his hands out of his jacket and opened Deena's backpack at his feet. He shuffled through what little there was; just trinkets, candy wrappers and paper. "Nothing. Not a fucking thing. Except of course for your useless tracking device that I'm assuming is woven into this thing somewhere." He stared at the faded tag inside that said where to return it, if someone found it.

Wallace slammed on the brakes and brought the vehicle over to the side of the winding road. "Listen. If it weren't for my "useless" trackers we wouldn't be this far and we'd have no idea where the girl has been at this point." He stuck his finger in Morgan's face. "What the hell have you done? Let's see, killed a couple of people that have nothing to do with this, and burned down a coffee house." He put his hands back on the wheel and sighed. "I say we call Marsh, tell him we found the bag, but no girl and we drive a straight line from here to L.A. and hope we find her before the law does, or some other interested party." He grabbed the gearshift and started to put it back in drive.

"Does this address mean anything to you?" Morgan held up the tag for him to see.

Wallace thought about it. "Tallmadge, California? That's where the girls are from originally."

"Are you listening to this?" Morgan's mentor growled from the back seat. "This incompetent asshole is deliberately trying to ruin this for you."

"And you didn't think to mention that? How far away is it?"

"No idea," Wallace said. He reached into his jacket. "Let me map it on my phone."

Mr. Hector yelled from the back seat. "He's got a gun. He's going to shoot you."

Morgan put his hand on Wallace's arm. "Just a sec."

"What?"

"You know their home town pretty readily."

"I have their files memorized."

"Their hometown would've been a good place to start looking for Deena. Why didn't you mention that earlier?"

"Fuck you. This should've been easy. Meet Ramirez at the train station and it's all over. There wasn't any reason to suggest other options. We *knew* where she was."

"Ly-ing…" Morgan's mom said from the back. Morgan turned to see her wedged in the seat with Brandt on one side and the monkey and Mr. Hector on the other. "What?" She said. "I can't have an opinion? I should just sit here and be silent?"

"Yes. All of you, shut up," Morgan said.

"Who are you talking to?" Wallace asked.

"*You* shut up." Morgan pulled one of his pistols and leveled it at Wallace. "You know that's where she is, don't you?" A thrill came over Morgan as he said that. Like a door had been opened to him that was locked before.

"No."

His ex-girlfriend joined in. "He does, you know he does."

"Why do you know about their home town?" He picked up the bag again and read the address. "4468 Southmoore Lane? You have everything at your fingertips up there in your mind. Ring any bells? Tell me." He felt a smile coming on.

Wallace shook his head no.

Morgan lowered the gun a bit and pulled the trigger. A bullet ripped through Wallace's right leg and lodged in the door.

Wallace cried out and leaned forward to clutch at the wound. A dark spot of blood quickly formed on his pants around the wound. Wallace continued yelling as Morgan got closer and leveled the gun at the man's head this time.

"There's a reason you know that stuff, isn't there?"

Wallace nodded his head before he cleared his throat. "We thought Avi and Deena had a thing going on. I planted trackers on both of them."

"Did they?"

"Yeah. They were meeting at the home where the girls grew up."

"In Tallmadge," Morgan said.

"Yes."

"Everyone but you knew it all along," Mr. Hector said. "Morgie was the last to know!"

It made sense to him suddenly. There was no reason for them to go. "So Marsh knew this. And, what, he already sent a crew there?"

"You and I can't be everywhere at once. He was just covering all his bases."

It felt good to shove the barrel of his pistol harder against Wallace's head. "I should've been able to make that decision. I have this gigantic brain in my head that I use to do my work. I make choices. *Not* you. *Not* Marsh."

"All right. What do we do now?" Wallace choked out.

"We? What we?" Morgan looked around the SUV. "Do you see anyone else here but me?" Morgan asked. He pulled the trigger, killing Wallace instantly in a brief cloud of crimson and gray matter. Morgan breathed a deep sigh of relief at once again working alone. It felt like a crowded room had just been cleared. He wiped his arm off where some of the blood had blown back on him. It took him a moment to recover his composure and once he did, he calmly and efficiently moved around to the other side of the vehicle, yanked Wallace out and tossed the man over the nearby guardrail. He watched for a moment while the body tumbled through the brush and the trees, before disappearing beneath the cover of the leaves.

Morgan sat in the driver's seat and rolled his head back and forth trying to work out a cramp in his neck. It began when he tensed up; waiting to make his move on Wallace was stressful, and it was bothering him to no end.

Mr. Hector looked up at him from the passenger seat. "Can't you just stop this? Walk away now before more innocent people get killed."

Morgan looked down at the little teddy bear now sitting in the passenger seat, with the buckle latched around him. "You think Wallace was an innocent bystander in this? He was just as guilty as anyone else. More so, if he was actually planning on killing me."

"You don't know that. You gave him the answers you wanted to hear and he fed them back to you. He had no choice." Mr. Hector looked as disapproving as a plush animal could.

"Don't listen to him," Brandt said from the back seat. "You did the right thing. Between this and the coffee shop, I think you're really starting to take charge here. You're going places now. You know exactly what the girl is going to do and where she'll be."

Morgan smiled. He did finally feel in charge of shit for once. Usually he took orders happily, that's how he made his living; he got a job, found the subject and killed them in the manner suggested by the client. Today he'd killed who he wanted, how he wanted and got the job done.

Still, the girl hadn't always done what was expected of her.

"Marsh is going to be very appreciative. He'll turn to you now," Morgan could see Brandt's face in his rearview mirror. "Better still, he'll trust you."

Morgan nodded again and activated the car's communication system. The small screen revealed itself on the dash. "Dial Mr. Marsh," he said. As the sound of the phone ringing began to emit from the speakers, he felt a smile of pride force the corners of his mouth open wide. He struggled to make his voice a little more somber before someone picked up on the other end.

32

Garrett gripped the seatbelt that crossed his lap. If there were any armrests, he would have held on to them for dear life. The plane was apparently too small for that. He took one glance at the California countryside sliding by below them and that was enough for him. He didn't need to look again. The prop plane dipped and rose against the air currents every other second it seemed to him.

"Don't tell me you're afraid of flying. That's crazy," Pel said.

In the cramped seat next to him, Pel was playing some game on her phone. "Shouldn't you shut that off? Don't they make you turn off phones when you're in an airplane?" Garrett asked. "Shut it off."

"Nah. We're fine. A little Angry Birds never crashed one of these things. Besides, I switched it to airplane mode."

"What the hell does that mean?

"We're fine," Pel said. "You seriously can't handle flying?"

"I'm fine with jets. Jumbo jets. Big planes. Widebodies. This thing runs on a tightly-wound rubber band." Garrett stared at the back of the pilot's head to make sure the man was watching where they were going. "I'm not cool with that."

After she closed the game, Pel brought up some documents on her tablet. "I did a little research into some things that Leonard was talking about," Pel said. "You know there are a lot of parasitic insects that can change the behavior of a host?"

"You're thinking someone put bugs like those into these people? On purpose? I don't know. That sounds far-fetched. Can't there be another explanation for this behavior?" Garrett asked.

Pel flipped to some images of bugs and enlarged them. "I don't know, but the bug thing is possible. Look at this one. It's a Maculina Rebeli." She handed the tablet to Garrett. The screen showed a beautiful butterfly with bright, colorful markings on its wings. "This thing? It puts out some kind of smell that makes ants think it's one of them. It's so effective, that the ants will take care of the butterfly's larvae."

Garrett looked at the butterfly and considered what something like that could do if applied to humans. Could a person be fooled into not knowing who their friends and enemies were?

"This one's my favorite. It's really gross," Pel took the tablet back and flipped to a new picture. "This is the Emerald Cockroach Wasp. She's kind of nasty. She paralyses a cockroach with her sting, and then stings it again in a specific part of the brain. The wasp then chews off part of the roach's antenna and completely hijacks its brain. The wasp makes the roach go back to her nest, lays some eggs in the roach's stomach which later hatch and the young eat the roach. The whole time? The roach doesn't care. Doesn't act like anything is out of the ordinary."

"Just lets it happen?"

"Just lets it happen," Pel said. "Something about the sting to the brain."

The image Pel pulled up was pretty gross. It showed a wasp chewing on a roach. Garrett wasn't really interested in seeing the video that Pel offered to show him. "So, you think this gives credence to what Leonard said? The fact that there are some nasty bugs that can make other bugs do stuff?"

"I don't know. There seem to be enough examples to show it could be possible." She started flipping through the file some more. "There's another bug in here that tricks rats into not being afraid of cats. That's weird, right?"

Strange science was one thing, but plausibility in humans was another. "Yeah. Definitely weird. Hard to prove though, if everyone dies when the thing is taken out of them."

"But, I mean, can these people be held accountable if they're being pushed to do these things?" Pel got silent as she flipped through the pictures and played the videos she'd saved. Her face contorted in disgust, but she kept turning to the next and the next. Garrett wanted to laugh at her, but he'd grown to accept and enjoy his younger partner's idiosyncrasies. A sudden drop in their altitude brought Garrett back to the here and now. "What? What happened? Are we going down?"

"We just changed altitude by twenty feet or so," the pilot yelled. "Not a big deal."

"How the hell does this generic agency not have a private jet? What kind of budget do they have that we have to fly in this sad excuse for transportation?" Garrett checked his seat belt one more time.

Pel put her tablet away and leaned over. She talked louder over the rattle of the plane's engine. "Where do you want to go first when we land?"

When we land. Garrett liked the sound of the words. "I think we should probably get a ride to the crime scene. I don't know how long they'll keep the train there on the tracks."

"They'll take it to the nearest train yard and we can look at it later. I'd imagine the coroner will need to take possession of the dead guys, though."

"Yeah. But if they don't have Deena's body on the train, it likely means she's on the move. Maybe we can find some idea which direction she went. Right now, she could've gone anywhere. And she's got a good head start." Garrett looked at his watch. "How long 'til we land?"

"No idea." Pel tapped the pilot on the shoulder. "How much longer?"

The pilot scanned the control panel and turned around. "If we don't hit any turbulence or anything, maybe an hour and fifteen minutes, maybe an hour and twenty."

"Turn around," Garrett said to the pilot. "Just turn around and fly." He looked at Pel again. "Don't bother him. He needs to fly this plane."

"What a baby."

"Just hand me Deena's file. And let's go over it again. Maybe we can find someplace logical for her to run to."

33

Her greatest joy in life used to be making fun of stupid people doing stupid things, and here she was, in a yoga class while the better part of the criminal underground searched for her.

Deena crossed her legs and stared off at the wall. She tried to make her mind a blank slate, tried to clear the thoughts that surfaced every time she needed to control her power. The Shadow Energy began to spread across her arm whenever Harper or Avi pushed their way into her thoughts. But it wasn't working, she tried to picture beautiful meadows and sunlight rippling off serene ponds, the mountains in the background, but all she could see were the black streaks lurking in the weeds and the strange dark currents just underneath, however light, seemed to be growing louder.

She regretted breaking her cover and stepping into the community as soon as she'd done it. She figured there would be some way to calm herself here in the little train stop town of Chemult, Oregon, but there wasn't much. On the corner stood an old-school coffee shop with red plastic booths and a mini jukebox at every table. The kind that served actual coffee with cream and sugar; exactly what she didn't need right now. But the coffee called to her, the way it always did—mocha, dark roasted, whatever. It was all good.

Chemult had a tiny police station that she avoided even though she didn't see any police cars out front; she supposed that every member of law enforcement this close to the train incident would probably be helping in one way or another. Scattered amidst the closed storefronts with newspapers taped to the windows were the town garage/gas station combo, some fast food places, jewelry store, coffee shops and the Paul White community center. She wandered into the community center just in time for a half-empty yoga relaxation class. No one said much to her, though they looked her over real good when she sat down. The instructor just smiled, introduced herself and got to business.

Deena opened her eyes and found her hands were balled into fists and turning black as the darkness migrated down her arms. She needed to release. She stood up quickly and grabbed her bag as she left the room. She saw a couple of the other women's eyes snap open to watch her retreat.

In the hall, she slung the bag over her shoulder and folded her arms so no one would see her hands. She quickly moved toward the exit, wondering what her next move should be. There was no way she could get back on a train, and she doubted the little town had a car rental place she could hit up.

"Hey, was it something I said?" the instructor whispered from the doorway of the classroom.

"Oh, no. Thanks. I was just having trouble focusing," Deena tried to keep walking, but the instructor advanced as she spoke, trying to engage Deena.

"Everyone has a little trouble the first time. You just have to work through it."

The stairs made Deena stumble and she put out her arm to steady herself. She was relieved to see the hand wasn't darkened nearly as bad as it had been. She hoped the woman wouldn't notice. "Look, Taylor was it? I'm just not in a frame of mind to relax now. I'm…"

"Anxious about something? It shows," Taylor said. She looked around the empty hall like she had a secret. "Look, I don't usually mix relaxation classes with the others I teach, but come here for a second." She nodded her head for Deena to come back.

Deena's lip twitched. She wanted to leave before something bad happened. "I have to get going."

"Look, I'll show you what I'm thinking. I have a place where you can take your time getting into a better state of mind, all by yourself. I have to get back to my class. I'll leave you alone, you can stay, you can go. Whatever," Taylor shrugged her shoulders.

Deena looked down at her feet. One was on the first stair. The other was on the second. She could say no and keep going. But she could feel an outburst building within. "OK. Two minutes." She stepped down and walked back to follow Taylor.

"I, uh," Taylor looked at the door to the classroom they'd just come from. "I also teach a kickboxing and self-defense class at night. Some of my yoga students get all weird about that for some reason." She smiled wickedly. "A girl can't be peaceful and kick some ass? Come on."

Deena smiled weakly. She had the ass-kicking thing down. A peaceful mind and body would be a nice addition.

At the other end of the hall, Taylor opened a door and leaned in to flip on the light. "This is the practice room. Most of the ones I've seen other places have some padding on the floor and mirrors all the way around," she stepped in and waved her hands around. "Never understood that. People need to see themselves in the mirror to make sure they're in the proper stance, suppose. Seems unnecessary to me. Mirrors break. I'd rather have it like this and be able to crash into walls and stuff."

The entire room was padded from floor to ceiling with light blue practice mats; not so soft that you couldn't walk on them, but soft enough that you wouldn't break a shoulder if you were thrown into a wall. In one corner was a boxer's heavy bag hanging from the ceiling and in the other, a speed bag.

"Plus, with all the padding, the room is pretty darn soundproof," Taylor stepped past Deena and started down the hall again. "If you decide to stay, have fun."

Deena couldn't stop staring at the room. A workout wasn't exactly what she needed, but it gave her a place to lay low and figure things out for a little while. She was sure people would be looking for her so she didn't really have time to pause for long. She worried she might destroy the place if things got out of hand though. "Look, I don't know…"

"Whatever you want to do, do it." The instructor's blonde ponytail bounced as she disappeared back into the classroom.

She needed rest and she need to get ahold of herself but she could almost smell the people that were tracking her at this point. Police. Feds. Marsh's goons. Still, she was no good if she kept lashing out with tendrils of magic constantly. Deena decided to take some time to get a grip and she let the door swing shut behind her as she stepped into the room.

Deena paced like some zoo animal for the first ten minutes or more. She went from one corner to the next, to the next, without a coherent thought. Images flashed in her head. She saw Avi and Harper, Marsh, Morgan and Ramirez, and then the parade of victims that died at her hands. It was a loop that started again, once she'd exhausted the list. After the first ten minutes, she added a punch at the speed bag and a kick to the body bag as she passed each of them. Soon the pacing became quicker as she went back and forth and the anger built in her. It became two punches on the speed bag, and a kick plus and elbow on the body bag, until it accelerated to the point where she was just going from one bag to the other and not even walking the room.

She feared that she was sliding back to what she was: some sort of zombie following orders without question and killing on demand without remorse. When she'd killed Mike, it was out of a fury she couldn't control, but she still felt something afterward, she'd been aware of what she'd done and known it was horrible. But the next time she took a life, when her power first revealed itself, had seemed like nothing.

It faded from her memory almost immediately. The man on the plane? She would've forgotten about him already if he hadn't been the catalyst for this change.

But what made her what she was? Was it Marsh? The first time her power came out, he was there. Did he do something? Was it the power itself that somehow made her blindly follow him?

As she settled in to punching the heavy bag, obsidian spikes poked from her knuckles and she tore into the bag with punch after punch, blow after blow. The thick canvas shell gave way quickly. Long, vertical rips in sets of four showed up with each swipe and sawdust began to fill the room like flurries in a mild winter storm. Deena could smell the oaky aroma of the chips flying as they passed close to her face. She ignored it. She ignored everything and struck out blindly releasing the anger and the fear that had built up. She didn't care if the Shadow Energy drained her again; she'd revert to a baby and work her way back to her twenties, kicking and punching the whole way. No one would expect a baby to rescue Harper, would they? She leapt at the bag and cut it in half with a sharp edge that had grown out of the side of her foot.

34

Deena at 17 the first time around

Being a waitress was hell for Deena: the long hours, the dull tasks, the jerks that didn't tip, the assholes that got handsy when she walked by. The smell of the strange combinations of foods would make her nauseous from time to time. The Nimbus Lounge wasn't a dive per se; Marsh kept it up and kept it respectable, but he didn't exactly pour money into it. He made it acceptable to a decent crowd and left it at that. No high aspirations, which meant no big tippers, ever.

Harper, however, loved it, or so it seemed to Deena. Harper seemed sure that they were always a day away from selling their bodies on the street, so working tables for the lecherous manager seemed like a welcome relief in comparison. Harper took their tips and squirreled them away, doing what she could to make the money last. It gave her something to occupy her time when she wasn't working. She bought groceries with coupons from the newspapers she got free at work when diners left them. Deena couldn't be bothered with it. She went to work, did her job and went home. If it weren't for Harper, the lights in their apartment wouldn't have stayed on.

True to his word, Marsh set the sisters up in a studio apartment a block away from the Nimbus. It was all as it was advertised—one room with two beds, a stove, a small television set that worked most of the time. The bathroom included a shower, at least. That was a treat. The temperature of the water couldn't be predicted from day to day, however.

They managed to get into somewhat of a routine after they'd been there for a little over six months. The cycle of work, home, eat, sleep was becoming ingrained, interrupted by frequent trips to a nearby gym that Marsh owned. Deena needed to vent aggression some way, and the gym worked perfectly. There certainly wasn't room to exercise in their little apartment, not even space for sit-ups without knocking into something. So Deena went. It got her out and, usually, got her away from Harper. There was something to be said for the healing power of *not* being near her sister. They saw each other at work, at home, everywhere. And it reminded Deena of their situation and how they'd landed there. Deena looked back at that day in the forest with Marsh and had a hard time believing she'd readily agreed to, even pursued the possibility of working for Marsh in any capacity. She chose to dwell on that when she was working out, not the fact that she herself had killed someone. Or was it two someones? The incident got cloudier the more time that passed. While she was hitting a heavy bag, Marsh's spectacled face appeared before her, his old man cologne filled her nostrils. She hadn't seen him since the incident and yet, somehow he was still fresh in her mind.

Occasionally, Harper joined her at the gym. It was a dirty, filthy old place where boxers and fighters went to work out, it wasn't a trendy place where people wore their yoga pants and went to feel the burn. Certainly not somewhere in Harper's comfort zone. At least not her former comfort zone. Deena was impressed with how her sister let things go now that their situation was dire. Harper had opened to new, cheaper, foods that she'd never have bothered with back home. The time on the run probably got her started.

When Harper came to the gym, Deena worked out on the other side of the building.

On a Tuesday night, Deena and Harper were working at the Nimbus with Ron, the manager, Troy, the "head chef" and another waitresses, and Amanda. It was close to quitting time, and Harper was helping Ron with the day's receipts. They sat at a table in the middle of the dining room while everyone else cleaned up. The nightly ritual was usually just an excuse for Ron to look down Deena's blouse or attempt to back her into a corner for a pat on the ass. She was getting more adept at avoiding that, much to Ron's chagrin. Harper's newfound skill at taking care of the bills and stretching a dollar made her more likely to volunteer to help with the daily tally, allowing Deena to slip from Ron's gaze nightly.

"You girls going anywhere tonight?" Ron asked, thick fingers stabbing at the calculator in front of him. Though he was sitting with Harper, he raised his voice for Deena to hear.

Deena knew it was another lame attempt to get her to go out with him. She pretended not to hear him and kept wiping down the tables.

Harper took the bait, though. "Yeah. Home."

"Come on, you girls are no fun. Christ. Live a little." Ron puffed blue cigarette smoke out of his mouth absently. It drifted up and joined the usual cloud that gathered near the ceiling.

"You want us to loosen up and experience life? With you?" Deena laughed. "Where are you headed? Some old dude club or something?" Ron wasn't that old, really. He was just old enough for Deena to be creeped out by him.

"I know some places that you'd enjoy."

"I'm sure you do. Like your place, for instance?" Deena asked.

Harper continued to count, making tics on a piece of paper for each stack of bills she set aside.

Ron smirked and poked at the calculator as he leafed through the tabs.

From out in the lobby area, the bell that rang when the front door opened tinkled repeatedly.

The clock on the wall read 11:56. Four minutes to closing time.

"Someone's cutting it close for their late-night slice of pie," Ron said.

"Want me to go?" Deena asked, hoping for a reprieve from the stench formed from the cloud of smoke, meatloaf and Ron's odor of sweat and what she referred to as his Chuck Norris cologne.

"Please, your sister and Amanda can get rid of them. They may be useless otherwise, but they know how to drive off customers."

Harper gave him disgusted look. "I'm right here. I can hear you."

"So go." Ron took another drag off his cigarette. "Deena, carry the money to the safe with me."

Harper got up and walked toward the lobby with Amanda.

Deena squeezed out a sponge into her bucket and came over to help Ron. She could feel his gaze on her ass as he followed her. She didn't know why her arm started to ache and her back stiffened. She could feel his breath on her neck as he got a little too close when they passed into the main office.

In moments there was a series of thuds from the other room and a scream that Deena recognized as her sister's. She moved toward the door but Ron caught her arm before she managed to turn the handle.

"Wait," he said, and as she watched, he walked around his desk and pulled a pistol from the middle drawer on the left. He then quietly walked back around to Deena and let her go ahead and open the door.

In the dining room, Amanda lay sprawled out on the counter, dead. Blood still poured from several wounds in her chest, but her eyes stared blankly, unblinking at Deena.

On the other side of the counter, near the hostess station, four men pointed guns at Harper and Troy, the fry cook. They all looked over as the office door opened and Deena stepped out. She didn't feel Ron emerge with her.

"Hey, look. Here's another one." One of the men pointed his pistol at Deena. "Come on out and join us."

"This is a bad idea," Deena said. "Do you know who owns this place?"

The man smiled. "Yeah. Everyone knows who this dump belongs to. Why do you think we're here?" He motioned toward the cash register and one of the other men pulled a shotgun from under his long coat. He pumped the gun once and fired, blowing the register apart. Harper screamed again. "We're thinking the owner might keep a little extra cash on hand somewhere."

Deena took a step forward and shook her head. "I'm going to say it again. This. Is. A *bad* idea." She didn't want to look at her arm, it was throbbing, and oddly cold. It was beginning to feel like cement; hard to hold up and thick. She wondered what Ron was going to do. He hadn't exposed himself to the assailants and was silent in the room behind her.

"Are you going to make us sorry we're here, little girl?" The man with the shotgun said. "Maybe your manager had a gun in the office back there and you've got it tucked in your belt or your frilly apron? Is that it? You gonna shoot us?"

The first man smirked, but looked slightly concerned. "Maybe you should put your hands up, just in case."

Deena did as she was asked, slowly lifting her hands toward the ceiling. Her gaze fell on Amanda's body, lying on the counter and her confidence faded. There was something in her mind that was nudging her to attack the men, but there was another part that told her she would end up just like Amanda; dead on the floor for no reason other than stupid happenstance. OK, she knew she didn't work for Marsh by happenstance, but it didn't seem fair. She looked at her arms and the sides that were facing away from the men had begun to darken with black and blue half-moons like scales. She didn't know if it was a trick of the light, but it seemed something flew over her, blocking out the lights and creating a shadow that drifted across her whole body, then disappeared.

The man with the shotgun walked past the counter and approached Deena with a wary glance. "How about it? What're you hiding? Barretta in the apron? Little one-shot Derringer? Maybe you think you can stick me with a steak knife or something?" As he approached, his coat wafted open and Deena noted a pistol in his waistband. Up close, the shotgun seemed huge and even more frightening than at a distance. It wasn't like an old double-barreled model; it was a huge black weapon that made Deena shiver just a little.

She shook her head no. The scales forming on her arms began to rise up above the skin, creating ridges. Somewhere in the back of her mind, she pictured fish hooks, like the ones she and Harper had used to catch carp in the lake when they were on the run. She tried not to react when those ridges became hard, curved points across the skin. It hurt. Not like the first time she'd had the darkness expose itself. That time in the woods had happened so fast and she'd been so excited with adrenaline that it didn't seem to hurt at all. Now that she had time to see it and think about it, it felt like razors on her arms.

"Hmm…" The man leered at her and checked her up and down as he approached. "You could be hiding all kinds of things in that outfit." His free hand glided across her stomach and lingered there.

Deena suppressed a snarl, keeping her lip from curling up in disgust.

It happened quickly. At least in her own head. It seemed there was little thought about what she was going to do from the moment she walked out into the dining area. Maybe she'd been analyzing the situation from the beginning without knowing it. Whatever it was, there was no time at all between when she decided to punch the man and the time the man was on the floor bleeding from multiple slashes across his face and neck.

With the incident with Mike, it had been something that rose in her until she jumped on him. Her sudden strength had surprised her then. Deena had seen her sister in distress and reacted in a way that came naturally. She hadn't planned that. It just happened. It was the same here, only she was more shocked by her own speed this time. Her body reacted to things in the environment faster than they registered in her mind.

As she watched the man's head hit the floor, she was moving toward the others. Her hands were wet with his blood and his shotgun was in her hand. The men's smirks hadn't left their faces completely before she was upon them. She planted the butt of the shotgun in one man's nose, and then swung it like a club, cracking it on another's skull. Her fist raked across both men's faces in quick succession, pulling skin as her jagged knuckles connected. She turned to attack the last man, only to find his pistol just inches from her nose.

"I don't know who the fuck you are, this is over." His jaw was trembling as his anger rose. The whole thing had happened so fast that Deena was fairly sure he didn't realize his friends were down.

The shot that was fired didn't come from his gun though. Everyone trembled as Ron's .45 fired from the office and he stepped out. The last attacker jerked to the left as the bullet struck him on his right side. He stumbled a few steps and then went down on the floor. He immediately tried to get up but fell back down, moaning. No one else in the room was watching him though; their eyes were on Deena, the dark scales on her arms and hands, and the blood that still dripped from her appendages.

"Ron? Thank you for your help," Deena said. She was sure she could have somehow fought off that last man, but that point was moot now. Still, she was emboldened by how she'd managed to handle the rest of the situation. Everyone staring fed her ego more than she realized. "But don't ever grab my ass again."

"Done." Ron moved back into the office and in seconds, everyone could hear him on the phone. In a shaky voice, he recounted the events of the last few minutes.

Deena looked over at Amanda, and then the men. She anticipated some horrible breakdown of emotion, some outpouring of anguish, but it didn't come. Everything that happened seemed like it had happened to someone else in a terrible movie from the seventies or something. She paused to make sure those emotions weren't just taking their time in bubbling to the surface. When they didn't arrive, she walked over to the table she had been cleaning, grabbed the sponge and wiped the blood from her arms, the spikes and scales were gone, leaving just a bold blemish in the shape of a small hook.

35

Stanley Yuko stood in front of the men at the door. He held up the grocery bag and waved it around. "Just bringing her some food and stuff."

"Why?" The first guard said. "She's not going to be around to enjoy it for long."

Stanley rolled his eyes. "Yeah. But Marsh felt it was a good idea in the meantime. I mean, if we can't prove Harper's alive, Deena may never come in."

"I don't think a day without a meal will kill her."

Stanley pulled out his cell phone. "Look, you want to ask Marsh why he wants her to have food, feel free. I'll give you his assistant's number." He held out his phone to the man then pulled it back quickly. "Oh. Wait. That's me. I'm his assistant."

The guards both shifted uncomfortably.

"Would you like me to go ahead and put you through to him? I'd be glad to. I'm sure he'd love to explain his actions to you." Neither of the men said anything. "No? You sure?"

The men opened the door without another word. Stanley reached into the bag and pulled out a couple of small bags of chips and handed one to each of the men. "Cheer up, guys. I'm sure you'll get to rough someone up soon enough." He stepped into the office, closed the door behind him and looked at the men standing on either side of Harper. "Good day, everyone."

Harper was lying on a desk, using a sweatshirt for a pillow. "If you say so."

The grocery bag landed with a thud on another desk. Stanley had dropped it slightly harder than he'd meant to. "I brought something to eat. Figured you'd be hungry." He took out some chips and sodas for Harper's captors and put them on the desk, then put the bag next to Harper. "There are some things in here for you as well."

"I'm not terribly hungry," Harper said.

"You need to eat." This whole thing depended on Harper helping out. Stanley hadn't had much time to think about a real plan. He hadn't received any further instructions from the feds and couldn't get them on the phone. Stanley was concerned that he hadn't correctly conveyed to them the dire circumstances Harper was in. If they wouldn't save her, Stanley would have to. He calculated his odds at successfully freeing her at well over fifty percent. "A drink would probably be refreshing right now. It would most likely change your whole outlook on things."

"Are you saying you have a beverage in that paper bag that is so good, it would make me look forward to getting whacked by these goons?"

Stanley looked at the men. "Possibly."

"Pass."

One of the men stepped toward Stanley. "Look, I'll take her snacks. I'm starving. What'd you bring?"

Stanley held out his hand. "Just. Just stay there. Harper? I really think you should drink this."

Both of the men guarding Harper looked at each other, both still eating their chips. "What's the deal here? Why are you so concerned with this?" One of them said.

"What's in the bag?" The other asked.

Harper was still lying down, but looked up at Stanley with a raised eyebrow.

"Soft drinks." Stanley tried to wink at Harper, but found he couldn't.

"What the hell?" One of the guards asked.

Stanley hadn't thought things through quite as well as he thought. "I need to take her downstairs." It was an awkward statement and he knew it. He had planned to stick to his script, but the new lie just flew out of his mouth.

"What?"

"Marsh wants to talk to her about the bus job."

The guard set his chips down and reached for the gun that was in his waistband. "Bullshit."

Stanley pointed at the man. "Don't do that."

"Or what, you'll go all Bruce Lee on me?"

The Asian reference angered Stanley. He was an accountant, not a thug, so the violence was all new to him. "First of all, I was born in Korea." He reached into the grocery bag and pulled out two handguns—one in each hand. "Second, I have always been partial to John Woo."

The guard grabbed his gun from his belt and raised it toward Stanley. He hadn't considered the fact that he would have to shoot anyone; it made sense that they would surrender rather than be killed for such a man as Marsh. "Stop."

"Shoot them," Harper said. Stanley saw her drop from the desk to the floor. "Shoot."

He did. Stanley pulled the triggers—alternating from one gun to the other. The automatic pistols roared to life and the stinging smoke of their discharge filled his eyes. He kept shooting and saw that some of the bullets found their target, though more seemed to dot the wall behind the guard.

Harper rolled toward the man as he fell then grabbed his gun. She turned and shot the other guard twice since both of Stanley's guns had run out of ammunition.

"Did you bring more ammunition for those?" Harper asked.

Stanley hadn't.

"The two outside guards are going to come in, and more from downstairs." Harper pointed her gun at the office door.

As he held the guns up to his face, Stanley went over his statistics. It should have taken him just a couple of shots for each guard. And yet he had emptied two eight-shot clips on one man. He began to recalculate their odds when the door flew open.

36

Two hours later, Deena opened the door and stepped out. The hall was just as empty as when she left it. She bent to the water fountain and took big gulps. She was starving, with no idea how she was going to get ahold of nourishment in the foreseeable future. She'd thought she could make it home a little faster than this. She sucked down more water and hoped that would sustain her until she figured something out.

She walked quietly past the closed door where Taylor had been teaching class and then bounded up the stairs as quickly as her exhausted legs would carry her. Deena wanted to thank Taylor, but also didn't want to impose on her any more than she already had. She also didn't want to draw more attention to herself.

Deena reached out and shoved the door open. Outside, the air was cooler than she thought it would be. She was sure there would be an oppressive humidity that would slap her face as she stepped out, but there was nothing but a light breeze.

"Oh thank God. I thought I was going to have to put this stuff down," it was Taylor, coming around the corner from the parking lot, her hands full with a giant cardboard box. "Could you hold that door, please?"

Deena stepped out of the way to let Taylor by.

"I was beginning to think you weren't coming out of that room," Taylor said. "Must've been even more full of stress than I guessed."

Deena stood with the door in her hand as Taylor got down the steps to the hall. "Yeah. Thanks so much. I feel a lot better."

At the classroom door, Taylor stopped again. "Uh, I hate to ask... but?" She motioned to the door with a free finger.

While she wanted to leave, Deena felt if she opened the door, maybe she'd be even with the woman for her help and she could walk away with a clear conscience— as clear as it could be after Deena had destroyed the training room, anyway. Maybe she could send some money to the center to cover it once she got settled. "Sure." She walked down the stairs and grabbed the door for Taylor. "What's all this stuff?"

"Oh," Taylor put the box on a table. "There's an open house tonight. In an hour or so, actually. I just have some decorations in here." She started pulling things out and placing them on the table. "Some flyers on the programs I do. A couple of boxes of crackers, some cheese. I don't go too crazy. Hardly anyone ever shows up for these things."

"That's too bad." Deena tried not to stare at the cheese and crackers.

"Eh. The other instructors get some traffic. This is a small town, so Ed, the guy that teaches karate, usually gets some parents and their kids. Helen teaches art classes down the hall, she gets some older people looking for something to do in their retirement. The tax guy is always popular." There was a sound in the hall of the door closing. They watched as a middle-aged woman in black tights and legwarmers walked by. "Hello Denise," Taylor yelled. "That's Denise," she said quietly. "She teaches the exercise classes. She keeps the place open, there's always a ton of people that want to lose weight." She tore open a sleeve of crackers and nibbled off a bit of the corner. "She's kind of a bitch, though." She held the crackers out to Deena.

"Oh, I don't think…"

Taylor gave her a "come on" look and Deena pulled one of them out and accidentally shoved the whole thing in her mouth without thinking.

Deena managed to score a couple of slices of cheese without seeming too desperate while Taylor was setting out her decorations and then announced she was on her way out. "I really need to get going. I'm hoping to catch the next bus. That should be coming up pretty soon."

"You got a while yet. Tickets ain't going to sell out or anything," Taylor said.

"Still," Deena said. "Thanks for the crackers, though."

The other woman smiled.

"Sorry I can't stay for the open house, you have some pretty cool decorations."

"You worked up quite a sweat, you're certainly welcome to use the showers in the locker room," Taylor said. "Hate to stink out the passengers on that bus."

There was no discreet way for Deena to smell herself, so she pressed on. "I'll be fine. Thanks, though."

Taylor pulled out a flyer and handed it to Deena. "Here, if you ever find yourself out this way accidentally again, you're welcome to stop by and beat the hell out of the padded room."

"Thanks," Deena nodded and walked through the doorway. She tried to hurry, so she wouldn't get caught up again and feel guilty for not staying. She ran up the steps as fast as her weary legs could take her. At the top, she saw Denise coming up with her decorations and she nearly rolled her eyes. Would she ever get out of the building? "Can I help you?" she said as sweetly as she could to the woman in the tights.

"Little late, honey. This is the last of it. Where were you ten minutes ago?" With that the exercise queen of Carbondale, California shoved past Deena, bumping her as she went.

Deena could see why Taylor wasn't fond of the woman.

Cutting across the parking lot, Deena noticed a little red sedan with a personalized license plate that read "WERKIT" with the trunk was open. She assumed it was Denise's. She stared at the car for a moment, then looked around to make sure no one saw her staring. She was on the way out of the life of crime. She'd kept telling herself that since the plane. She'd already done a few things that weren't anywhere near legal since she decided to go straight.

There weren't a lot of other vehicles in the lot. A dented pickup truck, a van with the community center logo on it, and a small sport utility vehicle were the extent of her choices.

She looked around for any pedestrians and considered how lucky she'd been since the train. Marsh's men and various law enforcement agents had to be closing in on the town, even if it was for a cursory glance. Stealing a car from a mildly annoying exercise queen would probably draw unwanted attention. Still. It would be harder to escape if she were walking. She stared at the car and found her reflection in the window. She looked like hell. Her hair was flattened with sweat and she had no make-up to speak of.

The car actually belonged to a person, however unsociable. That person would have to go through considerable time and effort to recoup their vehicle or its cost. Plus, if Deena stole it, she'd have to find a way to pay for gas. If she had the keys, it would be easy to take off with the vehicle, but she'd learned to hotwire long ago.

Suddenly, there was a thin black vein winding out of her index finger, no thicker than a piece of thread. Whether she'd been serious about it or not, she'd pictured a key and the Shadow Energy responded.

She watched the reflection up to the point where the dark line came in contact with the car window. From there it spread itself flat and climbed up the window, stopping only briefly at the top of the glass where it met the door. After a pause, Deena could see the blackness on the other side the glass. It dangled down, remaining in contact with the larger portion, enveloping the lock in darkness. Deena heard the click of the door unlocking and then another sound and the door opened slightly. The material tugged at Deena's arm, then the door opened more, using the tension between the door and Deena for leverage. Before Deena could decide what she thought of this, more of the blackness wrapped itself around the steering wheel and with a click, the car roared to life, its engine idling high.

Denise was a bitch, wasn't she? Deena thought. She reasoned that she could return the car when she was done, if she had to. What was a few hundred or thousand miles more on the odometer anyway, right? It wasn't like she was killing Denise. That's what she would have done in the old days. Was there a distinction between her old life of crime and casual use of her Shadow Energy?

Baby steps.

Deena closed the trunk, got in and, rather than flooring it, quietly drove out of the lot and onto the road. She let the exercise lady's GPS device guide her to the nearest road that paralleled a major highway and took off at a sensible speed. She reached into her bag for the phone to try to keep in touch with her sister and was pleasantly surprised to find a sleeve of crackers and some slices of cheese wrapped up in a paper towel. She was not as excited to discover that she couldn't remember if she'd taken them, or if Taylor had placed them there.

She crunched a cracker and let the crumbs fall all over Denise's seat and floor.

Baby steps.

37

Stanley picked up the revolver just as the other guards burst into the room. Harper fired two shots and one of the men fell. The other slid himself behind the reception desk. Stanley pointed his gun in that direction.

"Don't shoot unless you see him," Harper said. "Don't waste bullets."

Stanley nodded emphatically, showing her he understood. Despite her reputation as a screw up, she'd been through a number of successful jobs and had only received that reputation due to a couple of unfortunate turns. He looked to her to think of a plan on the fly.

The second man popped up and Stanley pointed his gun. He watched as the man pulled the trigger, sending bullets flying Stanley's way with a roar. The sound of those bullets embedding themselves in the wall behind him brought Stanley some solace, but his analytical mind began to compute the odds of all three of the shots missing him at such a close distance. He heard Harper behind him shout and Stanley accidentally pulled the trigger. He marveled as his opponent fell to the ground until he realized the man had simply dropped for cover. Stanley saw the wisdom in that, and fell back down himself.

"What the hell are you doing?" Harper said.

Stanley had no real answer. At least not one that didn't involve him admitting that he'd stopped to figure out the statistics of victory and dodging bullets like some character from *The Matrix*. "I'm new at this."

"Well it's going to get old real fast if you don't start shooting back at this guy," Harper stood and fired, then climbed over the desk and crouched low as she advanced toward the reception area.

Stanley stared at the reception desk that the last man was hiding behind. He knew the company wouldn't have ordered a good desk; they always used cheap furniture in offices other than Marsh's personal suite. Stanley figured that the furniture was thin, cheap particle board or worse. Its bullet stopping power was probably next to nil. He pointed the gun at the spot where the man had ducked. After thinking over the odds that the man was still there, Stanley opened fire and continued to fire at the same spot until the gun ran dry. And he waited.

A second later, the man popped up at the other end of the desk, and Harper shot him in the face. The man fell backward, his arms flailing unguided. He landed with a thump, out of sight.

The hot stench of gunfire made Stanley's eyes water and his nostrils burn. He stood with the gun still pointed at the same spot, and sulked at the miscalculation. He'd never been in a gunfight and the real-time variables confounded him.

"Thanks for flushing him out for me," Harper said.

Stanley felt a sudden surge in his stomach and he vomited all over the plastic desk chairs nearest him.

38

Morgan slept for an hour at a roadside rest stop off the highway. He'd been going nonstop for too long and all the soda and coffee in the world couldn't have kept him awake. Not after Mr. Hector had begun to sing "Twinkle, Twinkle, Little Star." Morgan had grown to hate that bear.

In the restroom, Morgan splashed water on his face and noticed a couple dots of blood dried on his face from when he shot Wallace. He chuckled to think what would have happened if he'd been pulled over for speeding or something. How would he have explained that to a state trooper? Shaving accident?

"You would've told them it was a shaving accident? But the blood is on your forehead." A familiar voice came from inside one of the bathroom stalls. After a second, Wallace stepped out. "That seems like a lame excuse. What then? Kill the trooper, like you did with the coffee shop kid?"

Another stall opened and Brandt stepped out. "Why not? He could handle killing one more person, right? It's what he does. He's a man."

"Both of you just shut up," Morgan said. He turned back to washing his hands and scrubbing at the blood, trying to get it off his face and fingers.

"Awww. Out, out, damn spot," Morgan's mother said. Morgan saw the other two give her a quizzical look. "What? It's Shakespeare. Don't you guys read?"

"This is the fucking men's room," Brandt said. "This is where *men* talk."

"And where they take a piss." Wallace walked closer to Brandt and looked at Morgan's mother. "Now, if you'll excuse us."

From the last closed stall, the monkey's cymbals started to clang.

"Is the monkey a boy or a girl?" Mother asked. "Just wondered. Wanted to make sure it's in the right bathroom."

"You really think shooting me was a good idea? Marsh is going to shit cats when he finds out. You're screwed now." Wallace seemed satisfied with himself and folded his arms.

"I already called him," Morgan said. "He's fine with it. Especially after I told him you were working for Thorpe's criminal organization. Seems Marsh doesn't like traitors."

"I wasn't. I would never double-cross Marsh."

"Yeah, well. Who's he going to believe? Me or the dead guy?" Morgan grabbed a brown paper towel to wipe his face and then wadded it up and threw it in the garbage. "I think he prefers getting his news from the living." He turned and walked out of the restroom and back toward the SUV.

"This is your idea of chasing down a subject? Napping in parking lots? You should have her by now," Brandt said.

"I'm getting there."

"Make sure you wear a seat belt," Morgan's mother said.

Brandt pushed his way in front of her. "Getting there? Bullshit. Someone else will get to her first."

"Anyone want to ride shotgun? Wallace?" Morgan looked at Wallace and waited for a reaction. "No?" He backed the SUV out of the space and sped off toward the highway. In his rearview, Morgan could see the trio that had been bothering him still standing there.

39

It was a long drive for Deena all alone, but Denise's car was a wealth of surprises. First Deena found change for rest stop vending machines in the center console, then a twenty dollar bill in the glove box. Best of all was a gas card that filled the tank and bought Deena some much needed caffeine at the gas station's mini-mart. *Ahh coffee.* Deena had always consumed vast amounts of it when she was working. It got her going like nothing else. Not food, not sleep, not anything. Deena bought a mug so giant that it didn't fit in the cup holders. She didn't care. She kept it in her lap.

Denise's taste in music was appalling to Deena, but at least the woman had satellite radio. The GPS was wonderful as well. Deena programmed in the address of her childhood home. She wondered if Harper had told Marsh about it, wondered if she and her sister truly had any secrets.

Of course, she'd spent a wild weekend there with Avi not that long ago, but she was sure he wouldn't have ratted her out to Marsh. Her mind locked up at the thought of Avi. She'd taken steps to force herself not to think about him—blocking anything that connected them—since his death on the train, but the drive was boring and his face flooded her memory frequently. She'd seen a number of people die and never given them a second thought, but Avi was different for so many reasons. She'd known him— *really* known him—in every sense of the word. She had to pull over and dry her eyes thinking about how much they'd been through. They seemed like the perfect pair from the start; both loving the violence that made up so much of their lives. Both being so good at it.

The looks Avi gave her on the last day lingered in her mind. He was horrified to see what had happened to her. How she'd regressed. She couldn't blame him for being terrified of sitting next to a teenager that was once his twenty-something lover.

Deena pulled the rearview mirror down to look at herself. She had a hard time judging how old she looked to others; she always seemed like herself, no matter the age. She guessed people would thing she was twenty. Maybe? It looked like her slow progression back to normal hadn't been interrupted by using her powers on the train or the outburst in the community center.

She pulled the car back onto the road and concentrated on making her way to her childhood home. It was odd for her to feel so conflicted about going back. She had no idea when her dad had left, if he'd ever come back, or even if he would be waiting there when she arrived. She had no contact with him since she'd left and she assumed her sister hadn't either. But again, did the sisters have any secrets?

The house was more or less as Deena had left it. It appeared no one had been there since the last time she'd managed to sneak off to unwind here. The lawn was overgrown, the tree branches were hanging low and the siding needed power washing. She drove along the gravel and pulled the car around back, so it was out of sight if anyone else came up the drive.

She lifted the garden gnome from the overgrown flowerbed and pulled the spare key out before returning it to the proper place. She let herself in through the back door and shut it behind her, snapping the deadbolt in place.

As Deena walked through the house cautiously, she listened for the sounds of anyone else that might be lying in wait. She heard nothing, but still walked through the living room, down the hall and thoroughly checked each bedroom and the bathroom. She then drifted back to the living room and sat down on the couch, which was just about the only piece of furniture left in the house. Everything was in its place.

She took deep breaths and closed her eyes. The last time she was here was with Avi. Months ago, they'd snuck away to blow off some steam and have some alone time after the Albany job. Their time together was always closely guarded, and carefully concealed. If Marsh or any of his people figured out there was something going on that might interfere with the handler/killer dynamic, they'd be reassigned.

Now, she questioned her feelings for Avi. Everything that drew them together was predicated on what the Shadow Energy did to her, how it controlled her. That was what brought them together: the thrill of the job, the excitement of the criminal life, the planning, the execution. Were there ever really any feelings between them?

The spot on her arm had settled itself into a shape vaguely resembling a compass. It didn't ache, didn't feel heavy and certainly wasn't moving at the moment. She wasn't sure she'd gained control of anything, but hoped for the best. Maybe she'd somehow worn it down, subdued it, even if just for the time being. If she was going to be any use to Harper, she had to have her shit together before she went storming into Marsh's den.

She looked around again. Why was she even here? In the early going, her wobbly teenaged brain felt like it would be the safest place, the most logical place to go. But it quickly became obvious to Deena that it wasn't. The most logical place to go would've been to help Harper. She questioned her loyalty to her sister and her mind started to become addled again. She had to keep herself focused. Unconsciously, she wanted to go hang out in her old tree house and watch the traffic from the highway. That always used to calm her. Back when she actually was a teenager. She pushed away childish thoughts and moved on to look at the bedrooms.

Empty. The house had an old couch that Deena barely recognized in the living room, a few cups in the kitchen by the sink and some rolled up sleeping bags in the bedroom that she and Avi had used the last time they were there.

The place was just as much of a dead end now as it had been years ago.

40

Deena at 20 the first time around

The first time Deena and Avi made love, it was a frenetic and frightening experience for both of them.

Five years before the incident on the plane, when the Shadow Energy shorted out Deena's shit, she had just completed a job in Miami, an easy target that required very little in the way of her power. She used her bare hands, enhanced by the terrible energy within her and strangled a rival hit man named Ford from another organization. It was her first major solo job that didn't involve plain old stealing or breaking and entering. Her heart was pounding the entire time and sweat was streaming down her neck from the heat and the fear that enveloped her.

And it was exhilarating.

After she felt the last rise and fall of Ford's chest, she watched the focus leave the man's still-open eyes. Something about it satisfied a need inside her that had been steadily building since she was in her early teens. She looked at Ford one last time and felt the stiffness in her arms release. The dark shapes receded and forced themselves back into a tight circle that resembled a smiley face.

Deena had taken the man, as planned, to the men's room of an upscale Italian restaurant under the guise of some wild sex act that Ford had readily and eagerly agreed to. She left him dead in a stall and walked as calmly as she could out the front door. From there, she ran to the rendezvous point in the back alley, out of breath and shaking with excitement. Avi pulled up and took her away like clockwork, the way all his plans tended to work, and they raced off to the nearby hotel they'd reserved; a good hotel for a change.

On the brief ride, they said little except to confirm the successful completion of their task. A small time crook with high hopes of walking away with a piece of Marsh's territory was no longer breathing. It was all business and clinical.

"Hungry?" Avi asked.

"Starving."

Avi stared ahead. "Want to stop for something, or get room service?

"I'm thinking room service." She was starving, but she wasn't thinking about food. She couldn't help but stare at Avi as they drove the streets of the city to the hotel. He had been forced to work with her and be her handler when she moved on to more complex jobs. Earlier on, she'd worked with Harper doing the petty stuff under the supervision of Wallace.

The elevator whisked them up to their floor in record time. Avi slid the key card, and tossed his things on the floor when they stepped through the door.

A suite. They both said it would be good for their cover, but they were actually sick of the rat holes and roach motels they were used to hanging out in. Sure, it drew less attention, but it was nasty. This time they were going to stay in style.

Deena grabbed him immediately, kicking the door shut behind her.

Avi tried to say something. "Deena, wait…" But Deena's mouth was already on his. The adrenaline of the evening's activities coursed through her veins, stronger than the Shadow Energy that had pushed her along from day to day. She pinned him against the wall and kissed him harder, not wanting to break the contact between the two of them. After a moment, Avi began to kiss back just as urgently.

Deena had been working with Avi without really thinking about him in anything other than a professional manner. They'd been working together for nearly two years and there had been tension between them, but everything had always been playful and mostly harmless. Everyone flirted with Deena and she loved flirting back. Occasionally it had gone somewhere, but never anything serious, or memorable. She'd been far too nervous about making sure she pleased Marsh with the way she conducted herself in every aspect of her criminal endeavors. Besides, the men who made unwanted advances were aware that there were consequences.

Tired of waiting for him to do it, she had both of their shirts off by the time they made it down the hall to the main bedroom. As she watched him unbuckle his belt, she began to have feelings she hadn't had before—she didn't think they were really sexual, but more like the ones she had when she got excited about fighting and attacking someone. They were overwhelming and she ran to grab Avi. The momentum knocked him, pants still around his knees, onto the bed with her on top of him.

"Christ, you're going to play rough, are you?" Avi asked.

Deena didn't answer, she couldn't. Her body wasn't reacting in any way that she could control. A line of shooting pain briefly made its way up her spine and as she tried to focus on Avi and what they were about to do. She could feel a bubble of darkness emanating from her and enveloping them. She couldn't hear anything or see anything outside the shroud that surrounded them, only the very startled and frightened Avi that was trapped inside with her. She couldn't pause to decide if the bubble was real or something she was imagining and she didn't want to. She also wasn't sure if the look on Avi's face was pleasure or terror.

If it was fear, he got over it.

41

Deena stared at the inside of the front door of her childhood home and felt weird about standing there without her sister. The home wasn't the same without her. Harper was always the responsible one, the one who got the good job that put food on the table when Dad didn't remember to come home and make dinner. Deena had the label of flake long before that. In school she was in ballet, then theater, then a punk band, then she started painting. That was just the first half of freshman year. Before working for Marsh, she'd never held a job long; most of the time it was just a few months at most. And here she was quitting again.

She'd thought it through this time, though. It wasn't like when she left the burger place because the manager was a skeev. Or when she quit the copy center because the ink smelled nasty. Those were high school jobs, gigs she had when she didn't have a care in the world, or responsibility.

She stood up and sighed deeply. She was pretty close to being back to normal and when she was recovering she couldn't help but feel the fleeting thoughts of her youth. It wasn't that she lost her memory of events and thoughts; she just couldn't help but feel different as she snapped back to her proper age she. Usually, the magic only took a few months, maybe a year from her. This time it was a decade and a half, and as she got closer to her real age, her attitudes were not what they were. It was like a do-over.

The sound of tires on gravel made her move to the window and look out. Down the long driveway she could see a plain white sedan winding its way toward the house. The dull car didn't look like something her sister would drive, but it certainly wasn't one of Marsh's hulking SUVs either. At this distance, she couldn't see who was in it, and the dust didn't make matters better.

Just to be on the safe side, Deena grabbed a set of steak knives from the kitchen and tucked them into her belt behind her back. She hated to carry weapons, guns especially, but it felt good to be almost fully recovered and she didn't want to think about using her power.

The car outside came to halt and Deena peered out through a crack in the blinds of the kitchen window. The car was a good distance away from the garage, as though the driver had stopped that far away on purpose. Deena could only see the outlines of two people inside.

Deena's cell phone suddenly rang and she answered it. She heard her sister's voice on the other end.

"Hello?" Harper sounded winded.

"Hey. Is that you outside? Are you coming in or what?" Deena laughed when her sister answered.

"What?" Harper asked.

Deena watched the two figures in the car move about, gathering up their things before the doors started to open.

"I said are you going to sit in the car all day or get in here?" She realized that neither of the people getting out of the car had a phone up to their ear.

"Deena, I'm still at Marsh's office. Stanley just freed me. Where the hell are you?"

Deena ducked back away from the window just enough so she could see the two men rising out of the sedan. She saw the dark clothes and she wondered if they were policemen, detectives, maybe. Their car was the right make, but they weren't all stealthy or tactical like cops would be. They looked around and headed up the path that led to the front door. One of them, the tallest, seemed familiar and she wondered if she'd seen him somewhere, like Marsh's office or the apartment building. They were briefly out of sight as the path wound behind some trees.

"I'm at our old house. And someone just pulled up." She didn't take more time to wonder who they were or what they wanted. She reacted by moving as far away from them in any way she could. Deena could hear the high-pitched noise of her sister emanating from the phone. She picked it up and whispered, "Someone unfriendly is here. Are you going to be OK?"

"God, no. We are at the top of the building basically. There are a whole lot of people between here and the front doors that would like to kill me," Harper said.

"I will deal with these guys and drive straight for you when we're done," Deena said. And she hung up. She felt bad for leaving her sister hanging, but she'd call her back when this was over.

Deena slowly backed into the shadows of the hallway toward the bedrooms, still with her eye toward the picture window in the living room, waiting for another glimpse of the men. Did the police find the stolen car where she'd hidden it? She slipped one of the steak knives from her belt and let it rest in her hand, feeling the weight.

The silhouettes of the men appeared again through the front curtains, advancing slowly along the walk toward the front door. Her right arm ached and throbbed where the blotch resided. She looked down at it and found it had formed the vague outline of a dagger. She thought about how she would've handled such a situation in the last ten years. Just unleash her powers and end it all quickly. It would be so easy to cast a little spell to help her out, but she couldn't bring herself to do it. She tried to think of baseball stats to keep her mind off of using the darkness, but she knew none, tried to recite poetry, but couldn't remember anything but "Mary Had A Little Lamb".

A firm double knock came from the direction of the front door. There were a few seconds of silence and Deena tried to hold her breath because it suddenly sounded so loud in her ears. She heard something else then, from the other direction, a snap behind her, not in the bedrooms but in the back yard. It was subtle, and if she was breathing normally, she might have dismissed it as imagination. As she tried to zero in on what it was, the knock at the front door became three quick pounds.

"Deena Riordan?" one of the men shouted. "This is the Ellis County Sheriff's office. Open up, please."

Deena thought about the noise out back and wondered if she should cross over to the kitchen. If there was one person out back, there could be more. There was another sound behind her, which she imagined as someone trying to break open a locked window without making a ruckus. Whoever was back there wasn't horribly good at being stealthy.

"Sheriff's office. Open the door or we will break it down."

In the dark hallway, Deena looked at the crack at the bottom of the closed door, waiting to see if whoever broke in was using a flashlight or fumbling their way through the dark in the unfamiliar terrain. She didn't see anything shining through. At least this guy was smart enough to know that.

She took one more pause to consider who these people were. They certainly weren't as trigger-happy as most of Marsh's men, but they could really be cops for all she knew. Her instincts said they weren't. Then again she'd been rather messed up for the last several days and her decision-making abilities weren't all they once were. Seemed strange to Deena that the sheriff's office wouldn't send more men, at least a few in uniform, to apprehend someone that they must consider to be a very dangerous fugitive. Surely they would've sent squad cars and deputies and, if handy, tanks. Police would be smart enough not to try to enter a house they didn't know. What if their fugitive were lying in wait for them? No, that wasn't the general law enforcement strategy.

The floorboards creaked in the master bedroom and Deena made the choice to stop thinking about anything but survival. She pushed the door to the bathroom open and stepped into it. She paused there, waiting for something, anything to happen. She had always hated reacting to things; her preference was to be in charge of what was going on. Initiate and control the situation. This meltdown with her powers, though, had made her react, and react poorly, to everything that had happened since the plane. She could be back in control soon enough, she figured.

In the darkness, she gripped the knife loosely.

The door to the bedroom opened slowly and a man in a black jacket walked out. The jacket was a windbreaker. Deena grinned. Never wear windbreakers. They swoosh when you move. Stupid people.

The man appeared as the pounding on the front door started again. The windbreaker guy was short and held a shotgun in his hands. First the windbreaker, then the shotgun. Stupid people doing stupid things. The shotgun was a dumb move given the situation. She'd never been big on guns, but would've gone with a pistol in this case, due to the space constraints of the hallway. More maneuverability. Of course, the shotgun could kill everyone in the hallway with the blast radius, whereas a pistol could only hit in one specific area. But, if you were good enough, one shot was all it took. She hated that thoughts like that entered her head so easily still.

Another man came out of the bedroom behind the short man, and she recognized him as a nobody named Rollie. He handled collections for Marsh on the south side. Deena did the math in her head: Marsh's people were here to drag her back, NOT the cops with some questions and NOT her sister come to collect her. It was someone else with guns sneaking up on her in the darkness.

She could feel her breathing get slower; felt a calm fall over her body. She moved by instinct, as if she were in a trance or performing some intricate dance that she had memorized all the steps to. She moved behind the half-shut door and waited. Within seconds the barrel of the shotgun appeared in her line of sight, as she knew it would. When the man was fully within her view, she kicked the door shut, leaving them in near darkness with only a shaft of daylight streaming through the windows to see by. Not that it mattered. The man tried to swing around to shoot Deena, but didn't have enough room. The shotgun took up too much of his turning radius.

Deena used to the man's sudden confusion to stab him below the armpit with her knife. The pain caused him to pull the trigger involuntarily. In the tiny bathroom, the roar was amplified in the confined space and the toilet exploded, baring the full brunt of the weapon's discharge. Deena cursed herself for not being better prepared. She'd judged the man for bringing a shotgun into a confined space, while failing to make a plan for herself. Now she was alone in a bathroom with a shotgun-wielding man and at least three other men somewhere outside the door.

In the plus column, the man had taken his hand away from the trigger because of her stab which forced him to let go. Rather than drop the gun, the short man tried to swing it at her, hoping to do some damage that way. It was a clumsy jab and Deena used his momentum to bring her elbow up into his nose, causing a terrible crack.

Out in the living room a crack of another sort exploded forth. Deena guessed it to be the front door being kicked in by the men out front.

As the short man tried to recover from the blow Deena dealt him, he slipped on water and pieces from the shattered toilet and fell, taking Deena down with him. Deena grabbed at the shotgun, trying to wrest control of it from the man, not to use, but to keep him from getting off another wild shot that would either blind them or deafen them. Her hands slipped off, covered in blood from where she'd stabbed him. She managed to point the weapon away from herself and toward the door. The man flailed for control as well, with just as much luck.

The door flew open and Deena could make out the face of another one of Marsh's men standing in the doorframe with a 9 mm pistol in his hand. Much wiser than his friend. She gave up her play for the shotgun and reached for another knife, the first had been lost in the melee somewhere. As she did, the short man took the opportunity to regain his weapon. He managed to grab the stock but only with his weak hand. As he moved for the trigger, his hand slipped and the gun went off. The blast caught the man in the doorway square in the chest.

The short windbreaker-clad thug let out a cry when he saw what had happened and froze for a second before he moved toward his accidental victim.

Deena took the opportunity to pull the steak knife across his throat. It was easy. It was natural. She was suddenly afraid she wasn't as free from the darkness as she'd believed. The short man dropped to the wet floor among the shards of porcelain, bowl water and blood. She got herself into a crouch and listened. She could make out the shape of the other man's body, which had fallen into the hall and the pistol he'd dropped just inside the bathroom.

"I think we got off on the wrong foot," someone yelled from the living room. "You might as well come on out and talk. The place is completely surrounded."

She knew it wasn't. If there were that many of them, they would've swarmed the little ranch-style abode easily and overwhelmed her with sheer numbers. Or hosed the place down with gunfire. Better yet, they could've stayed out completely and given her the ultimatum from the safety of cover. Odds were good there were only the two of them left, though more could be coming. They probably couldn't bring themselves to send many people to subdue a girl, even when they knew that girl was dangerous. Like the men on the train, they most likely were spread thin to find her, hold her, and wait for help.

Deena stepped forward, shards crackling beneath her feet until she was within reach of the gun. Slowly, quietly she grabbed it, looking for shadows on the hallway wall the whole while. The pistol felt odd in her hand. Not that she didn't know what to do with it; she just hadn't used one in a long time. She hadn't needed one. Her arm throbbed like a migraine. She checked the chamber of the gun and quietly removed the clip to make sure it was loaded before locking it back into place.

42

"Please tell me you have an escape plan," Harper said. She knelt behind a desk and looked to the door for the men that she knew were on their way.

While Stanley's plan wasn't nearly as thorough as he'd believed. He certainly had one thing in place. "I have a key card for the freight elevator. It's locked down on this floor and waiting for us. We should be able to jump on and take it all the way to the bottom without stopping."

"And then?" Harper

Stanley was confused. "We run out the door. Marsh doesn't own the whole building. His men wouldn't try anything in full view of everyone."

"Wouldn't they? You've worked for him for a while. You know better."

Stanley knew his boss took serious efforts to make all of his businesses look legitimate and keep a buffering layer between the criminal aspects and himself. But that most likely went out the door when he kidnapped Harper and held her so close to his headquarters.

"We could take the elevator down."

"To the parking garage? And where from there? If the gates are locked, nothing gets in or out," Harper said.

"No vehicles. We could still leave through a side entrance." Surely it would be easy to slip out in the crowds of innocent people that came in and out of the building daily. Harper didn't look convinced. "How long will it take your sister to get here?"

Harper's brows fell. "We can do this without her."

"But it would be easier *with* her, right?"

Down the hall, a number of voices began mumbling at each other. More of Marsh's men had come to investigate the sounds of gunfire.

"Deena is a couple of hours away. It sounded like she had her own problems."

It was hard to tell from the side of the conversation he'd heard, but it sounded to Stanley like Deena had more than just ordinary problems. It sounded like she had the same kind of problems he and Harper were currently experiencing. "Can't we find a place to hole up in this building for a couple of hours? It might be easier than running."

"And what do we do when she arrives? They could kill her and then get back to finding us. It might only prolong the inevitable."

"Or give us time to come up with a new plan."

Harper went through all of the dead men's clothing, looking for guns and ammunition. She made sure to hand Stanley a pistol. He figured she'd chosen it because it was the easiest to use and reload. Point and shoot. She filled up one of his coat pockets with extra bullets. He watched as she tucked a gun in her pants behind her back and loaded a second weapon. "Stay behind me and watch where the hell you're shooting that thing. We're going to head out to the hall, check to see who's coming and then make our way to the elevator. Got it?"

They both looked down at the gun in Stanley's hand. It shook as Stanley tried to come to grips with what was happening and what he might have to do. Harper looked at him with a raised eyebrow. "Maybe you shouldn't be behind me after all."

"I can do this."

"You've worked for Marsh for how long, and now you're getting squeamish about killing?"

Stanley tried to force his hand to stop, but it wasn't working. "I do spreadsheets. I make appointments. I have nothing to do with killing people."

"Don't you?" Harper asked. They poked their heads into the hallway. Voices could be heard coming from the right.

"We can head left to get to the freight elevator," Stanley whispered. Harper motioned him on and followed, watching their backs. They quickly arrived at the elevator without encountering anyone and stepped in.

Harper kept her gun ready as she backed into the elevator. They could still hear voices further down the hall, and Stanley imagined they'd be approaching the office. "See?" He smiled, satisfied that he'd managed to affect a daring rescue despite his obvious lack of action hero skills and training. "We'll be fine from here."

Harper didn't look convinced.

Stanley pressed the button for the third floor. "He shouldn't have any men on three. We can figure it out from there." He leaned against the back of the elevator and crossed his arms. "There's a couple of storage rooms we could hide in."

The door didn't close.

Both of them stared at the numbers above the door and then at the button that was lit up for three. Stanley laughed nervously and leaned up and pressed three again. When the doors didn't close, he pressed the door close button numerous times.

The door still didn't close.

"Shit," Harper said.

The voices in the hall sounded closer.

"Don't you have to push the key card all the way in for it to work?"

Stanley looked over at the buttons and knew she was right. He'd left it in the lock position, so the elevator wouldn't take off until they were ready. He reached up and switched it, then pressed the third floor button again. The door slowly slid shut and the elevator began to move again.

"Sorry," he said.

43

Deena knew the longer she was trapped, the better the chances were that reinforcements could show up to help the thugs and make things much worse for her. She crouched, tried to stay as still as possible, afraid the noise would give her movements away. There were large chunks of the mirror littered across the tile and Deena took one in her hand. She slowly leaned forward, jutting the shard into the hall, using its reflection to see where the men were. Both of them had stuck their heads out to see her as well. They opened fire on her and she ducked back into the room. At least she had managed to find out the men were in the living room on opposite sides of the hall entrance and neither of them were far away. It wasn't a happy thought.

She started to move forward again and her foot accidentally nudged something on the floor. The shotgun. She looked at it for a moment before deciding on her course of action. If they weren't going to come to her willingly, maybe she could push them along.

She placed the pistol on what was left of the sink and quietly checked the shotgun's ammo situation: six shells. Plenty. She stepped away from the wall and pointed the gun near the corner of the room. She tried to gauge exactly where the assailant was on the other side of that wall. She turned her head a little to try to avoid any shrapnel and pulled the trigger.

The blast was loud in the small room and Deena's ears started ringing immediately. Plaster, drywall and other scraps pelted her from the impact. A light layer of dust flew up and when it cleared, she saw that while the shot hadn't penetrated the wall, it had torn away almost everything on her side.

She racked the slide and tried again.

The results were better this time. When the dust and debris faded, she could see light streaming through the wall from the other side. One of the men let out a scream and she saw his shadow move past the light, followed by footfalls leading toward the front door.

She racked the slide again. She felt like she was trembling, but when she looked down the gun was steady. Her right hand was black; the dark tattoo-like blemish had spread out during the action. What appeared to be sharp ridges had formed on her knuckles and she hadn't felt a thing. She whispered the opening of a calming mantra she'd developed from a stupid exercise show she liked to make fun of when she didn't feel like getting off the couch. The floor creaked as one of her attackers approached in the hall.

Her assailant's shadow across the floor clued her to his exact movements and she waited for him to show himself so she could fire and have it done with. His shadow lingered and she gave him credit for not running headlong into a room with a girl holding a shotgun. As she finished mouthing her words, she heard his breathing. He hadn't been running, or lifting or anything else that required exertion but he was breathing heavily. He was scared. The man had seen what had happened to his friends, and he didn't want the same thing to happen to him. There were coins being tossed inside his head to decide if running was the better idea. After a few beats, Deena heard him move closer. It seemed his better judgment was on the losing end of the toss. Stupid.

She was staring at the open door, waiting for the right second, but unable to stop looking back at the man lying dead in a pool of blood in the hall. She yelled out to the man that was still alive. "Are you looking at the same thing I am? Are you looking at your buddy out there bleeding on the carpet, all full of holes?" She paused and listened to his ragged breathing a little more. "Are you thinking, 'That's not going to happen to me?' or are you wondering if you can run out the front door and still save face?"

It was quiet enough that Deena could hear the man lick his dry lips.

"Your other friend didn't seem to have any trouble running off," she said. The words caused her to involuntarily look back at the hole in the wall where she'd clipped the other man. She could see a form block the light there and a pistol appear near the hole. The runner had returned.

Deena started moving just as the pistol let out a roar that chipped the tile behind her. She dropped the shotgun as she charged the doorway, watching the shadow in the hall start moving again. The man appeared with his own handgun ready to point into the room, but she managed to grab it before he could get a shot off on her. They struggled and it was quickly evident to her that the man was taller and much stronger.

She used what skills she had to duck under the man's arms and punch him as hard as she could. He howled in pain and she punched again. Her hand felt wet and she was suddenly aware the other man was there too, his arms reaching out for her. She was thrilled that the first goon wasn't impeding her at all as she swung at the new target. She didn't look at this one's face, or stop to size him up, she just kept going.

After half a minute, Deena couldn't be sure if the men were even swinging back at her. The rest was a flurry of her own fists wildly flailing. She stepped back, and the men slumped against the wall and fell to the floor.

She looked at the three men lying motionless on the floor. The two she'd just fought were covered in scratches and gouges, all bleeding. She looked at her fists and found the ridges that had formed had risen even more, like seashells, jagged and sharp. They were dark with blood and the ink beneath them. She could feel her hands returning to normal slowly. They pulsed with retreating energy.

As she got hold of herself and calmed down, she noticed a small pile of debris in the middle of the men. She leaned closer and discovered it was her cell phone. It must have fallen from her pocket in the fight and gotten trampled or shot in the melee. So much for calling Harper back.

In the silence, she listened for the telltale sounds of anyone else coming for her. A silvery glint caught her eye. One of the shotgun blasts had blasted away part of the wall behind the shower. Deena tried to look into the hole to find the source of the light, but couldn't make anything out. She grabbed the crumpled tile and plaster and pulled, making the hole larger. She tore away enough to stick her head through and see a staircase leading downward.

In all the years she'd lived there, she hadn't known about a basement to their home. She looked up and guessed that the entrance had to be somewhere behind the living room closet. Deena broke more of the wall away, tucked a gun into her waistband and climbed over the debris to step down onto the wooden steps.

There was light coming from a bare bulb hanging above her.

44

The treehouse was safer than Morgan had expected and made a great vantage point from which to watch all of the proceedings at the house. He could have joined in and helped Marsh's men as they stormed the house to get the girl, but he figured that would have just gotten him killed like the others. They entered the home like it was just an average criminal proceeding. They had no idea what they were opening themselves up to. Each did things their own way, rather than working as a team. That's what got them killed. It was a small house. They could have easily covered every side and waited for more of Marsh's men to come and make it a slam-dunk.

But no. They made pigs of themselves in order to have the bragging rights. The One Who Brought Down The Witch.

So Morgan stayed out of it. He set up his rifle and focused the scope wide, to take in the whole house. He couldn't see the back from the treehouse, but anyone leaving would have to run for a few seconds in the open and he could nail them then.

"You just going to let those guys have all the fun? All the glory?" Brandt asked. "You're sitting up here with your fucking thumb up your ass. It doesn't look good. You look like a pussy."

"This is what I do. You know that. I prefer the long distance call. Let those guys get their hands dirty and their faces bloody," Morgan said. "If they are lucky and grab the girl? I'll just pop them in the head and take her for myself." Morgan felt pretty pleased with himself until he realized who he was talking to. "Now, who's the pussy?"

"Look, you can rationalize it all you want. You're still afraid to do anything yourself. Can't handle a little physical contact. Never could."

Morgan's college girlfriend pulled her way up the crude ladder. "You can say that again. He had trouble with all kinds of physical contact back in school. Technically, I guess I had trouble getting any contact in school, if you want to be honest."

Morgan rolled back over his stomach and repositioned himself and his rifle. He peered through the scope and refocused it on the door, then pulled out so he could see the whole house. Once he had both framed the way he wanted them, he focused back in and then out, getting used to going from one extreme to the other quickly. He settled on the wide view where he could see everything. He wanted to be ready just in case the girl and her friends tried to sneak out the back or if there was a car parked that he couldn't see.

"What if they go out the back and head through the weeds into the low trees? You'll never see them. You'll be sitting here all Goddamn night and never know they've gone," Brandt said. "There has to be a better spot. Hell, go lay in the tall grass. Better than this shit."

The smell of the trees and the swaying grass filled Morgan's head. He did city jobs. He liked city jobs. Concrete. Exhaust fumes. City smells.

"Aww. Is Morgan getting homesick?" Mr. Hector sounded genuinely concerned. "Maybe we should just go home. You can take a nice hot shower and crawl into bed. It'll all be better in the morning."

Morgan took a deep breath and focused on the scope in front of him. He stayed as silent as he could and strained, but he could faintly hear the traffic from the highway as it zipped by on its way to anywhere that wasn't here.

"He probably could use a nap, the pansy," Brandt said. "You gonna fall asleep waiting for any action to come your way clear out here? You're going to be waiting a good Goddamn long time, I can tell you that."

Mr. Hector walked up to the barrel of the gun and leaned on it. "Is that what you need? A little rest?"

"Fuck off." Morgan listened for the traffic and it pulled him back into the now and grounded him in what he had to do.

45

The basement wasn't much more than a large room with cinderblock walls and a bare concrete floor. Whoever the decorator was, they didn't put much work into it. On the opposite wall, there were three large plastic-and-metal containers the size of refrigerators lying on their sides. At one end, they had plastic windows to see inside. In several places on each wall were larger power outlets with room to plug in a half-dozen electric appliances at least.

Deena looked into the containers through the dust-covered clear panels, but they were empty. She walked along one of them, dragging her finger through the thick layer of dust. She noted that she, and just about anyone else, could fit easily inside. Fumbling with the latches on each end, she quickly figured out how to open it. She swung the lid up and confirmed it was empty inside. There were no knobs or dials or readouts, no levers; nothing that might operate the fridge. Deena did manage to uncover several ports that a computer and power source might plug into. There weren't any computers or displays or tablets in the room, however. The containers didn't look familiar to her.

As she walked through the room, Deena was blown away by the idea that directly above this area were the bedrooms, the bathroom and the living room. Had it been here all along? Did her dad know about it? Was it his? Or had it been a secret even from him? The cobwebs in the corners were pretty thick, but the dust didn't look that bad.

On the opposite wall, Deena noticed a panel cut into the concrete. She put her hands on the metal sheet that covered a hole and slid it aside. Inside was so dark, she couldn't see anything. Couldn't even make out the size of the room.

Above her, floorboards creaked in what must have been the living room.

"Deena Riordan? This is the FBI... er... the FEI."

Not this again, Deena thought. Another fake set of law enforcement? What the hell was the FEI? She looked down a narrow passage just as wide as the panel she'd moved. She couldn't tell how far back it went.

"Miss Riordan? This is Agents Garrett and Pelligrino with the FEI. If you're here, please identify yourself."

Deena looked up and considered trying to shoot them through the floor, but that wouldn't fit in with her whole "baby steps" thing to becoming a better person. After all, it was possible that the people upstairs were actual agents and killing them would be wrong. It was a long time since that thought had crossed her mind. Someone might be innocent and worth saving.

Deena reached into the passage and took a couple of steps forward. The wall wasn't nearly as far as she thought. On the other side was a set of metal rungs that led upward. Deena assumed it was a secret exit to the back lawn.

"Deena? This is Agent Pelligrino. We're aware of your situation." It was a female voice this time. "We'd like to help."

Deena opened some boxes she found in the corner, but they were all empty. "What situation is that?" Deena said it out loud almost by accident. She'd been mulling over her long list of problems, crimes and situations from the last few years. Were they talking about the latest situation? The developer in Tuscon that Deena had killed last year? Did they mean the car that ended up in Lake Michigan with a missing lawyer in it? They'd obviously needed to be more specific.

There was more creaking from upstairs as the man, Garrett, spoke again. "Look. I think we're aware of most of your history. We know about Marsh and the work you've done for him. We're also aware of the power you have. The Ink... uh... dark gift... or whatever you want to call it?"

Dark gift? Who had this guy been talking to? Deena wondered. "Sure. I have a *gift* let's call it. What about it?"

There was another creak from the floor above her. "We know how it's out of your control," Pel said.

"How about you just stand where you are and talk to me," Deena said. The longer she could keep them upstairs, the more time she had to figure out her next move. In the past, she probably wouldn't have given a second thought to fighting and possibly killing someone in law enforcement. Things were different now. She was trying hard not to be one of those stupid people she made fun of. "Sounds like you know a lot about me. Who've you been talking to?"

"The government detained a man named Leonard with the same sort of powers as you," Garrett said. "He had some interesting information for us on his condition. We know that your behavior is out of your control."

The name didn't ring any bells for Deena, and she'd never met anyone else with her powers before. "Go on."

"He talked about his thing hijacking his body and making him do what he was told," Pel said. "He said it was like being trapped in his body with no say in what he did. Is that how it is for you?"

Marsh's orders had been the catalyst for everything she'd done throughout the last decade and no matter how she'd fought it, she couldn't stop herself from doing the horrible things he'd told her to do. She'd loved it on some level. She'd loved making him happy. "Something like that."

"Marsh? Was it his orders you had to follow?"

Deena cautiously walked back toward the stairs. "Look. Cut to the chase. You want to help me? How?" In the years that Deena had been working for Marsh, no one had ever offered to help her. No one had suggested what she was doing was wrong.

Except her sister. Harper had been terrified in the early months and years of what they were doing. She didn't have the benefit of the Shadow Energy running through her and numbing her to the horrible things she was doing.

46

Pel stood next to Garrett at the end of the hallway, pointing her gun in the direction of Deena's voice. "What happened here, Deena?" she asked. "Are you all right?"

Garrett examined the bodies on the floor near the bathroom. It was a bloody mess and it was obvious that Deena had gotten the better of them. From the bullet holes in the walls, Garrett was surprised that the girl had walked away from the fight. But, if everything he'd heard about Deena was true, he imagined she could handle herself.

Deena went silent.

"Please answer me, are you OK? Do you need medical attention?" Pel asked.

Garrett pointed to Pel and motioned for her to keep talking. He felt Pel might have more luck keeping the girl engaged. She and might trust a woman more than a man in a hostile situation.

"Are there more attackers in the house, Deena? We're walking around up here to make sure no one is going to take us by surprise. Are there more wherever you are?" Pel looked around the living room but her gaze quickly came back to Garrett.

It took a moment, but the girl finally responded. "No," Deena said. "I think that's it."

Garrett stood still, not wanting to rile Deena up. If she wanted them to stay still, they'd do it, at least for a little while. He was actually surprised that she'd decided to speak to him. He took it as a good sign.

Crouching just outside the bathroom, he took stock of the dead men and the rest of the scene there. The bits of sink and tile were overrun with blood that flowed easily from the men there. He didn't recognize any of them, but he imagined them to be more of Marsh's goons. He'd received a report from the train that at least one of the men found there was confirmed as a "foot soldier" for the organization.

It took him a minute, but Garrett noticed that the hole on the far wall was deeper than it should be. In the dim light of the room, he noticed a faint glow on the other side of the wall. He pointed it out to Pel, but said nothing.

"So, what is the grand plan here? If you know my situation, you know I have to go help my sister. Marsh has her. I would hope you at least know that," Deena said.

"We know, Deena." Pel replied. "We should have a warrant any minute and our task force will go in and get Harper. Harper will be fine."

Garrett liked how Pel had begun to work Deena and Harper's names into the conversation. It implied that they cared and personalized the conversation. Hopefully it was doing something to ease Deena's fears about trusting the agents. However, they had a long way to go before the girl walked out the door with them.

"No. Marsh will worm his way out of it. He'll get out before you can do a thing about it and my sister will die," Deena said.

Pel looked at Garrett but he had no other angle for his fellow agent. They had to wing it and hope to talk Deena into surrendering somehow.

"Look. You have to know that if you go in there that Marsh is going to kill you both. You just can't do this alone," Pel shrugged to Garrett.

"That's what you went with? You're going to die anyway?" Garrett whispered.

"You didn't seem to have any other ideas," Pel responded quietly.

"Listen, you want me to surrender peacefully? We do things my way, and once my sister is safe, I'll do whatever you ask. You help me. I'll surrender no problem and do what you want. I just want my sister to be OK. I got her into this."

"I don't know if we can do that. We want your sister to be safe, too. But you're both wanted criminals. We know you have been doing this work against your will, but we still need to prove that. And your sister..." Pel stopped.

Garrett thought about the bus bombing that Harper was responsible for and wondered if Deena had even heard about it. There was no way that Harper was walking away from the situation unscathed, assuming she lived. At the very least, Deena had the Shadow Energy to blame for what she'd done. As far as he knew, Harper had no such excuse.

47

"Jesus. Looks like a couple of feds," Brandt said. "Getting awfully crowded in that little house."

Morgan nodded without meaning to. He'd guess the man and woman were federal agents, just by their clothes and the way they approached the house. Their suits were tasteful, but off the rack. He watched as they walked together, checking out the side of the house, watching each other's backs and moving strategically.

"A girl? That one agent is a girl," Mr. Hector said. "You like killing girls, don't you? How exciting. Hope the man doesn't give you too much trouble, though. He looks like he might work out."

"Are you implying that I can't handle men?" Morgan didn't want to show weakness and hated that he let the apparitions get a reaction from him. "I've killed plenty of men."

"From a distance."

"I've killed men with my bare hands. Just because I prefer to do it from a distance, doesn't mean shit," Morgan said.

"Just sayin'."

"Well stop saying it." His orders were to catch or kill Deena Riordan. There was nothing that suggested anyone from the federal government. If he killed her with them present, his escape could become problematic. They would pursue him and surely an unwanted conflict would ensue.

Brandt didn't allow a silence to set in. "You're not worried about a couple more dead people are you? Come on. You're right at the finish line. Kill them all and you'll have everything. You'll be Marsh's right hand man, with all the work you ever want. Hell, he may even move you out of the field and into the office with him," Brandt said. He was leaning against the side of the treehouse smoking a thick, noxious cigar. "You'd be in line to take over when he leaves the organization."

Nadine spoke up from the other side of the treehouse, but Morgan didn't turn to see her. "Then, you can get all the girls you want. And they'll *have* to do all the kinky shit you want them to."

"What kind of stuff are we talking about?" Brandt asked.

48

That wasn't the answer Deena had hoped for. She hadn't really anticipated the agents would accept her offer, even though she meant it. She was ready to put it all behind her and pay for what she'd done, but she couldn't leave Harper. Not after all she'd done to try to protect Deena. Not after Deena had dragged her into this hell.

"Look. Get me to Marsh's office before that warrant gets served and I'll surrender to the agents when they show up. Both of us will. Harper and I will do it willingly. It'll save us all a whole lot of pain and headache," Deena said. If she didn't make some sort of a deal with the agents, Deena knew she'd be hounded the rest of the way to the city and she just didn't need more distractions. She was being honest about turning herself over. No matter what abilities she had, she couldn't see putting Harper through more time running away and hiding. The question was whether her sister would feel the same.

"We can't make that deal," Pel said. "You know we can't do that without causing all kinds of problems for ourselves. That kind of thing is *way* over our heads."

"Then are you going to chase me some more? Who has time for that? Get me to the city and give me a head start." Deena checked the pistol in her waistband. She didn't need one. Not right now. But there would come a time, when she got to Marsh's place, where she'd have to decide whether she was going to go back to using her powers or keep them in check. So far, that hadn't worked. They'd emerged no matter what.

"I'm putting my gun down and coming out to join you. Let's talk about this." Deena put the gun on the steps and began to cautiously make her way up toward the top. "I'm coming out of a door behind the closet and I don't have a weapon." Not a gun, at least.

Deena fiddled with a latch at the top of the stairs and the door swung in. She found herself inside their hall closet. She turned around and closed the door and examined it. Unless you knew what to look for, you'd never see that there was a secret door there. She turned and opened the closet door slowly. Outside, two people in dark suits pointed guns at her. "Agents Pelligrino and Garrett, I'm assuming?"

"Turn around," Garrett said.

"There's no need for this." Deena twirled slowly for the agents to prove that she didn't have another weapon of any sort. "I left my gun back there, like I said."

Garrett pulled out his handcuffs and looked at them for a moment. It seemed he wasn't sure what to do next.

"Are those really necessary? I mean it's not like you can hold someone with my power anyway," Deena said. She didn't know if she could escape from cuffs or not, but she figured they didn't know it either.

"We have a suspect back at the office that would beg to differ with you. He's been incarcerated for a year or so." Agent Garrett stepped forward and closed the cuffs on one of Deena's hands then moved it to her back to attach it to the other arm.

"I don't know who you have, but you probably don't have him quite as tight as you think you do. Not if he has my power." The more Deena thought about it, it seemed like it would be easy to break the restraints if she wanted, if she just let the Shadow Energy run wild like it did back on the train, but she knew they'd never cooperate if she didn't lull them into thinking she was under control.

Once she was cuffed, Deena saw both agents visibly relax. She watched as Pel moved down the hall, checking out the scene in the bathroom, and then disappearing into the bedrooms. When she stuck her head back out she said, "No more bodies or lurkers that I can find. Let's call Rivers and let him know what's going on. I'm sure he can send a team out to go over the whole place more thoroughly. But I'd like to suggest we hit the road again." She crouched down and started going through the pockets of the men in the crowded hall.

Garrett directed Deena to the living room and sat her down on the couch. "Wait here," Garrett headed for the kitchen before reappearing with a wet handkerchief to wipe off Deena's hands. "Are you all right? You never really said." He looked at her torn shirt and pants.

"Most of the blood there isn't mine, I'm fine." Deena didn't bother to say she'd been recently shot on the train. It had already healed and didn't even ache anymore.

Pel pulled a water bottle out and held it up to Deena's lips. "Drink. You look awful."

Deena drank the water and stood up. "Thanks and everything. But you're right. We need to move before more of these guys crawl out of the woodwork. If you found me, they can find me." Deena held her hands up as best she could. "And I don't want to be all chained up if someone comes shooting at us, OK?"

Deena watched as Garrett opened the door to let her walk out. "Let's get moving, then. We aren't really equipped to fight a bunch of thugs right now."

Deena stood and followed. "Give me the keys. I'll drive."

Pel turned and looked at Deena. "That's OK. I'll do it. Thanks for the offer."

"Yeah. She can sit in back with me and we'll talk," Garrett said.

"Let's just get out of here. Time is running in short supply here," Deena said. "Especially for Harper."

49

Deena at 18 the first time around

Harper smacked Deena on the back of the head as she walked past. "Get up. You've gotta be downstairs in ten."

"I don't want to train anymore," Deena said, swinging her leg over the arm of the couch. "I'm tired." She'd been up late the night before, watching movies. They'd managed to finally afford basic cable and Deena wasn't about to waste a moment of it.

"This is your shit. You wanted to do this. If you piss off Marsh now, there's no telling what will happen." Harper went through this every morning since they started working for Marsh. Harper got up at five, gathered things together and pulled the covers off of Deena, screaming at her to get up. Deena would immediately bury her head under her pillows and sigh. Harper would try again every ten minutes until six or so. At that point, it was always time to fight dirty. "We could have just stayed at the diner."

"Not after the robbery."

"And whose fault was that?"

"You act like I have some kind of control over this. I don't. It just happens," Deena said. She'd found she could control it to a point. Her thoughts were a direction for the power, like a suggestion.

"Wah. Some of us have to make it without that crap. Let's go. We have to be downstairs at this warehouse at six-thirty." Harper set a bag on the table. "I packed your gym bag, extra clothes, a snack. You're ready to go. I don't know exactly what my role is going to be in all of this, but I'm thrilled to be your valet. To no end."

"Seriously? You packed me a snack for our first day of work with the mobster? Christ, you're not my mom," Deena said. "I can do it myself."

Harper flipped her off. "You know, screw you. You can do it yourself, but you don't, do you?" She tossed the blue bag at Deena and took off toward the door. "This is all fun and games for you, isn't it? You made this bed, but we both get to lie in it, don't we?" She opened the door and started into the hallway.

"You're so dramatic," Deena called after her. She grabbed the bag and followed her sister. She had to take long strides to catch up.

Harper lowered her tone in the hall and Deena knew she was afraid one of the other tenants would hear. "We're living in a Goddamn high-rise with murderers, thieves and other horrible people, learning to be just like them, and you think I'm being dramatic?"

Harper punched the handle to the stairwell door and knocked it open. She slung her own pack over her shoulder and started down the 576 steps to the main floor. Step after step, she picked up the pace, obviously trying to out-distance her sister and work out some of the anger that was brewing.

The two of them had been living inside each other's personal space for the last several months. They went to the diner at the same time, they came home at the same time, worked out in the gym together, did laundry, slept and rode the bus together. Deena thought about that as she heard Harper's feet pound on each step, louder and louder. Harper spun at each landing, barely touching it as she continued to the next set of stairs.

Deena had been threatening her sister as subtly as she could. She suggested Harper would be held accountable in some way for what Deena had done to Mike. That she would be implicated in what Deena had done to the stick-up men in the diner, or the killers in the woods. So far, it was enough to get Harper to keep running. There was some inherent guilt in Harper, but the shock of all of the events piling up on each other kept her running. Deena didn't feel good about what she was doing to her sister, but the lure of the criminal life, the thought of working for Marsh, had a hold on Deena that she couldn't break and she would do anything to make it happen.

Still, she wondered where that would leave her sister. What was Harper's breaking point, and what would happen when she reached it?

Deena skipped the last two steps, passed Harper on the landing and slammed into the door, shoving it open and kept going to the street. They both turned on the sidewalk and moved down the alley. "What are we doing? Will they take us to Marsh's office?"

"How the fuck should I know?" Harper asked. Deena knew her sister cussed more when she was nervous. "Let's go to damn gym and find out." She pointed down the alley. "All I know is Ramirez'll blow a gasket if we're late."

Deena rubbed her arm and watched her sister disappear around the corner of the building. The gym where they worked out was not a fancy, upscale city gym where women went to do Pilates and ride exercise bikes. There was a woman who did the books and another who came in and cleaned a couple of times of week, but other than that, Deena and Harper were a rarity. Deena didn't mind the smell so much after a while and Harper had finally learned to stop complaining about it, but the smell of sweaty, bleeding fetid men continued to make her nose visibly curl every time they entered the facility.

There were limited options for anyone who wanted to work out. They had heavy bags to pound, speed bags to punch and weights to lift. Some jump ropes and medicine balls rounded out the facilities.

In the workout area, Deena found the usual assortment of men who hung around with seemingly nothing to do but lift weights and run laps. Six of them this time, which was about average. The sisters had been using the facility for a while and had never seen the place crowded, but it was also never empty.

Once both sisters were in the room and had placed their bags on the floor, Ramirez entered, his face twisted in its usual scowl. A man they'd never met followed Ramirez.

"Good morning, girls. Nice of you to show up," Ramirez said.

A searing pain erupted on Deena's arm and she saw the line, like a shadow, sweep down her arm. "Hey." She was immediately on guard and wary of the new person.

This is Mr. Danny Englewood," Ramirez said. He pointed to the disheveled man who had moved closer to the main door. "Until approximately twenty-four hours ago, Danny was in prison upstate."

Harper looked at her sister and then back at the wiry Mr. Englewood. "What was he in prison for?"

"Don't ask, because you really don't want to know."

Englewood smiled, revealing a crooked line of yellowed teeth with a number of gaps. His eyes were red and bloodshot. He walked with a confident swagger and Deena assumed he was high on something. He seemed very pleased with himself.

"Danny's the kind of man you're going to be working with here in the organization. I just thought you'd like to start meeting your coworkers now, rather than later. Just so you know what you're getting into," Ramirez seemed pleased with himself.

Englewood dropped his jacket on a chair and began unbuttoning his thin white shirt to slowly reveal the tattoos that littered his upper chest and torso. Images of eagles and skulls were interspersed with the American flag and a fiery pair of eyes near his neck. There wasn't a space anywhere from his chin down that wasn't overlaid by the ink work. Deena thought about the little spot of blackness on her arm that had put them in this situation and she worried that Mr. Englewood might be some kind of strange sorcerer like herself. She looked closer to see if any of his artwork moved like hers did.

"Like what you see little girl?" Englewood caught her staring. "You'll get your chance soon enough." He started toward them with a disturbing confidence. "Ramirez here told me all about you girls. He says you like to party."

The girls looked over at Ramirez. He was smiling wide and had a number of the men in the room gathering behind him near the door. It seemed everyone in the room was smiling except Deena and Harper.

Deena's body tensed and she felt a cramp forming in her stomach to go along with the pain in her arm. Deena didn't answer, but something inside her started assessing the distance to objects around her that she could use as weapons. There was a scale in her mind that was slowly dipping down toward violence. And she was beginning to look forward to it. Just as the violence in the woods and at the diner had thrilled her, the anticipation of it here was overwhelming her brain.

"Oh. I think you'll find out that I like to party, too. I'm a regular party guy," Englewood said. He was slowly circling the girls and getting closer as he did.

Harper held up her hands. "Look, we're not…"

She didn't get to finish as Englewood lunged forward and punched her in the jaw.

Harper stumbled backward and tipped over, falling to floor, only to be caught by Englewood. He grabbed her by the shirt and pulled her so close that Harper had to be able to smell his breath. "Enough Goddamn talking. I've had nothing but talking for the last ten years. I'm done with talking."

There was a cheer from the men assembled to watch.

Deena reached for Englewood but was blocked by a young boxer named Dane who grabbed her from behind. He had a tight grip on her waist and dragged her backward while another man quickly grabbed one of her arms.

It was hard for Deena to focus, as blind rage brought the familiar shadow across her body. She could see that the blow had really jarred her sister and she was only standing because Englewood was holding her up. She feebly tried to raise her arms but just couldn't muster the strength.

"OK, we get it. You're in charge here and you don't like us," Deena told Ramirez. "But we've made a deal with Marsh. He wants us to work for him. He made a deal with us."

"Jesus Christ. We don't need to do this," Harper mumbled. "Marsh asked us to be here. He told us that we were here to work." She was on the verge of tears, but was still too shocked to cry.

"Yeah? Marsh asked me to be here, too. Seems he's not convinced you're an asset," Ramirez said. "He put me in charge of you to do whatever I thought was necessary.

I decided that you're no good to him if you can't handle yourselves. You'd be pretty worthless to him, wouldn't you say? Your careers as ruthless criminals would be wildly short lived. And that's not a good thing."

"We don't have to do this," Deena's voice pierced the encroaching blackness.

Ramirez's response came like a whisper from the void. "Oh, we do. We most certainly do have to do this."

Englewood grabbed Harper's shirt with both hands and ripped it, revealing the girl's black sports bra underneath. The men cheered again.

"Stop." Deena's voice shook within her chest. She closed her eyes and thought about the spikes that had protruded from her knuckles in the past. She waited a moment as she felt her arm become thick, filling with darkness. Immediately, the man holding her arm screamed a high-pitched cry. They both looked down to see thorny protrusions had emerged from her arms and into his hands, the largest of them came out the other side of his wrist. He tried to pull away, but was stuck fast. Deena took a swing and connected with his nose, causing an audible crack. She released him from the spikes and he fell on the floor.

Deena was still held around the waist by Dane, who squeezed her tighter and lifted her off the ground in an effort to gain control. The other four spectators weren't laughing, and they moved in to help Dane. Ramirez stayed where he was, seemingly confident that the men would handle her, and Englewood stayed with Harper.

It was hard for Deena to get any sort of angle to grab Dane, as he continued to squeeze from behind. She twisted and turned, but his grip was too strong. Her breath was getting short as she struggled to take in more air. The ends of her fingernails became sharp black claws. She plunged them into Dane's arms and dragged them up from the wrist to the elbow. The cuts tore a gouge that flayed the skin and immediately dripped blood. Dane let go.

Free to move again, Deena stepped toward Englewood and Harper, but was blocked by the remaining four, who encircled her. Deena was about to warn them of a dire fate if they didn't let her pass, but decided not to. She didn't have the capacity for coherent language and they were grown adults. Stupid ass adults.

There wasn't much of a fight. The men had size and strength, but Deena had energy in her body that crept out like murderous shadows. There was no grace to Deena's fighting; she'd never had much call to practice. She attacked like some feral animal cornered and afraid for its life. The men's size worked against them, as they couldn't get out of each other's way fast enough to react to her slashes and kicks. They were all down in a matter of minutes.

"Whoa. OK. We need to dial this back. It got out of hand real quick," Ramirez said. He held up his hands to try to calm Deena. "This wasn't supposed to go quite this far. We were just going to get a little rough and teach you a lesson." He looked over at Englewood, but distanced himself from the man, slowly taking steps away.

Harper was pinned beneath Englewood, who had barely noticed what was going on around him. He was tearing at Harper's sweatpants and nuzzling his face into her neck, nearly salivating as he went about his work. Harper's shirt lay in tatters and her black sports bra shined in the harsh gym lighting.

Ramirez tried to get Englewood's attention, but stayed away from him. "Christ, Englewood. Stop." Deena ended his plea by swinging her arm in his direction. She didn't look at him, only thought of a meat cleaver as her arm made an arc across his body.

Ramirez's scream finally got Englewood's attention. He turned to see that he was the only one unscathed in the room. He staggered to his feet and took a moment to quickly button his pants back up. "What's this? What the hell is this?" His eyes were glassy as he tried to focus on Deena.

"What *is* this? What *is* it?" Deena growled. She took steady strides toward Englewood. "You started it. You tell me."

A switchblade appeared in Englewood's hand, produced slickly from his back pocket. "I don't know what you…" Deena punched him in the jaw before he could finish. He staggered back, swinging the blade in front of him to prevent Deena from a quick follow up blow. "Look bitch. I am here to teach you a lesson." The knife settled between the two of them. "*That's* what's goin' on here." His words were wet with the blood that was dripping from his lips."

"Get the fuck away from my sister," Deena said. She saw what she thought was a shadow pass over her whole body and it spurred her on. She thought of a handcuff and a line of the blackness shot out of her and wrapped itself around Englewood's wrist, immobilizing the knife he was holding. He struggled as Deena pulled him closer with the dark restraint. Realizing he couldn't use the knife, Englewood swung at Deena with his free hand.

"I think today's lesson is about over. Don't you?" Deena asked. She thought about the knife drawer at home and immediately, her fingers elongated with Shadow Energy and flattened into the likenesses of the sharp and serrated things that she kept in her kitchen: steak knives, a paring knife, bread knives and other sharp cutlery.

As soon as he was close enough, Deena sliced Englewood. She'd considered letting his wrist free, just to give him a chance, but didn't. He hadn't given Harper such a chance. Deena brought her razor-sharp fingers across his chest, cutting through the fabric and leaving rows of deep gashes.

She suddenly felt nauseous. It wasn't a reaction to the blood or what she was doing to Englewood, it was something internal. Her grip on him weakened and the tendril that had wrapped itself around his wrist was beginning to loosen. As she struggled to maintain her grip on him, her body rebelled with spasms of sharp needle-pricks of pain. She felt light-headed and stumbled. Englewood saw an opportunity and tugged his arm free. He swung at Deena with the knife and managed to cut her across the arm. The pain gave Deena enough of a jolt to keep herself in the fight. She pulled her arm back, and shoved all of the blades that had grown from her hand into Englewood's chest and then pushed as hard as she could. She stumbled forward and knocked Englewood to the floor, falling on top of him and shoving the blades in with all her weight.

The last thing Deena heard before passing out was Englewood's piercing scream.

She awoke the next day in the crappy apartment she shared with her sister. Harper had dragged her there after the fight and nursed her to health as best she could. Deena had no scars, no bruises, not a single scratch. But Harper made a point to hand her sister a mirror. What Deena saw there was a sight that made her sit up and look again. In the mirror, she saw herself three years ago. It was subtle, sure. But the definition, the shape was different in her cheeks and chin. "It's a good thing, right?" Deena said to her sister. "I can use this power and stay young forever. That's the best power, ever."

Harper stared at her with pale, vacant eyes.

"What?"

"You've been asleep since yesterday. I've been sitting here waiting on Marsh's men to burst through the door and kill us," Harper said. She nodded over to the coffee table. There were two automatic pistols resting there with a scattering of bullets next to them. "I took them from the gym. I thought I was going to have to use them."

Deena rubbed her eyes as she stared back at the mirror. "Why would they come for us? They gave us a test and we passed. Why would they have a problem?"

"You killed most of them. You killed Marsh's men. Why *wouldn't* they?"

The thought of what happened yesterday was hiding somewhere in her mind, but wouldn't fully reveal itself to Deena. "Back in school, they didn't penalize you for passing a particularly hard math test, did they? That wouldn't be fair." Deena pushed her hair back, to look at her neck and ears. The changes in her body were so subtle.

50

Morgan took a deep breath as he saw the figures through the picture window. They were moving towards the door.

"Here they come. You're going to kill them all, right?" Brandt's words felt hot on Morgan's neck. "Goddamnit, if you don't do it this time, I'll lose my shit."

The Russian SVN-98 sniper rifle felt right in Morgan's hands. It was fast becoming one of Morgan's all-time favorites, even though the experimental model was still new to the market. He'd adjusted for the light breeze, calmed himself and controlled the rising and falling of his chest. As they moved away from the window, he zoomed in closer to the door, anticipated it opening and waited for the first of them to walk out.

"Do you need a breath mint?" Brandt asked.

Morgan's mom spoke up in her soothing tone. "Juice box?"

"Are you comfy?" Mr. Hector sounded sincerely concerned. "We just want to make sure you handle this right. Your whole future's riding on it."

"After all, if you miss, everyone will think you're a dick," Nadine said.

"No pressure," Brandt added.

With his breathing still in check, Morgan waited a few more moments for something to actually happen in the house. The door swung open slowly and his scope was suddenly filled with targets. The blonde agent came into view first, followed by Deena and finally, the black agent bringing up the rear.

"Cookies, maybe? I can make you a nice batch of oatmeal raisin. You used to love those." Morgan's mother stepped close enough that her feet were visible next to him as he looked into the scope.

"No. Knock it off, I don't need anything."

"Just shoot all of them," Brandt said.

Nadine leaned close, her breath, stinking of beer and cigarettes, was wet in his ear. "Get this over with, so they don't come back to haunt you later."

"Yeah. Hate to see them come back to mess you up." Morgan could hear Wallace's voice outside the treehouse, somewhere below them.

"You really shouldn't have killed Wallace. He was such a nice man." Mr. Hector suddenly seemed very sympathetic to a man that everyone agreed would probably have killed Morgan, given half a chance. It was pretty much par for the course. The teddy bear could turn on a dime.

"Shut up, he deserved what he got," Morgan said. "There's no room in Marsh's office for both of us. I did what I had to. Ask Brandt, he knows. I was just securing my future."

Mr. Hector started to laugh and Nadine joined in almost immediately. "Aren't you supposed to be quiet when you're sneaking up on someone?" Mr. Hector asked.

Morgan realized that he'd taken his eye from the scope in order to admonish a teddy bear that wasn't even there. He'd never let his demons distract him from doing his job in all the years they'd been coming to him. They'd faded into the background the moment he'd locked on his targets and he'd successfully completed each job despite their interference.

He leaned back down and put his eye to the scope.

51

The warm sunlight felt good on Deena's face as they stepped through the doorway. The fresh air was a welcome change from the musty house. She'd miss the place. The city was great for a murderous thug, but that wasn't her life anymore, she hoped. No. She wouldn't go back to that. But with every contract killer and murderer suddenly knowing her address, she didn't see any chance of moving back into the old house. Maybe a nice little cottage in the woods, or something. That would be nice. Something by a stream. Good Lord, she was losing it. How was that childish fairytale ending ever going to happen? She was handcuffed and being led to a car that would deliver her to prison, where she'd live in a cell no bigger than her old treehouse. It wouldn't be so bad actually living in her treehouse, but to have to be behind bars would ruin it. It certainly wouldn't have as good of a view.

Deena looked up to see if her former hideout was still on its perch and in good condition. The sides had mostly fallen off, but the floor itself seemed to be hanging in there. Imperceptibly, she saw movement on the platform; the outline of a man was clearly visible laying down and turning.

"Get down," Deena lunged, knocking Pel forward. As she did, the report of a rifle rang through the woods and an area of the doorframe splintered from the impact of a bullet. She saw Agent Garrett drop to the ground, the bullet landing just a few inches to the right of him.

Strength rose within Deena's body and her arms felt like granite. She struggled to pull them from the cuffs, but saw that Agent Pel was still exposed to the gunman. Without much thought, Deena stepped in front of the agent to shield her from the sniper's next shot. "Get inside," Deena said.

The young agent didn't need prompting, and was already scrambling back toward the door. When her foot hit the porch, another shot exploded from the hidden assassin.

The white-hot pain that ripped through Deena's shoulder threw her backward. She'd managed to maneuver herself between the gun and Pel, blocking a bullet that most likely would have found the agent had Deena not been there. Deena stumbled back and fell to her knees. Behind her, the agents had pulled out their sidearms and were firing back. The bark of the firing handguns hurt Deena's ears, with the weapons so close to her head.

Pel grabbed Deena around her uninjured arm and pulled her inside out of danger. Another shot from their assailant tore a chunk off the doorframe.

"Are you all right?" Pel asked. She examined the wound, pulling Deena's shirt away, to get a better look. Pel's hand immediately went over the wound to try to stop the blood.

It hurt like hell. It was a burning sensation that was unlike the last time, when she got shot on the train. She wondered if the bullet had broken a bone, or severed something important in the shoulder or collarbone.

"Jesus. Garrett. Look," Pel said.

They all turned to see the blood seeping over Agent Pel's hand had turned black.

"Don't worry. That's perfectly normal." Deena was having success in getting her breath and staying calmer this time as the dark substance leaked out and went about its work. "Take your hand away. It'll be OK."

They watched as the wound did the same thing it had last time. The blood stopped flowing, replaced by the black ooze, then that also stopped and the wound became just another dot. The difference this time was that it still burned inside. She suspected that would pass, but it was hard to say. She'd never been this terribly injured when she was under the Shadow Energy's control. She thought of it like that now. It wasn't a power that she'd been wielding all that time; the power was wielding her. Now that she was free of it, how would it affect her and how long would it still work?

There were two more shots from their unseen foe, before it got quiet again.

"What other exits are there?" Garrett asked.

Deena considered a tactical perspective that she'd never applied to her home. "Back door, bedroom windows. And I just discovered a trap door out of the basement."

"Our car is so exposed out there. How are we going to get to it?" Pel snuck a look before crouching and moving to the next room to look out the window.

"I have a car out back," Deena said. "Should be easy to get to. I mean, if you want to stay here and track this guy down, I get it, but I'd rather put some distance between us and this place. What do you think Agent Garrett?"

Pel motioned toward the area where the gunfire originated. "He's already out the back and circling in on the guy. Give him a second."

Deena could feel the agent's gaze. "I'll be fine. I think." She touched the area where the bullet had penetrated, which was now nothing but a streak of blood and grime. "I got shot on the train and it feels just dandy now."

The blonde agent didn't look terribly convinced. "If you say so." Pel looked back out the door. "Here we go."

Agent Garrett had made his way around and was moving from tree to tree for cover. Deena could see him slowly moving forward, pointing his weapon at the treehouse, pausing to watch for movement before moving on again. As best Deena could tell, nothing was happening. After a couple of minutes, the agent made it to the old hideout and looked up from below before climbing up the old wooden rungs. He shook his head for Pel's benefit before pulling out his radio. "There's some blood up here," Garrett's voice crackled from speaker. "Not a lot. I'm going down and have a look around. See if I can figure which direction he went."

"Got it, I'll stay with Riordan," Pel replied. Her partner climbed down and moved off stealthily in the woods again.

"He's long gone," Deena said. "Hard to tell how far he's gone or if he'll be back, but he's gone for now."

"Friend of yours?"

"Not anymore, I guess." She looked out of the window for Garrett, but couldn't find him in the tangle of trees that surrounded the house. "If you didn't know who we were dealing with before, you know now. They want me dead and they don't care who gets in the way. They'll kill you, your partner, my sister…"

"Look, not to be indelicate, how do you know they haven't killed her already?"

"I get the feeling Marsh believes I'll come in, change my mind and things'll go right back to normal," Deena said. "That I'll take one look at his wrinkled old face and fall back under his spell."

"That's not going to happen?"

"Nope." Deena tried to rally her voice to sound as sure as should could to the agent. The reality was she wasn't positive of anything. She didn't trust her instincts and still found herself drifting into teenage thinking and flawed logic. "Look, if you don't think your partner will let us go after my sister, I can run out back and jump in my car and zip off to the big city by myself. It's not really my car; I stole it from a bitchy exercise lady. It's a little car, but it's peppy, it moves like you wouldn't believe. "

52

It was quiet in the car for the longest time as Garrett drove down the interstate toward Los Angeles.

"Soooo…" Pel was in the backseat with Deena.

Garrett had already made up his mind that he wasn't calling in anything to Rivers or Rice. They should've let the agents know they had Deena, they'd been attacked, hell, there were any number of things that they should have told their superiors, but they didn't. Deena had saved them from that sniper's bullet. Garrett really didn't see any reason to draw attention to their situation. As far as he knew there weren't any other killers, monsters or freaks following them and there was no reason to think otherwise, so he didn't want to ask for backup.

No one responded to Pel, so she dropped the question, such as it was.

Garrett himself hated the silence, hated driving these stretches of highway. All the flat fields and cows. He let the silence go for ten more minutes, which allowed him to count six more tractors and two dozen sheep.

"So where are we going?" Deena asked.

It was quiet for another moment.

"I think we need to start back at Marsh's office," Garrett said.

Deena's statement was simple. "Yeah. That sounds about right. We need to finish this one way or another I guess. But I can't put you in danger again. I think I should go in alone."

"The only reason we're going is because I'm letting you. We should take you straight in and put you in a cell," Garrett said. "Let's not talk too much about it. We'll go in with you, and if anyone gives us shit, we'll make up some excuse."

"Thanks."

"Are you sure you're going to be able to handle Marsh?" Pel asked. "This imprinting thing might kick in and make you want to keep working for him."

"Just worry about your own ass. He obviously has reacted poorly to finding out I'm no longer his favorite puppy. He's going to want to eliminate everyone involved in order to cover his trail," Deena said. She held up her wrists and jiggled the handcuffs. "You're going to take these off before we get there, right? Can't do much with these on."

It was something he knew they'd have to do eventually, if they really wanted to help her here. "You know much about his organization?" Garrett watched the road, but he kept eyeing Deena in the rearview mirror.

"Enough."

Garrett questioned his choice again. Someone that valuable shouldn't be walking into a situation where they could be killed. If her information was substantial enough to shut down Marsh's organization, she should be in a safe house, or a jail cell, or in a highly guarded convoy headed in the opposite direction from Marsh. Here he was, driving her right into the path of danger. Still, she'd never talk if he let something happen to her sister.

"We need to do this my way, though. I'll direct how we enter and how we handle Marsh's men. There may be a way yet to get out of this with minimal conflict," Garrett said. "I want you and Harper to come out of this intact, so you can tell us all about the fun things Marsh is doing."

"Garrett?" Pel said.

"If we can put that smarmy bastard away, it would truly make my day."

"Garrett?"

"Maybe you should start filling us in just a bit. You don't have to spill it all."

"She's asleep."

"What?" Garrett looked back up into the rearview mirror and saw that, indeed, Deena was leaning back in her seat with her eyes closed. She was even snoring lightly. "Guess she's had a rough day."

"We've all had a couple of busy days."

"What? You want to nap too?"

Pel leaned forward and talked over Garrett's shoulder. "Later. Look. I'm worried about making promises to her. We don't have the authority for any of that. That bus bombing her sister pulled is still fresh and the press is going nuts with crazy speculation."

"We've been on the move constantly since that happened. How do you know what they're saying?"

Pel waved her phone in front of him. "Seriously? You need to learn how to use this. They're saying it was a terrorist attack, but they can't agree if it was homegrown or foreign. They're all over the map."

"Figures. That's the first thing everyone would think in a situation like this," Garrett said.

"And it isn't going to go away. When they find out we've grabbed the prime suspect, they're going to want her and they're going to want to parade her around in public and show everyone its safe again. And let's face it: *we* know she did it." Pel messed around with her phone and shoved it in Garrett's face. He swerved as he tried to look from the phone to the road. "And look," Pel said. "Our old boss is even all over the news making statements."

A video played of Harris at the crime scene with a dozen microphones in front of him. He made a quick statement that was non-committal, but said they had leads. It was full of vagaries that said absolutely nothing about what was actually happening. Anyone with half a brain could tell that he knew nothing.

"That was *our* case," Pel said. "If Rivers and Rice hadn't pulled us out, we'd be the ones making the statements and we'd be the ones without a freaking clue what was going on." Pel sunk back into her seat.

It was true. The bombing wasn't going to go away. Unfortunately, being so far out of the loop made it tough for Garrett to know what exactly was going on with the investigation. What did they know? Was Harper Riordan even on anyone's radar back at Garrett's old office? Maybe the video Pel had given to Rivers and Rice was the only evidence anyone had on the girl.

"I think we take this to Rivers and get his take on things," Garrett said.

Pel paused for a minute. "Is Rivers the one in charge? I thought it was Rice."

"Rice is the nice guy."

Pel shook her head. "See, I didn't get that at all, he came off as kind of a jackass to me."

"They'll both take some getting used to." Garrett started rehearsing a conversation in his head. It was a discussion he wanted to have with Rivers about how Deena might actually be able to help the FEI without being locked up.

55

There was only another half hour or so until they'd be back in the city, but Deena felt like crap. She'd slept for a good hour and change, but it hadn't helped her. That last little healing trick, combined with all the other action of the past few days had completely done her system in. She'd fought sleep out of fear of what trouble was going to erupt within the car if she closed her eyes. She was paranoid that they would just take her in to some prison, despite their assurances that they'd get her to Marsh's building. Still, she'd slept and nothing happened. "I could use a coffee," she said.

"I have no idea where we are, or where to find coffee," Pel said. She'd taken over the driving from Garrett while he went over some files. Paper files. No one did that anymore, did they?

Garrett looked at the upcoming exit sign. "I don't think it matters where you stop. I'm pretty sure it's a law now that every city, town and hamlet has to have at least one coffee shop."

"Federal mandate?" Pel asked.

"Yep," Garrett answered. "Damn government has their hands in everything these days."

Pel guided the car off the highway and followed the signs to the center of a small town. "There's gotta be a gas station with a coffee maker somewhere here in Mayberry." She circled back toward a filling station on the other side of the square. As they got closer, she let out a yell. "Hey! Is that a picture of a coffee cup on the side of that building?"

"Yep. Looks like you're in luck, java fiend," Garrett agreed.

"I'll go get the coffee for you," Pel said. "I really need to stretch my legs."

"Let's all get out," Garrett said. He pointed to some picnic tables in the town square. "We'll meet you over there."

"Sure," Pel started toward the convenience store.

"Grab me a soda?" Garrett called.

Pel shook her head. "How about a water for a change?"

"No. And beef jerky?"

Pel grimaced. "You're joking. How are you still alive?"

Garrett looked around as they sat down under a shelter house. The picnic table was beat up and defaced with graffiti. Deena put her hands on the rough tabletop and sighed. She wished she'd just stayed asleep in the car. Her head felt like it was caving in.

Using a napkin he produced from his pocket, Garrett wiped off his side of the table and the bench before sitting down with a groan. "I hate being in the car this much. Hate traveling. I'd rather be in the office or at a crime scene. I feel like I'm getting nothing done." He took a second to think. "Driving's better than flying, I guess."

Deena watched him as his gaze fell on everything around them, except for her. He was making small talk. She was flattered, until she realized he might just be wasting time before Pel got back by talking about inane things. "So what is the story?" she asked. "What's the deal with you and agent ponytail?"

"What do you mean?"

Deena dug at some of the loose splinters of wood on the table. "I mean, you seem to be a long way from the city. Are you on some special mission to bring me in?"

Garrett turned and looked over at the gas station. Deena supposed he was searching for his partner to help. "Something like that. We just joined a little group called the FEI"

"Did you say F*E*I or F*B*I?"

"Yes, 'E'. The Federal Entity Index. They… We… chase people like you, with powers that tend to cause mayhem and destruction." Garrett thought about how badly he wanted to suggest his bosses change the name of the agency. The FEI sounded so fake. Maybe something cool like the CAGE or Operation Thunder. Anything would be preferable. It was like drinking an off-brand of soda. Mountain Fog instead of Mountain Dew.

"OK. That's all you do?"

Garrett stood up as he saw Pel exit the store balancing three coffees and a bag of snacks. "Yes. That's all we do." He paused and waved to Pel, who'd already seen them anyway. He took a few steps toward her to help. "Hey. I was just filling Deena in on what we do."

Pel handed out the coffees and dropped a few sugar packets and creamer cups on the table. "And?"

"He hasn't gotten very far," Deena said as she tore the ends off several sugar packets and dumped them into her cup. "You guys hunt freaks."

"That's the very basic job description, yes." Pel took a drink. "But there's more to it."

"Is there?" Garrett asked.

"Are we going to discuss the research aspect with her, or not?" Pel took another quick sip of coffee.

Garrett didn't want to spook the girl and convey misgivings about the way the FEI treated their suspects and prisoners. If Deena got worried, she might lash out and bolt. They needed to keep her under control. "Look. We just came on board, but the Index has been doing what they can to make people with your powers normal again. They've tried to remove the thing that gives you power, but they haven't had any luck."

"We just want to make sure you get treated as fairly and humanely as possible," Pel said.

"Humanely as possible? I don't understand. I'm going to jail, right?" Deena looked up at Garrett.

Not even close, Garrett thought. "You'll be a prisoner, sure. But we'd like to find a way to make your incarceration more productive. Let us lay out what we're thinking. If you agree, we'll talk to our superiors and fight for the plan."

"Did you talk about the bugs and the dead guys yet?"

Garrett cringed at his partner blurting out the two main things Garrett wanted to keep quiet, or at least ease into with Deena. "No. No. We haven't gotten to that yet."

Pel took a sip and looked over at their prisoner. "Here's the thing. We have it on good authority that your powers don't come from any sort of magic. They come from something else. Possibly weird insects."

"Is she serious?" Deena asked.

Garrett felt himself blushing at the stupidity of what they were trying to convey to the young woman. "Well, that's kind of a working theory, we can't really prove it. And they're probably not insects. It could be…" Garrett wasn't surprised when Deena turned and vomited.

56

Deena at 19, the first time around

The lights outside the Piedmont Hotel were dazzling. They'd been arrayed in a number of colors—pink, yellow and white—to attract as much attention as possible for the charity event that night. They were honoring community leaders or raising money for the less fortunate in some other country or something, Deena wasn't too clear. But it was beautiful. From the lobby of the hotel across the street, she stared at the spotlights as they scanned the skies and drew more of the city's elite and wealthy to the event.

"One more time," Morgan said from behind her.

"We've been over it," Deena sighed.

"That's all part of the process. It helps you get prepared. Keeps the surprises from popping up. You have to talk it through in your head every time when you're alone, so let's talk it through out loud once again."

"Come on, Deena. Just do it so you don't screw something up," Harper's voice came across their earpieces. She was on the roof of the smaller building next door, keeping an eye out for the target.

Morgan keyed his mic. "You're here as a spotter. So shut up and do your job. You're not to speak until you see them approach. That's it. No other chatter. You'll get your turn soon enough. We need quiet so we can concentrate."

Deena wanted to stick her tongue out at her sister and laugh. It would be a natural reaction for the sisters if it weren't for the situation they were in. There was no way to explain, even to herself, why she felt so confident in her ability to stroll into an event uninvited, track down a woman she didn't know and kill her in the midst of hundreds of other people. Nothing in her mind made her question the possibility of a successful outcome. Not now, anyway. In the wee hours of the previous morning, as she sat awake in her bed and began to nod off, the surge that she felt every morning left her and she was suddenly aware of everything she'd done and what she was to do the next day. Her chest hurt and she began to cry. She was puzzled why she never thought that way before, how she could kill Mike and never bat an eye. She'd listened to her sister cry herself to sleep night after night over that, and out of fear for what was happening at Marsh's organization, but nothing in her own mind would allow her to feel remorse until that night.

When she woke in the morning, she lay with her eyes open and thought about those feelings but then her morning routine kicked in. There was a pulse in her mind and her thoughts were obscured. It was like shining a light in someone's eyes in the dark, the overload was too much and she stopped trying to think about it.

Another limousine arrived in the line and pulled up to the curb to wait its turn.

"Start," Morgan said.

Deena sighed. "Fine. The target is Lianne Hauk. Former councilwoman and potential Mayoral candidate. She is five foot, six inches tall and has shoulder-length brown hair. According to the papers, she'll be wearing a red sequined dress with spaghetti straps designed by Ester Lamont especially for the event."

"Good. She has blue eyes," Morgan said.

"I know that." Why the hell did she need to know the woman had blue eyes, when she had several good pictures of the woman and would now know her on sight?

"Then say that."

"She has blue eyes."

Morgan nodded. "Good. Details, girl. Details. Go on."

They'd done this exact thing a dozen times the night before. With maps and graphs and charts and weather forecasts and wind speeds and other shit that Deena saw as completely irrelevant to putting an end to a woman's life with a steak knife in the ladies' room.

"I'll be in constant contact with you if anything goes wrong, but if we lose communication for some reason, you need to be able to fend for yourself."

"I know."

"So let's have it," Morgan said.

I'd like to let you have it. Deena thought. "Harper will signal when the limo approaches, and I'll walk out to the curb and cross the street. Careful to use the crosswalk, with the traffic signal, so as not to attract attention to myself." That was one of Morgan's big things—he needed Deena to blend in. To become a part of the scenery and look like everyone one else.

"Then, enter through the front door, just like the rest of them." That was the part of the plan that Deena and even Harper had questioned. It was one thing to blend in and act like everyone else, but there were cameras and guards at the front door that would take Deena's picture and remember her from the moment she walked in. They'd know her, or at least have a picture of her if questions were asked later. She wondered if it was part of a plan to get something on her, to have something to hold over her head if they needed a scapegoat later. Morgan said to stick to the plan without a bunch of questions. He was the expert.

"Once I get inside, I…" She stopped as another limo approached and parked behind the others. "I then make my way…" something about the car that had pulled up caught her attention. As the rear door opened, Lianne Hauk stepped out onto the sidewalk, her head and shoulders visible over the top of the car.

"She's here."

Morgan turned. "What?"

"Right there." She pointed to the car.

"Fuck, that's her all right." He touched his mic. "Harper, what the hell? Where are you?"

"That's not the car we talked about." Deena heard her sister's voice over the earpiece.

"That's exactly the fucking car we talked about."

Deena moved toward the lobby doors. "I'm going."

"Stay casual," Morgan said.

Sure. Be casual about killing someone. Not a problem. She keyed her mic before she opened the door. "Harper? You're a dumbass."

She walked through the door, pulled her earpiece out and tossed the entire thing, microphone and all into the trash can at the curb. She looked both ways as she ran out into the middle of the street and then cut between two parked limos. She knew Morgan was watching and was sure he was pulling his hair out over what she was doing. She put one hand behind her back and gave him the finger, hoping he could see it through his spotting scope.

The red carpet was roped off and she found herself stepping into a crowd of gawkers and media that were watching the arrival of sports figures, actors and politicos to support whatever the cause of the day was. She carefully worked her way into the heart of the crowd, pushing and wiggling past the amassed idiots with their autograph books and cell phone cameras at the ready.

She didn't manage to make it up to the ropes, but got a good view from behind two excited girls wearing *Twilight* t-shirts who couldn't stop moving. It was like they were high on caffeine or something, they were so wired that they couldn't stop vibrating.

Deena spotted Lianne Hauk still standing near her limo. She'd been met by a half-dozen men in black suits with visible wires coming from their ears. They were the security that Morgan had babbled on about during the planning sessions. Most likely off-duty cops from the Los Angeles police force, though they could be private security. Not that there weren't plenty of the city's finest; uniformed policemen lined the sidewalks and were posted at intervals along the red carpet. The security men surrounded Hauk as they waited their turn on the carpet.

"Are you guys here to get the councilwoman's autograph too?" Deena asked, leaning over the girls' shoulders. They scrunched up their noses and then turned away, vibrating slightly less. Deena couldn't recall ever having a weird crush like that on a movie star or musician. Harper had John Mayer posters on her wall and crushed on him big time in middle school. She had posters, downloads and concert DVDs and anything else Mom let her get her hands on. Deena never understood it.

The procession surrounding Hauk started moving closer to the carpet and Deena began to wonder whether there was a way to take her out before she even made it inside. Morgan's stupid, elaborate plan was out the window, so she was trying to formulate a new one on the fly. The change in plan had nothing to do with Harper's little flub. Truth was, Deena had no designs on doing what Morgan said in the first place.

She looked at the pens that the girls were holding for their autographs and wondered if she could turn them into a weapon somehow and stab the woman to death. She dismissed it as a dumb idea, as she would have to get really close and then she'd have to try to escape through the wild crowds of people and law enforcement on either side of the carpet. It pissed her off that Morgan didn't just shoot her. That was his thing—he shot people from a distance and he was good at it. Apparently this was "the only way she'd learn," according to Morgan.

With only a small purse at her side, Deena moved in closer, pushing through the people in the crowd. The girls resisted, the men let her move freely. It was most likely because the men were confused by her cleavage and the women were reluctant to give up their spots so close to the red carpet. When their celebrity crushes showed up, the girls wanted to be able to paw them freely.

"Watch it, bitch," a blonde spectator in a sparkly t-shirt shoved Deena backward. "Get back there with the rest of the skanks."

She had been in high school the last time Deena heard *anyone* called a skank, let alone herself. She looked at the girl with the bad dye job and tacky shirt and saw an opportunity. She sized up another girl on the other side of them and figured that girl was just as rabid a fangirl. Same sort of shirt, same look of breathless anticipation. Same fan, just darker hair.

"Skank? You bitch, take your hands off of me." Deena grabbed the blonde and swung her into the dark haired fan, knocking them both to the ground. When the brunette started getting up, Deena blamed the blonde. "Jesus, watch what you're doing."

The brunette shoved the blonde off of her. "Yeah, dammit."

The blonde shoved back and the two quickly squared off in a way that suggested they weren't used to fighting. Deena decided to help things along by punching the blonde in the stomach and pushing her back toward the brunette before backing away. People began to crowd around, reaching out to pull the girls apart. There were shouts to break it up from security manning the ropes. A few of the officers crossed into the crowd to see what the commotion was.

Deena extricated herself and moved to the head of the line. There were still officers there, but they were distracted by the fight, which had somehow grown rather than diminished with the presence of law enforcement. She looked down the red carpet to see the councilwoman approaching, shaking hands and wearing a big unnatural smile as she went. Two men in suits walked on either side of her with white ear buds prominently sticking out of their ears.

As Hauk got closer, Deena put on a fake smile of her own and stuck her hand out. The councilwoman made eye contact and put her hand in Deena's. What started as a quick, surface greeting went a little longer as Deena leaned in. "I'm so happy with everything you're doing since you took over your position." Deena yelled to be heard, but not quite loud enough. As Hauk leaned in to hear her, Deena let a long sliver of Shadow Energy slip from her finger into the councilwoman's side. It went in and withdrew so quickly, that no one around them could have seen it. Judging by the look on the councilwoman's face, she had no idea what had happened either. There was just the vague impression that she knew something was wrong. She actually kept walking for a few more steps and Deena waited until security had passed her before slowly moving back into the crowd.

When there were shouts that Hauk needed a doctor, people moved forward like a tide, leaving Deena beached on the sidewalk. She walked slowly and calmly to a nearby building and began following her preplanned escape route that she'd gone over and over with Morgan. She left the building, moved up a filthy alley and ascended the stairway of a parking garage on the next block. She would climb to the third level, meet her sister and Morgan in an old brown Ford Bronco and they would take a zig-zag route across town to a safe house where they would wait for the all clear signal from another of Marsh's associates.

Halfway up the stairs, Deena was interrupted by a voice from higher up. "What the hell was that?" As she got up a few more stairs, she saw Morgan and Harper standing in the concrete stairwell, in front of the 'L2' sign. "I had that thing planned to the letter for you. How did you end up with that mess?"

Deena opened her mouth to answer, but Morgan continued. "You were in a high profile area. Do you have any idea how many photographers were there to take pictures of celebrities and politicians? Do you know how many of them accidentally got your face in their shots? Holy Christ."

"I got it done." Deena was indignant now. She was there to learn from Morgan, sure, but she had an internal compass that seemed to guide her forward as she worked. It wasn't an elegant hit by any means, but she got it done. Marsh would surely be happy with that part of it at least.

"When you start working with a handler, they need to know they can trust you to do the work. They have to know you aren't going to fuck them over because you think you can do better than the plan they come up with," Morgan said.

Deena was still defiant, but waved her arms to placate the man. "I'll do better when we're in the field. I just panicked that's all."

"*We're* in the field? That's a joke. No chance will we ever work together again," Morgan started up the stairs and Harper followed closely, leaving Deena on the landing by herself. "I have no idea what's going on in that head of yours. It's like you can't control your impulses. It's not just this time, it's every time. When we met in the woods? Tell me you were thinking and not just reacting and doing whatever you wanted."

There was a flash in Deena's mind at that moment that suggested maybe he was right. Her head ached as she tried to remember what led her to deviate from Morgan's plan. But it was like being in a car accident: Every time she got near a coherent reason, a sudden force tugged her back, like a seat belt keeping her from going through a windshield. "Fuck you, Morgan. Job's done." She forgot what she was thinking about and the ache in her head went away.

57

In the little town square, Deena stood near a bed of beautifully arranged flowers and waved the agents off. She'd stopped heaving and convulsing after a few minutes and walked away from Garrett and Pel. Her stomach was under control, but not the rest of her body, not her mind. All these years of practicing magic that wasn't magic. Thinking she'd figured out some kind of key to casting her own limited spells and guiding some tremendous power, when deep inside there was a creature feeding off of her. Her body was wracked with revulsion. She looked at the blotch on her arm. It looked like an ordinary blemish at the moment and she wanted it out. Deena tore at it with her nails; slicing, scraping, she began to draw blood almost immediately. But it was nothing but blood, no black fluid or whatever it was.

"Jesus, Deena stop," Garrett said. He'd moved up next to her without her noticing.

"I want it out." Deena was angry with herself and whatever it was inside of her. She should have been able to figure out that she was being used all that time. "I need it out of me, now."

Pel was at Deena's side as well. "They're working on how to remove these things. They just aren't quite sure how to go about it yet."

"But tearing it out of your arm with your fingernails certainly isn't going to work." Garrett grabbed her by the wrist and held it firmly.

Deena was aware the agents knew what they were talking about, but it didn't lessen her dread of the thing insider her. And as she calmed down, the blood spilling over her wrist began to come out black. Instead of dripping down onto the bricks of the sidewalk, it turned to a tar-like substance before reversing itself and pulling back into the wound. In less than a minute, there was just a trio of scratch lines down Deena's forearm. Worms. Snakes. Spiders seemed to be running just under her skin. She couldn't let herself panic again, as much as she wanted to. She took deep breaths and closed her eyes as tight as she could. Her sister was still in danger, and Deena had ignored Harper for far too long. "Can we get out of here and get on with it? Let's get going." She could see the uncertainty in the eyes of both agents. "I'll be OK. Let me get something in my stomach while we drive the last bit and I'll be fine. My sister is waiting."

"We'll call our superiors at the Index and outline what we want to do and the ideas we have for you," Garrett said. "You need to pay attention and this call needs to go well."

"Let us do most of the talking." Pel still looked worried that Deena was going to implode at any minute. The agent helped Deena to the car. Deena let herself melt into the backseat. As they hit the road, Pel dialed her phone and put it on speaker. They had a conversation with two other agents called Rivers and Rice. It was all a little fuzzy and Deena felt slightly drunk as she identified herself and said yes at what seemed like all the right moments.

It was a short conversation that included some moments where Garrett took it off speaker and talked to the men on the other end semi-privately. She tried to keep her eyes open, but it was impossible. She was still exhausted, coffee or no coffee. As the call came to an end, Deena fell asleep again. It was like her mind just shut off.

Twenty minutes later, Deena woke up in the back of the car, with the agents talking about whether this was a good idea.

"Let's just go," Deena said. She stepped out of the car and walked around to the back bumper. The license plate, "WERKIT," failed to inspire her.

The three of them stared at the building as they sat in the car. Deena had been in the building numerous times and had never given it a second thought. Now, it seemed like a dark tower that reached into the clouds. Somewhere inside, Harper was probably sitting with a gun to her head. "Let's just get moving," Deena said. "Let's go find my sister."

"All right," Garrett said. "We can go in the loading dock, where they make deliveries. Probably less security. From there we can take the back stairs, all the way up. I doubt anyone would even blink if they saw us."

"You want to run up thirty-two flights of stairs and hope no one notices us?" Pel asked. "That's a hell of a lot of walking."

"I don't want to risk taking the elevator. We could easily get locked in there, or have the doors open onto a floor full of gunmen. The stairs are the best way of doing it without getting trapped so easily."

"Yes," Deena said. "You're absolutely right. You guys should take the stairs. I'll walk in the front door and take the main elevator up. They'll focus on me and ignore you. There's no way they could anticipate me showing up with the FBI."

"'E'. FEI." Garrett was becoming paranoid about the name. "The Index actually has a nicer ring to it."

Deena glared at the man.

The passenger door opened and Deena stepped onto the sidewalk. "I'll go in first and draw everyone's attention to me. You guys circle around to the loading docks and stay out of sight as much as you can."

"We'll meet you on Marsh's floor? What's to stop him from killing you on sight?" Pel opened her door and took a step out. "You know that's his plan here, right?"

"Yes," Deena said. "I have to guess he wouldn't do it here. And he wouldn't do it himself." Deena thought about it for a second and hoped her logic was correct. "And if he does, then you guys should have a solid case against him. Right?"

Neither of the agents seemed happy with that explanation.

"So, I guess you better get up there before that happens, right?"

"You don't think he's going to just hug you and let the whole thing slide, do you? I know you're joking, but the potential danger here is very real," Garrett said.

Deena finished getting out and leaned in the open window. "*Potential danger*. We're talking about Marsh here; you can drop the 'potential' part. I know what's happening here." They had discussed the plan, such as it was, and other contingencies on the ride to L.A. but Deena had left out a few things. She'd left out the part of Marsh's call where he said he'd let Harper go if Deena came back and worked for him. She was sure it was bullshit, but if it turned out to be the only way to get Harper out, she'd have to seriously consider it. "I'll take my time, but I think you'd better move it, if you plan on getting up those stairs." She slammed the car door and bounded across the street while the traffic was clear, just before the onrush of cars, so she couldn't hear if anyone responded.

She'd really never come through the front doors much, only when she took taxis or a car service. Usually, she came in through the underground parking garage and took the private elevator, but she'd used the front entrance enough to be able to get a nod of recognition from the large dark-haired man in the navy jacket at the front security desk and another from the almost identical man that stood near the bank of elevators with his hands behind his back. She continued past the elevators, followed the signs for the lobby restrooms and shoved the door to the ladies' room open. She took a moment to walk up and down the restroom stalls, making sure she was alone. The water from the sink was tepid, but she still splashed some on her face to wake up. She was right back where she'd been after the airplane job: feeling sick to her stomach in a strange bathroom. Her body still ached, her stomach was a mess and she still felt like an idiot teenager. The big difference was that she didn't really appear like one anymore. She looked in the mirror and watched the water drip off of her nose. The face was pretty close to normal for her correct age anyway. She felt thicker, slower, more aware of herself and her physique. At least she had that going for her.

There was another difference that cropped up in the last few hours. The magic that she'd guided and worked to control and employed to do her bidding was not actually magic. It was some sort of living thing feeding off her. The reality was, it had controlled her. It had taken her conscience, taken her will to choose her own path, destroyed her ability to tell between right and wrong, sucked her soul dry. Her power had been using her, not the other way around. Maybe she shouldn't have called it Shadow Energy, but a Shadow Entity instead. She stared at herself in the mirror and wanted to cut deep into her body with a steak knife and scrape around until she found it.

She looked at her arm and saw the blemish had become a squiggly line that looked like a black wave. She stared at it and thought of the beach. Slowly the wave started to roll, like water onto the shore. She wasn't cutting into herself until she got her sister out.

Deena left the restroom and walked back to the elevator bank, thinking she'd given Marsh's men enough time to be made aware of her arrival and react appropriately. She approached the elevators, seeing two burly men standing there, looking up at the numbers as if they were waiting for the next car. She assumed they were there to make sure she got to Marsh's floor without incident. Deena confidently punched the up button and then stared at the numbers over the three elevators as well, to see which one was going to arrive first. One of the men grunted after thirty seconds of waiting and began jabbing the already-lit button repeatedly with his forefinger.

"You saw me push that, right?" Deena asked.

The man was startled that she had talked to him. "Yeah."

"You know that once it's pushed, you're done? Pushing it again doesn't speed things up."

The man scowled and began pushing the button faster, staring at Deena all the while.

"Mature." Deena began scanning the red numbers that were slowly changing over the doors. The click-click of the man's button-pushing annoyed her and Deena reached out and batted his hand away from the button.

"Bitch, what do you…" He was cut off by the ding of the elevator arriving.

Deena was never so happy to see the doors slide open in her life. "Thanks for your help. I don't know how we ever would have flagged one of these things down without you. Nice work."

"Fuck you."

They all stepped into the waiting elevator car and when it closed, Deena stared at their reflections in the silvery surface of the doors. They stood a foot or two behind her and sized her up, their heads scanning her body, possibly checking out her ass. Either way, she could handle them. She pushed the button for thirty-two. "What floor?" she asked the men.

"Thirty-four," the button-pusher said.

Deena knew that floor was empty, with most of the rooms being renovated. They were definitely here for her. "Got it."

The elevator stopped on the second floor and three more men got on. They all needed to go to thirty-four, but none of them seemed to know each other, and they all stood behind her.

The doors closed and the elevator slowly ascended, but came to a stop yet again on the third floor. This wasn't looking quite as easy as Deena had hoped. The possibility of just walking out with her sister seemed more distant by the second. If burly thugs got on at every level, they might just smash her to death by sheer volume. She could overpower a lot of men, but she still didn't know the extent of her power now. Knowing it might be a living thing inside her, she was even more reluctant to call upon it for help. And she was more than a little creeped out.

As the doors opened on the third floor, she was greeted by two people pointing guns in her face. She recognized them both. "Harper? Stanley? What the hell?" Her sister and Marsh's assistant seemed rattled, but none the worse for wear.

"There they are," the button pusher said. He grabbed Deena, shoved her back against the elevator wall and charged off the elevator with another goon, tackling a clearly conflicted Harper. Any shots she would have taken might have hit Deena as easily as they hit the other men in the elevator who now surrounded Deena.

The elevator doors slid shut as one of the men put his thick hands on her shoulder in an effort to pin Deena.

58

Stanley was just as astounded as Harper to see Deena in the elevator. They'd given up on waiting and he and Harper were making their way out of the building by moving from air ducts and supply closets to bathrooms and empty offices. Unfortunately, the building was so secure that cameras and alarms thwarted their efforts to hide in place and wait. Stanley blamed himself for insisting the building security be beefed up after his initial threat assessment for Mr. Marsh in the early days.

The street seemed like the best shot at escape for the duo. They could run out the loading area and down the alleyway to the next street. The hope would be that some passing citizens might report anything unusual if Harper and Stanley were stopped and hauled back in by Marsh's employees.

Stanley looked above the elevator and watched as the number for the next floor up became red. "They're heading up," he said. The nearest man grabbed Stanley by the throat and shoved him against the wall, pinning him.

Harper punched the other man in the stomach and then again in the side. "That's not helping us right now."

The breath was quickly leaving Stanley's lungs and with thick fingers wrapped around his windpipe, he couldn't pull in more. He panicked and swung wildly at his attacker's face, but he was too weak to be effective. It took two swings to realize that he still had a gun in his right hand. He felt it slipping out of his grasp as black spots began to appear in his field of vision. Too beat to raise the weapon, Stanley put all of his efforts into pulling the trigger.

The roar of the weapon lit up the hallway and Stanley's attacker screamed as the bullet went through his foot. Stanley fell to the floor and felt the welcome rush of air fill his lungs. He coughed as he writhed next the larger man holding his foot and shouting.

As he recovered, Stanley looked over at Harper and her assailant. She was pounding the man, landing blow after blow, but it didn't seem to be slowing him down any, just wearing her out. She was already obviously tired, moving from place to place, on high alert, waiting for the next people to discover her and force the duo to move on. She was still alert enough to dodge the man's wild, uncoordinated punches, but it was hard to say for how long. As his strength came back, he raised his gun and pointed it at the man. "Hey." Stanley immediately began coughing and Harper and her attacker kept fighting. When he stopped coughing, he tried again. "Hey. Stop." He had to use short words to keep from starting another jag of hacking. "Now."

The goon stopped and looked at Stanley, giving Harper an extra second to punch the man in the throat and then the nose. He went down wheezing worse than Stanley had, with the added bonus of having blood pouring out of his nose.

Harper sat down in the hall to catch her breath and Stanley joined her. The two men writhing and bleeding next to them made the atmosphere less than relaxing.

"We need to move," Harper said.

"I'm tired."

"Me too, but we have to move." Harper didn't sound too terribly motivated. "We couldn't stay here if we wanted. There'll be more of these idiots showing up soon." She kicked the nearest of their assailants in the back of the head.

It was true, and Stanley knew it. There were still plenty of hired hands in the building that would be eager to get Harper. He looked over at the two sets of elevator doors. The one with Deena had gone all the way up to Marsh's floor. The other was down at ground level. "Want me to press the button, or are we taking the stairs?"

"Fuck it. We'll take the elevator."

Stanley slowly nodded his head. "Should I push the up button or the down button?" He wanted to know if they were still making a run for it, or if they were going to try to help Harper's sister. If he had a vote, it would be to run. Anyone in the building would probably be called up to fight Deena and it might be their best time to get out. If they went back up, there was no telling what mess they would be walking into.

"She fucked me over. If she hadn't just run away, we could've gotten out together. She left me twisting in the wind," Harper said.

"True." Stanley stood and moved to push the down button on the elevator.

"But she is my sister."

Stanley propped his head against the wall and let his finger hover over the down button.

59

At the loading docks, Garrett took Pel's hand and pulled her up. "This is dumb. We never should have made this deal, we never should have let her go up by herself, and we should have just waited for the warrant and went in with an army of heavily armed agents and officers."

"You know this is right," Pel said. She made her way into the loading area with confidence and speed. "She's not going anywhere. We'll be up in no time to back her up."

Garrett looked back at the street and the parking area, scanning to see if any of their friends of the federal persuasion had arrived. Rivers had assured them that the tactical team wouldn't be in place for another half hour or so. This was Marsh's place of business; surely some agency had a car or detail watching the place. But as he looked again, he found no one in the street or sitting in a car. He scanned the shiny glass of the nearby buildings and was pretty confident that someone had the smarts to be watching a criminal of this magnitude. He involuntarily patted his gun and felt at least a little better at the bulk and heft that he felt there. It didn't dispel the unease he felt about going in without a full squad, but it would have to do.

They left the maze of boxes and crates and shoved open a stairway door back in one corner. It was like they'd said; no one saw them and no one physically challenged them. There were cameras everywhere, which they couldn't avoid, but as long as they weren't challenged, Garrett was happy. It was both comforting and terrifying that they had simply walked in and hadn't been scrutinized. He was sure any guards in the place had been summoned to deal with Deena. "Let's go," he said. "We need to get going if we're going to make it up the stairs in time to help if they need it."

Pel put her foot on the first step. "They? Do you think Harper is still alive?"

"Mmmm." was Garrett's only answer. His world had been completely turned upside down in the last two days. He went from investigating a horrible bombing, to agreeing to protect and fight for the safety of the main suspect in that case. Oh, and apparently witches were real. Or something like that. In a way, he already missed the familiar safety of his desk at the federal building, where he was surrounded by agents who smiled and talked about their kids. He was running up thirty-some flights of stairs into a building filled with heavily armed, hardened criminals, trying to help a

girl who was a terrible villain herself until her miraculous turnaround just days ago. Plus, there was that girl's equally villainous sister, who may or may not want to be saved and could quite possibly try to kill them all, given the chance. Mmmm, indeed.

He placed his foot on the next stair and began to chase after Pel, whose footfalls were already echoing higher up in the stairwell. She was younger and in much better shape than Garrett, but he tried not to let it show.

"Are you sure we can't use another elevator?" he called up to her. "Maybe if we just make sure we're not on the same one as Deena, we'll lessen our chances of being associated with her and caught if she gets in a jam."

"Come on, you fossil. It's only a few more floors," Pel called.

"A few dozen more, maybe."

"Sissy."

"Seriously? That's the best you've got?" He saw her up ahead, as she rounded another set of stairs. "I'll beat you to the top and you'll eat your words."

Pel laughed and turned to watch him as he ran, which Garrett used to his advantage. She couldn't run quite as fast as she looked back. He closed the gap to within half a flight of stairs as they reached the next floor. "Hey. Tell me again how to back up my contacts to the cloud." He figured any distraction would help.

"How many times have we gone over that?"

"I'll get it this time."

They were laughing as the door on the landing between them opened and a man stepped out. Garrett's momentum carried him into the man and they both fell into the wall then to the floor. Pel stopped a few stairs above them.

"Christ, what the hell?" the man said. He picked a cigarette and lighter up off the floor next to him.

Garrett quickly disengaged himself and scrambled to his feet, extending a hand to help the smoker up. "Sorry, didn't expect you there."

"What the hell were you doing?" the man asked. His gaze drifted to the badges the agents were wearing. His eyes got big and he turned around to grab the door handle.

"Whoa, whoa. Just hold on," Garrett said. He grabbed the man's arm and tugged him away from the exit. "What's your name?"

"Me?" the man asked.

Pel was now directly behind him. "Who else would he be asking?" She got in close to the man and stared at the ID hanging from a lanyard around his neck. "James Marshall? Says you're in tech support?"

James stared at her.

"Is that true?" Garrett looked the man up and down. "Do you do tech support for the whole building? Or just one business?"

James continued to stare.

After a pause, Pel reached down to grab James' cigarette. She held it up to show her partner it wasn't shaped exactly like it should be.

"James? Were you sneaking off to smoke a joint? Seriously?" Garrett was more than a little amused. The man had terrible timing. "That's highly illegal."

"It's for my… back. It's medicinal," James said.

Pel rolled her eyes. "Right."

"Look. James, is it? Is your desk nearby? Let's go to your desk real quick." He was shoving James back inside. If James was in IT, hopefully he knew passwords and other technical mumbo-jumbo that Pel could translate.

"I don't think that's a good idea." James didn't stop anyone from pushing him, but he played along reluctantly. Garrett assumed it was to put on a show for anyone who saw him with the agents.

"It's a great idea. You and my partner can talk about servers and firewalls and gigabytes and jpegs… and… bookmarks…" Garrett started to trail off.

"Just stop," Pel said. "It's embarrassing."

The IT room was right next to the stairwell and the agents followed close on James' heels. The man's desk was cluttered with computer parts: screws and wires, scraps of paper and action figures. Three monitors, a keyboard, roller mouse and a webcam appeared to actually make up his functioning work area. Garrett wanted to believe the Wu Tang Clan poster over the James' desk was meant to be ironic, but judging from the man's recreational smoking, it probably wasn't. Pel sat down at the desk and looked up at James.

"She'd appreciate any passwords and such to get access to your important stuff like finances and whatnot," Garrett said. He looked around the room and noticed another man sitting silently behind another bank of monitors. Garrett nodded. "You need to use the restroom or something?" The man started to shake his head no, but switched to yes. "Then you probably ought to take care of that." The other techie left.

"Don't you need a warrant for that sort of information? I'm pretty sure you do." James bit his fingernails.

Garrett looked at Pel. "You know. We just started with a new agency. I'm not sure if we need one, do you?"

Pel shrugged in response. "How about you just do it and we'll worry about that later?"

James was still hesitant.

"Look. Your coworker is gone. It's just us here. Give us the passwords and we'll give you your cigarette back."

James' face lit up slightly as he leaned down and typed in a string of letters and numbers and then leaned away. Pel started typing, opening histories, and looking at directories.

"It's a start," Pel said. "At least I think I can get a good picture of some of their operations. Nothing horribly incriminating, I'm afraid. What do you want me to get?"

"Just save everything you can and let's get going," Garrett said. He looked over Pel's shoulder at the computer screen. "I wish we had Stanley here. He'd be a huge help. He has to know his way around these files like nobody's business."

"He isn't." Pel hadn't stopped nodding since she sat down at the keyboard. The device allowed her to access everything on the server and all the records in the cloud. What she couldn't get into, James shrugged over and said he didn't have access.

"I'm a little concerned about the girls," Garrett said. "Can we move this along?"

"Deena said they'd come back and I trust them." Pel was still typing and nodding.

Garrett wasn't so sure. He was putting his ass on the line by suggesting the deal with Deena and if she skipped out, he was screwed. "We just met this girl."

"I can tell. She wants an out. We are the only one available." She turned to James. "There's nothing we can use here. Numbers. Lots of numbers."

James shrugged. "I generally tell people to try turning their computer off and then back on again if they have a problem."

"We can improvise. Maybe we can match some payments up pretty closely with contract killings and more criminal endeavors," Pel said. "That should be worth something."

"Circumstantial." The computer talk had bored Garrett, but criminal investigation perked him right up. "We need more."

"Sorry, they didn't keep a 'People We've Killed' file or anything, as far as I can tell," Pel said. "It does seem a little counterproductive."

Even with Pel's assurances, Garrett still wanted to keep an eye on the girls. "Get what you can and let's go. I want to get upstairs in case they need help."

"I could be at this all day."

Garrett turned toward the door. "Don't."

60

Deena hit the stop button with her foot. There was no way she was going to reach Marsh's floor with her arms pinned by some minion and her feet dangling because he had her in a bear hug. The abrupt stop put everyone off balance and Deena saw her chance. She wrenched up an arm, elbowed the man in the face, and wiggled free, standing on her own two feet. She considered trying to summon the Shadow Energy, and again decided it wasn't something she wanted to tamper with. What would it cost her physically and mentally? The thought of conjuring help from a being that existed inside her was disturbing. She'd gotten free of its control; she wanted to stay that way.

Plus, it creeped her out.

While Deena had worked out at the boxing club and had occasionally had to fend for herself without using her powers, she wasn't really a brawler. Fistfights weren't her thing and the two men were much bigger and more muscular than she was. If she couldn't use her powers, she'd prefer a gun in her hand. Deena's only advantage was the tight environment of the elevator. The men didn't have much room to swing at her without getting in each other's way. As they advanced, she smacked the stop button again, putting the elevator back in motion and unbalancing everyone all over again.

"Are you gonna do this all day? Cause it's getting boring, quick," one of the men said.

"We're headed back up towards Marsh's office; I thought that was what you wanted." Deena backed away without putting herself into a corner. There weren't many places to go on the crowded elevator, so she tried to keep moving. The men looked up at the numbers over the door, watching the twenties light up one by one.

61

As each floor number lit up, Stanley felt his body tense. What awaited the two of them was a confrontation he had never thought he'd be around to see. At the next stop was Marsh's office, along with several bodyguards, thugs and hired killers. He assumed he'd be long gone when someone came after Marsh. He'd hoped he would be in a new city, with a new name, living in witness protection or something. He certainly didn't anticipate that he would be one of the idiots gunning for one of the city's biggest crime bosses.

"You're awful quiet over there," Harper said.

"Nothing to talk about."

"Isn't there?"

"Nope," Stanley tried to keep his focus on the numbers lighting up. His hands were shaking a little and nothing he did could stop them. He put them behind his back so Harper couldn't see.

"This could get ugly. Maybe you should stay in the elevator and let me and Deena regroup," Harper reached out.

Stanley moved just out of her reach. "If it gets ugly, it gets ugly. What's going to happen once you and your sister meet up? She's the one that got you into all of this. Not just the current situation, but she's the one that got you started with Marsh. I watched you. It took you years to finally break down and do the things Marsh told you to do. Until that point, Deena had done all the dirty work. She killed who needed killing, beat who needed beating. All for Marsh. But you held out. If it wasn't for her, you could've left any time."

"I wanted to leave. I did. But Marsh and Deena both fed me separate lines of bullshit. Deena said I was just as fucked as she was for all the crimes she'd committed and Marsh said he'd kill Deena if I tried to get out. She never once seemed serious about leaving with me," Harper said. She checked the gun and steeled herself for when the door opened. "Am I going to be happy to see her? I don't know. I just don't."

When the elevator doors finally opened at the top floor, they found the lobby empty. Stanley's desk was empty, and there was no one sitting on the leather couches in the waiting area, not a soul to be found.

Stanley looked at his desk warily, he wondered if someone was hiding behind it, waiting to ambush them and he wondered if he could dodge a bullet meant for the sisters.

Harper moved over to the elevators and watched for the car as it ascended. "Looks like we managed to make it here first."

62

The high-pitched sound of the elevator's ding rang as the car reached the thirtieth floor. "I take it I'm getting off first?" Deena asked the two men. They'd danced around in the elevator together, no one wanting to make a move. The men seemed content to wait out the clock and make a move on Deena once they'd reached their destination. They didn't know that Deena hadn't planned on using her powers, so they could be excused for not wanting to rush her and risk a black shadow cutting them to ribbons.

If the goons had expected help on Marsh's floor, they were disappointed. The shiny metallic doors opened slowly to reveal two people with guns aimed directly into the elevator. But Stanley and Harper weren't there to help them subdue Deena.

Deena ducked and the waiting duo shot into the elevator, filling the men there with bullets. When they stopped shooting, the elevator doors closed and the elevator started back down, floor by floor.

Deena pushed herself up onto her feet. She saw how empty the lobby for Marsh's office was. "Did you make an appointment?"

"Funny," Harper said. Her face was stony and showed no sign of emotion.

"I'm sorry. Mr. Marsh is booked solid until four. Maybe you could come back then?" Stanley's face was easier to read. He looked scared and shaky. Guns weren't his thing and neither was violence. As far as Deena knew, he lived and died numbers.

Deena looked at the door to the office. "Do we want to go in?"

"Why? Why would we need to?" Stanley said. "We're all together. Harper is safe. You're safe," Stanley said. "Let's get the hell out of here and let the feds or the police or the army take care of this now."

The noise in Deena's head didn't let her react. All of the years at Marsh's command, all of the horrible deeds that she'd done at his behest. It wasn't just the thing inside of her that had made her do terrible things; he had a big hand in it.

"I don't really want to go in there, OK?" said Stanley. "I don't want to have to look that man in the eye when he finds out how screwed he is and that I'm one of the ones who screwed him." Stanley talked in a low tone and kept looking at the door.

"I do," Deena said. "Buzz me in."

"What?" Stanley asked.

Pointing absently, Deena indicated the button on Stanley's desk. "The buzzer. Let me in."

On his way to his desk, Stanley handed Deena his gun. "You might need this."

The weapon felt heavier than she remembered in her hands. "Thanks."

As the buzzer began to scream, indicating she could open the door, Deena could feel her sister fall into step with her. She turned to see Harper, her face still blank and unreadable, standing almost next to her. They walked through the door together.

There weren't huge hordes of killers and cutthroats waiting to capture and murder the sisters. The office was the same as always, a huge space with minimal furniture. Tennis balls everywhere. The giant window that made up the western wall was bright and clear, showing the city beyond. The only actual furnishings were an oversized desk with a chair behind it and two uncomfortable chairs opposite for Marsh's visitors to sit on. Deena had felt her butt go to sleep on those monsters numerous times over the last decade or so. They made her squirm, though she hadn't realized until that moment that the chairs were probably chosen deliberately for exactly that reason.

Marsh himself was standing with his back to them, looking out over the city. He didn't turn; though Deena got the feeling maybe he could see them in the glass. He'd always seemed to know things he had no business knowing, arrivals and departures, facial expressions. As she got better at her job, Deena began to understand the tricks that people used to give themselves an edge in life. Using reflections in glass was just one of them.

"So, everyone's back safe and sound?" he asked. "It was a big empty building for a couple of days there, and now all at once everyone is back." He held up his hand and ticked off the names one at a time. "Deena goes missing, Avi goes after her, Wallace goes, Morgan goes, Ramirez goes. And oddly, we can't find Harper *or* Stanley. It was unnatural. It was lonely here without you." He turned and finally looked at them with a face of quiet, almost pleasant, calm. "But now everyone's back. All at once. What fortunate timing."

"Look," Deena said. "I agreed to come back to talk if you let my sister go. She was free when we got here, so I guess that deal is off."

"Hmmm," Marsh said. "I'm not sure how poor Stanley got involved. When Harper escaped, did she take him as insurance? Did she think Stanley could get her out of here?" Stanley was a wildcard in the whole thing. Deena wasn't sure how involved he had been in getting Harper out, but Pel and Garrett had assured her that

Stanley was integral in bringing a case against Marsh. It was impossible to know if Marsh knew about Stanley's overtures to the feds.

"Apparently *everyone* was getting lonely, Mr. Marsh. They all wanted me home just as quickly as possible, judging by the number of your goons that stopped by to see me at one point or another. Ramirez was out there. Was that Morgan that paid me a visit? Just one after another, your lonely employees came to say hello. They must have really missed me." Deena's throat felt dry suddenly. The words thick in her mouth.

"Well, I understand Avi isn't going to be joining us anytime soon," Marsh said. "That's too bad. Thankfully, he managed to give us your location and convey your plans to come back here before he died."

"That's crap." Deena was sure that Avi's help was genuine and that he hadn't sold her out. If he had, why would Marsh's men have killed him? It was all a ploy to throw Deena off, or a way to stall her until more men could show up to kill them.

Deena and Harper moved to opposite sides of the office, together with Marsh, they formed a triangle.

"So you're leaving me? After I took you wretched orphans in? You were living in the woods like animals and I gave you food, shelter and productive jobs." Marsh's tone was dripping with sarcasm, mocking Deena. "You'd be dead now if it wasn't for me."

Deena adopted a similarly insincere tone. "I'm grateful for everything that you did for us back then, but don't act so wounded. You took advantage of us in terrible ways, ways that I just can't take anymore. Something's changed in me this time." Deena looked more to her sister than Marsh for understanding. Still, Harper said nothing.

"Oh? You're a changed person? Elevated? Above killing to earn your living?"

"Yes."

"Humpf. I know of a little house in the mountains that is full of reasons why I find that to be bullshit. You know the house that I mean, yes? The old family abode? I understand things went on there, that prove you're still willing to do the job," Marsh said. "Don't tell me you haven't got the stomach or the skill for it, 'cause you really laid into those men. Oh, and the train? Do we want to talk about how unwilling you were to kill those men?"

Harper finally spoke. "So you went ahead and killed people even though you've been telling everyone you've changed?" Through the years, Deena had confided in Harper about the Shadow Energy, and the toll it took. She'd broken down numerous times describing the feeling of helplessness as her will slowly lost out to the power that pulsed through her body. Usually it was immediately after she'd killed someone, because the further from the event she got, the less it seemed to weigh on her mind. The fact that Harper chose to forget the pain it caused Deena, especially during the current conversation, made matters worse.

"I didn't have a choice. They were trying to kill me and they were going to kill you." Deena turned back to Marsh. "Did you send those men to bring me back, or to test me?" Deena asked.

Marsh's oily voice was calm and soothing. Deena could feel something inside of her melting just a little as he spoke. "My dear, I've loved you and your sister like you were my own children. I've loved you better than your own father. Where was he all these years?" He kicked a tennis ball lightly and watched it roll before continuing.

"You were testing me. You wanted to see if you could push me back to the way I was, didn't you?"

"Young lady, I've known what you were since the day we met in the woods. If you think I was going to give up on an instrument of destruction like you so easily, you're dumber than I thought."

"You knew? How? I didn't know what I was," Deena said.

"A girl gets in a fight and shards of blackness poke out of her skin, I do a little investigating. I ask questions. But undoubtedly, I see how I can put that power to work for me and my organization." Marsh looked back over the city. "But if you aren't planning on staying, I'm afraid our family will have to break up in a big, ugly way. I'm fond of you. But I'm not that fond of you."

Stanley came in the room and slammed the door behind him. "The rest of the men are here." He avoided looking over at Marsh.

"Which men?" Harper asked.

"*All* of the men."

63

Morgan squinted into the sighting scope and watched the scene unfold in the office 1.3 miles away. He watched the sisters pace back and forth in front of Marsh as he sat at his desk. They all periodically looked over at the office door, and Morgan had to wonder how many of the crime boss's minions were trying to bust in.

Once the feds took her away in their car, Morgan assumed she was going to jail and not coming back. Still, here she was.

He was positive that he had managed to at least shoot the little witch girl in the arm. Still, here she was.

Deena was consistently defying Morgan's expectations and it was getting on his nerves.

"Come on, you've got to admit this is the perfect opportunity to get in good with Marsh," Brandt said. "He's stuck, no one else is coming through for him. His guards are incompetent. Imagine the reward. He wants them gone and you can make that happen, no problem."

Morgan stepped away from the window and looked past Brandt around the empty office. No one would bother him, if he finished before the others showed up.

He flipped open the battered old suitcase and began piecing together his rifle. He stared out the window at the building that housed Marsh's office as he worked. The weapon nearly put itself together, parts slid into place from rote memory, not requiring his actual attention. He could feel the cold metal form into the gun, smell the welcome scent of oil. Without magnification, he could only see the distant building, not the people inside.

"So we're doing this again?" Mr. Hector was leaning on the suitcase the next time Morgan looked back. "Is this a regular thing now? He looked around the room. Where's everyone else?" He nodded at Brandt and scowled a bit. Brandt looked away.

Once he'd completed the weapon, Morgan flipped down the tripod and planted it on the windowsill. He put his shoulder to the stock and peered through the lens. He found the giant window of Marsh's office easily. He zoomed in on the figures still standing much as he'd left them, still talking.

"You know what he wants you to do," Brandt said. "He told you to bring her back, or kill her. And her sister. Now is the best time to do that. Nothing is stopping you."

"Ahem," the little teddy bear cleared his throat.

Brandt looked down. "You're going to stop him?" The man chuckled.

"Here's the glitch in your logic, Brandt." Morgan didn't move away from the gun. "He wanted me to make sure she came back, and she's back."

"Semantics. He wanted you to bring her back into the fold, back to work. She obviously isn't planning on working for Marsh again."

Morgan turned at the sound of footsteps in the lobby of the office. He paused, tempted to pull the pistol under his shirt. He quickly realized it was no one who could affect his work here and turned back to the window.

"You don't think I can stop you?" his mother asked.

"Great. The whole damn peanut gallery's going to make an appearance," Brandt said.

Morgan adjusted the scope for an even closer view, making Deena's head fill the entire circle. He could see the scratches and cuts on her face and neck in great detail.

"She doesn't deserve this Morgie," his mother said. "She's got a second chance here and you can't stop that. You're telling me you never wanted to start over?"

"This *is* him starting over, bitch." Brandt's voice was gruff and louder than it needed to be. Morgan looked away from his scope long enough to see Brandt get in his mother's face. "He was a milquetoast until I plucked him out of the sewer you raised him in and made something of him."

Another voice drifted in from the outer office. "That's crap. He was a pussy in college when I met him and I walked all over him until the day I walked out." Nadine said. "So whenever you made him into the magical love god we see today, it was way after that."

"I meant it metaphorically, whore. I meant that I pulled him out of the sewer where he was raised, metaphorically. Christ, did you actually graduate from that college, or was it too hard to study when you were on your knees all the time?" Brandt turned his attention from Morgan's mother to the voice in the hall.

CLANG! CLANG! CLANG!

The monkey with the cymbals rolled in a circle and bared its teeth at Brandt. "Jackass!" It whirled around again.

"I don't think there's really any need for name calling," Morgan's mother said. "We all want to make our point, let's just be civil about it."

Morgan tried to ignore them, tried to concentrate on the scene unfolding through his lens. He needed to clear his head and figure out the best way to handle this. He wanted Marsh's approval and the added prestige of saving his life. Not to mention what killing that witch would do to his reputation.

"Aw, Morgan. She's a magical being, she needs to live free and roam the earth happy. Let her go and give me a hug." Mr. Hector approached with his arms wide.

"No!" Brandt stepped forward and kicked Mr. Hector hard enough for the little doll to go flying across the room. "That bitch isn't magic, she's evil. She's evil and if you don't stop her now, she'll destroy everything you've worked for. If she kills Marsh, you're out on the street. You think Thorpe will take you on in her organization? Not after you've been a toady for Marsh this long."

The others looked at where Mr. Hector landed, then back at Morgan. "You bastard," Morgan's mother said.

"Now, now. Let's watch our language," Brandt chuckled.

Morgan's mother exhaled loudly through her nose and her face screwed up in rage. She stepped toward the still-smiling Brandt and punched him. Brandt stumbled back. As he regained his balance, the monkey began beating his shins with the symbols.

Brandt lashed out, knocking Morgan's mother against the wall. He kicked at the monkey, trying to get the thing away from his feet.

A wild cry echoed through the office. "Arrrr!" Brandt turned in time to see Mr. Hector flying through the air at his waist.

Morgan turned away from the scene and looked again through the sight. His mind was racing through the last ten years he'd spent in Marsh's organization. He knew all the people, all the big clients. He'd done jobs big and small, things he'd distained, but they were duties he'd performed to learn the business. The words Brandt said came to him again—*If she kills Marsh, you're out on the street.*

Morgan ignored the cursing and scuffling behind him and got into his firing stance again. His finger rested lightly on the trigger and the stock fell neatly into the groove in his shoulder. He looked at all three of the people in Marsh's office, then zoomed in on the individuals, he could see Deena clearly again.

"You are all thinking way too small," he said. In the next breath, the room fell silent as everyone stopped to question what he meant.

In the breath after that, the room shook with the percussion of a gunshot.

64

Deena heard the pounding of the men trying to get into Marsh's office. She stood with the gun at her side, feeling its weight in her hand. The culmination of a dozen years of working against her will began to seep into Deena's consciousness and her jaw ached from holding it so tight. But it had to stop somewhere. When she was fourteen, the Shadow Energy within pushed her hard enough to kill a young man in the name of helping her sister. Now, she knew what it was, and she might even have a say in how it was used or *not* used.

"This is getting us nowhere. If you aren't going to shoot him, let's go. Let's walk out while we can," Harper said. "Maybe we can still fight our way out." When Deena didn't move, Harper got more forceful. "You ungrateful little bitch. It's always been about you, everything has been about you, and now you won't even bend to do one thing for me? Let's go."

"One thing? More killing? That's the little thing I should do? Give up my sanity and keep ending people's lives to make it out? I think that's more than a little thing." Deena noticed that Harper tightened her grip on the gun.

"You embraced this life like a religious calling. *That's* crazy. You dragged me along with you and guilted me into staying. *That's* crazy. I sacrificed and sacrificed for you." She raised the gun and pointed it at Deena. "Mr. Marsh? You know I've been loyal to you from the beginning, you give me the chance and you'll see what I can do. I can be every bit as good as she is." She cocked the gun. "Say the word and I'll kill her for you."

"What?" Deena asked. Her sister sounded serious and her face showed grim determination. Deena shifted her gaze from her sister to Marsh, tracing the lines in his face, looking for some sign. She waited and wondered what was going through his mind. "Harper, this is insane."

"Put down your gun," Harper said.

Deena set her weapon on the ground, not wanting to provoke Harper any more than she had to.

"This is some situation, yes?" Marsh seemed to breathe a little easier. "Two girls I'd like to see dead are standing in my office. One is offering to kill the other. What to do, what to do?"

"You don't want to do this, Harper. I had no control over what I was doing. The agents say it's some kind of parasite that controlled me. Let's leave and we can talk about it. You and I can leave here and start our lives over." It was a lie. There was no starting over. Not once they met up with the agents and they went into custody. Even if the compromise they'd discussed actually happened, it wouldn't be freedom. It would be living in someone else's cage. "There are agents on their way to arrest everyone on the other side of the door. We can wait it out."

"I doubt that would happen," Marsh said. "Start over? After the bus incident? You'll have every cop, agent and sheriff after you for the rest of your life. They may call out the Texas Rangers and the Marines as well."

Deena looked at her sister and Marsh. "What bus incident? What are you talking about?"

Marsh feigned surprise. "You didn't tell her? My. My. I thought there were no secrets between sisters."

"Harper?" Deena asked. She knew about every job Harper had done, except for anything that might have happened while Deena had been chasing her last mark around the country. The job that had shorted out the hold the Shadow Energy had on her.

It got quiet in the office while Deena waited for someone to either fill her in on what she was missing, or shoot her in the head.

"Your sister was a little too zealous in trying to take care of a witness for us. She… She got a few unintended targets," Marsh said.

"It was an accident. He told me to send a message." Harper's nostrils flared.

"Not the message that we're incompetent." The smirk on Marsh's face lingered as his voice trailed off. "And I had such high hopes for you both. Your father spoke so highly of you."

"Our father?" Deena felt her jaw tighten. "What the hell are you talking about?"

"You don't think I just accepted a person with talents like yours without a little investigation, do you? I asked a few questions, and it seems your father is the foremost authority on whatever that destructive force is that courses through your pale little body," Marsh said. "Isn't that a coincidence?"

Deena was stunned into silence. She thought about the things she'd seen in the basement: the mini-lab, the containers. None of it was familiar to her, but was it possible that her father was responsible for putting some vile creature inside of her? She shuddered.

The silence of the moment was broken when the window shattered and Marsh fell backward, his body hitting the wall with a thump.

Deena and Harper both fell to the floor, trying to make sure they weren't hit by any follow-up shots. Deena crawled toward the side of the window, hoping the metal frame would block any further shots into the office. She peered around the corner and out into the city, seeing nothing but birds, open sky and tall building after tall building.

She saw her sister across the room, still in the open but slowly crawling toward the desk. Marsh's body had disappeared behind it with nothing but a bloody streak on the wall to show he'd ever been standing. Harper was headed in that direction, weeping as she went.

With all the death and mayhem she'd seen and caused, Deena was surprised her sister had the ability to shed tears about death. And about Marsh, one of the most notoriously violent criminals to walk the streets of this city, the man who'd pushed them to become thieves and killers. There were questions that Deena never thought to ask, and she saw how her sister was right in a way, it was always about her. It was always about what Deena wanted and needed. She wondered how far Harper had gone to make a place for them here with Marsh's organization. She shuddered, wondering whether that unknown variable might be far worse than all of the things she actually knew about. She watched her sister place a hand on the side of the desk and push herself along. "Harper. Forget it. Let's go. Let's just go. He's got to be done for." She wanted to run over and grab Harper, take a running leap and fly out the window, off to the mountains, back to the house and hide there until winter covered their world and their tracks. "Don't you get it, we can go. There's nothing holding us here."

If Harper heard, she didn't acknowledge as she disappeared behind the desk.

65

Morgan turned to the figures frozen behind him. "I think all of you are thinking way too small," he said.

Mr. Hector, the monkey, Brandt, Wallace, Nadine and Morgan's mom all stood with their noses pressed against the glass looking out across the city toward Marsh's office. Morgan wondered what they expected to see without the aid of a scope or binoculars. He supposed whether they could see anything or not wasn't the point.

The monkey let out a low whistle.

"My God, boy," Brandt said quietly. "What have you done? You killed Marsh. You'll be hunted by every member of that little fucker's organization. They'll string you up. This isn't what I told you to do at all."

Morgan let himself smile. "The big picture, Brandt. The big picture."

The teddy bear was the first to look away from the window. "Uh oh. This is bad news. Morgie screwed up again."

"Morgan, it was bad enough when I thought you were going to kill another woman, but this can bring you nothing but more and more trouble," his mother said. "I don't know what to say."

Brandt spoke again. "Jumping Jesus on a Tuesday. What in hell made you decide to shoot Marsh instead of the girl?"

Morgan was still looking through the scope at the office. Deena had disappeared from his view fairly quickly and Harper slowly made her way behind the desk where Marsh had fallen. His smile faded. "Instead?" He squeezed the trigger. "Let's see if we can't start with a clean slate."

66

Chunks of the desk exploded into splinters that showered the room. One shot left a gaping hole in the front and Deena heard Harper scream.

"Harper!" Deena stood and left her cover as part of the wall exploded bits of plaster near her head. She ran to the desk and tried to hide herself in the useless cover there. She first saw Marsh's lifeless body in a pool of blood, his eyes wide and unseeing.

Harper was next to him, holding her left shoulder. Before Deena could ask, Harper said, "I'm fine, it'll be fine."

Deena wanted to ask if she could check it but the sound of more bullets impacting the room interrupted her. She looked around and saw that the gunfire was concentrated at the door on the other side of the room. He's toying with us, she thought. If he wanted us dead, we would be. Like Marsh.

There was some thudding from the hallway and the door crunched in two. Deena realized the door had been weakened enough that Marsh's men could knock it down. Still in a crouch and using the desk for cover as long as she could, Deena hurried toward the doorway. Two men came through and looked around the room, apparently bewildered at the destruction. Another man entered it with an automatic pistol and leveled in her direction. Deena figured he wouldn't have time to zero in on her and fire fast enough, not with his friends in the line of fire. She wished she'd kept a weapon, a pistol or something, so she wouldn't have to fight the men so close up. She could feel the Shadow Energy moving on her arm, expanding up her veins. It hurt more than ever. She'd hoped she would be able to fight without the help of whatever it was that dwelled within her. As with so many other times, she didn't have a choice. No chanting, no calming words, no yoga or screaming would make it stop now.

She covered the distance faster than she'd expected, faster than the men anticipated as well. They barely had time to look at her before she was there. Her fist was coming down on the first man's face, she knew him, had seen him in the office many times, but his name didn't come to her. She brought her knuckles down squarely on his nose, and heard a thick crack with the impact. She pivoted her body so that her back was to the men, using the swiveling motion to build momentum to plant her elbow firmly in the next man's neck, she didn't bother trying to remember whether she knew this one, she just let him fall with his hands at his throat as she turned toward the man with the Uzi.

As quick as she'd been, the man was still a few feet away with his gun trained on her. She could hear more people coming in the hall and somewhere in her mind, she figured it was over. Even with that knowledge, the entity within wanted her to keep going.

A single shot rang out, and Deena dove to the side to dodge it before she realized the man hadn't fired. Once she hit the floor, she turned to see Harper standing by the desk, holding the gun Marsh had threatened them with. The Uzi man went down.

Several more thugs ran through the doorway and Harper dropped them before Deena was even back on her feet.

Deena pulled a pistol out of one's hand and aimed it toward the door. There wasn't a sound in the outer office and she couldn't decide if that was good or bad. Were more waiting, hiding? Or was the way finally clear? She put her back to the wall and peered around the corner.

She only got a glimpse of Agents Pel and Garrett in the outer hall before she heard a thud and another scream from her sister. She'd fallen to the ground close to Marsh again, but this time things didn't look as superficial. Harper wasn't moving and as Deena approached, she could see blood trickling from her sister's body. There was a gaping hole in her side. Deena's hand curled in rage.

She looked out at the city; the myriad buildings, skyscrapers and rooftops came into focus then blurred. One by one, they disappeared from her view as though they didn't exist. One building, on the other side of the highway glowed a bright yellow to her and she saw a shadow fall across it, as though a cloud was blocking out the sun. As she focused on it, one floor near the top began to pulsate red until a window in the middle turned dark.

Without another thought, Deena raised her hand and pointed to a far-away window that she couldn't even see. Flames of blackness erupted into a ball around her hand; the room was silent, at least to her, as she let the power do what it wanted. She didn't try to control it, or guide it in any way. Her arm jerked and she remembered the sensation of firing a shotgun at the men in the house. It was a strong kick that made her stumble after the energy discharged. She recovered enough to see a circle of darkness the size of a softball disappear toward the building she'd focused in on. She didn't try to follow it to its destination, just turned to tend to Harper. She weakened as she felt the cloud of the Shadow Energy's control fade. She was suddenly tired, each step a chore with leaden feet.

Deena knelt next to her sister, trying to decide what to do. No ambulance or paramedics were going to make a run to this office right now; no doctor was going to make a house call. Harper's eyes were open only in slits, like she was falling asleep.

"Harper?" Her own voice was growing quiet, catching in her throat. So much so that she barely heard the words coming from her sister's mouth.

"Everything that happened here," Harper paused and swallowed. Her lips dry and sticking together. "It's your fault. All these people, this blood, all of it, because you couldn't control yourself. I only wanted to watch over you." Her eyes flickered and closed for a moment. She opened them again and tried to speak, the eyes couldn't quite focus.

Tears rolled down Deena's cheek and her arm began to ache. "It wasn't me. I couldn't control anything." The hand throbbed and Deena looked at it as if it hadn't been there all her life. Another part of the desk disintegrated in a hail of wooden debris but she didn't flinch. Dark thread-like tendrils began to accumulate and wiggle at her fingertips and she began to speak words that she knew wouldn't calm the force, but antagonize it, encourage it. A tendril began to extend beyond her index finger, like a drip of paint with a mind of its own. She moved her hand over toward her sister's body, which was now heaving with the effort to breathe. Deena tried to pause and think through what was happening, but thought better of analyzing the situation. No one was going to help Harper if she didn't try something, she knew that, but she had no clue what the material would do or how her sister would handle it.

Harper suddenly looked up and saw her sister's hand coming toward her and shook her head. She raised her good arm and pushed weakly against her sister. "No," she said softly. Her eyes widened a bit, but she didn't seem to have the strength to fight or move away.

The drop of blackness fell free; broke apart from Deena completely and fell into the gaping wound below it and disappeared.

Harper screamed with strength that Deena was sure her sister hadn't had moments ago. Harper's body convulsed and Deena did her best to prevent her sister from moving for fear that she would injure herself further. "Don't fight it," she told her sister. "Fighting it makes it worse. I've been trying to fight it all my life."

She heard sounds in the outer office and reacted without realizing it. She grabbed a gun and pointed it at the doorway without leaving her sister's side. A moment later, Garrett and Pel burst through into the room. She had the presence of mind not to shoot.

"What the hell happened? You were supposed to wait for us." Garrett looked around the room at the destruction and death and then looked back at Deena. "Are you all right?"

Deena was glad he was here. She wished like crazy that he'd been here minutes ago to help, but she wondered if the shooter would've targeted the agents as well. "I'm OK. Harper's been shot, and I didn't know what else to do."

"What do you mean, what else? What did you do?"

Deena could hear the concern in his voice and she hesitated to explain. "I…" She held up her left hand, still black with the subsiding power.

Pel stepped over and looked at the wound. It was no longer dripping blood, but instead, seeping black matter. "This is like what happened when you were shot at the house."

"You used the power on your sister? After all the pain it's caused you, after everything that it's done to you?" Garrett's brow furrowed. "What the hell is going to happen to her?"

"What other choice did I have? It just happened on its own. What would you have done?" She started to grab Harper's hand, to try to comfort the girl, or comfort herself, but she couldn't bring herself to touch her. She heard Garrett inhale deeply and she thought he might pursue the argument further, but he didn't. Instead, he pulled out his radio. "Rice? Where are you? We are inside and there has been a massive amount of gunfire." He waited for a response before adding. "I repeat, shots have been fired. Request assistance."

"Is the shooter neutralized?" Pel asked. "Do you know where they are?" She moved to cover as best she could and pointed her weapon toward the window.

"I think I got him," Deena said.

67

Blocks away, Morgan had only a split second to wonder what the blob was that darkened his telescopic sight. He'd been focused on Harper for a moment, and by the time he nudged the rifle scope over to where he'd left Deena, the missile of blackness was already near. The streak shot into his telescopic sight, shattering the lens. The sound of the destruction barely registered with Morgan before the dark blob burst through the second lens and embedded itself in his right eye. His head jerked backward and he fell to the floor, his hands instinctively going to his eye. He uttered what would later be described by his ex-girlfriend as a very unmanly and quite school-girlish scream as he writhed on his back. He fought to get up and figure out what was happening, to get himself away, but the pain was a shooting crackle of heat that penetrated his skull thoroughly. He passed out with the dull outlines of several figures gathering around to peer down at him.

"That doesn't look good," Mr. Hector said.

Later, on the floor, he could hear bits of glass tumbling off his chest, and the wind streaming in through the window. Unfortunately, for the moment, he could only hear it. When he opened his eyes, there was still nothing but blackness in his field of vision. His right eye, where he'd been struck, hurt horribly whenever he opened it, so he stayed on the floor with both eyes shut for as long as he could. He wanted to get up and make his escape, though he was fairly sure no one from Marsh's office was going to travel across the city to get him anytime soon. He was far enough away that it was a good bet the police wouldn't make the connection for some time.

As light slowly seeped into his left eye, he found the right one wasn't improving. He couldn't keep his right eye open for more than a second or two without it shutting involuntarily. He tried to sit up, but felt ill immediately and rolled on his side to vomit. When it passed, he looked around the room, blinking constantly. "Hello?" He was alone.

He crawled over, grabbed his rifle, pulled his suitcase next to him and closed his good eye to rest it. From memory, he disassembled the weapon and put each piece carefully in its designated place inside the hard-sided case, including the shattered telescope. When he was done, he opened his eye again, got on his hands and knees and picked up every spent shell and every little bit of the shattered lens he could find and put them in his shirt pocket. He pulled on his jacket and removed sunglasses from the inside pouch and slipped them on. It hurt, but the light was making everything hurt worse. From another compartment he pulled the ear nub for his cell phone and shoved it in his left ear. He decided that no matter how dumb it was, he couldn't handle the stairs. Since his first job, he'd taken the stairs whenever possible and crisscrossed from stairwell to stairwell on the way down, to avoid any pursuers. Today, he knew he couldn't handle forty flights of steps, so he stumbled toward the elevator.

68

Garrett ran ahead of the group and into the parking garage to let Rivers and Rice know that the girls were on their way and prepared to cooperate. He hoped he was right. Harper seemed to be hanging on by a thread. He wasn't sure what her death would do to the deal they'd worked out and how it would affect Deena's temperament. "Let's not get too crazy about this," Garrett said. "Nice and easy. No need to scare anyone."

"Don't worry. I'm not going to upset the weirdo with scary powers, *or* any gangsters with automatic weapons. Not that stupid." Rivers put his hand on his gun and unsnapped the holster. "Think they'll actually show up, or try to make a run for it?" Rivers asked quietly.

Garrett was sure they were coming down the escalator to the lower level of the parking garage. They had little choice, with the condition that Harper was in. Pel could handle them and the deal made sense to everyone. It wasn't ideal, but it would do some good for everyone. "They're on their way. Pel's good with Deena."

"This better go well." Rivers stood with his arms folded the whole time. The only reason he'd gone along with the plan on the phone was that he saw some gain in bringing Deena in without a fight. At least not a fight that involved the FEI agents.

They stood in plain sight so the sisters could see there was no ambush. The agents soon heard voices coming nearer, talking low. Garrett could count four people coming up the ramp. "I wasn't sure you were coming back," he said. "You OK, Pel?"

"I'm fine, but we need an ambulance or something for Harper."

With a slight nudge, Harper pushed the agent away. "Actually, it just kind of stings." She pulled her hand away from her side and everyone saw that there was little more than a scratch where she'd been bleeding before. She looked concerned and turned to her sister. "What's happening?"

"I don't know. It just happens."

"Does anyone other than Agent Pellegrino still have a weapon? If so, drop the guns and kick them down the ramp." Rivers stared at them, and appeared fully prepared to shoot if they did anything he didn't like. Pel had her hand near her own weapon, but didn't pull it. Garrett and Pel had both been sure they were doing the right thing with Deena; it was her sister that was the variable in the situation. As he sized Harper up, he noticed she didn't seem to be carrying a gun.

"Whoa, whoa. Wait a minute." Stanley stepped between the two opposing groups. "Deena said you wanted to talk, let's talk. We were just coming to talk."

Garrett felt his finger twitch on the trigger. The accountant was harmless, but Rivers and Rice didn't know that. "Stanley, we'd be more inclined to believe you if you didn't have two guns tucked in your waistband."

Stanley looked more embarrassed than scared. "Oh."

"Now everyone put your guns on the ground and kick them away," Rivers said. "We had a deal, Deena."

Everyone grew quiet but no one moved.

"And that deal is still in place?" Deena fought her instinct to fight and run away. It wouldn't work this time.

"Yes," Rivers said.

"We can take these guys," Harper whispered. Her hands balled into fists.

Garrett sighed. "I'm standing right here, Harper. I can hear you. Don't make any sudden moves or we'll shoot."

Harper turned slowly to Stanley. "You sure you trust these guys?"

"Yes, I trust these new guys, the other two are kind of dicks," Stanley said. "But, at least I think these two have their hearts mostly in the right place."

"I can fix that," Harper said. "Where would you like their hearts? Floor? Ceiling?"

69

Deena put her hand up to calm her sister. She'd never heard Harper get so aggressive. "We've talked to them. They're trying to help, that's all." Deena slowly bent down and placed her weapon on the ground, knowing full well she could defend herself without it. She kicked it lightly down the ramp.

Stanley did the same with his weapons.

Harper stood there for a moment, eyeing Garrett, and it was obvious that he felt uncomfortable, like maybe he didn't have the situation in hand the way he thought he did. His hand hovered near his holster.

"OK," Harper said. "Talk."

"All right, let's all head back to the office and we'll talk out the details," Garrett said.

"What's there to talk about?" Stanley looked over. "He's dead. Marsh is dead. The organization's done, right? I testify. They testify. Done."

"Not exactly. Someone else'll take over. They'll re-organize, move around. Hell, they may just take over Marsh's legal holdings and rebuild. They'll make things difficult for us. We might get a few of them here and there, but the bulk of the people will make it out unscathed."

"That's a bitch," Harper said.

"Well put," Pel agreed. "I managed to get a crapload of dirt on Marsh's organization, but I don't think it'll be enough to really close the place down for good."

"So let's talk here." Harper folded her arms. "Otherwise, I guess we're going to have to renegotiate this deal."

Garrett looked around. "We can't do it here. I'm assuming there are some very dead hit men on the premises, and that your gunfire has attracted the local police. Once they arrive, there's going to be a lot of explaining to do and I'm not sure I can keep this deal on the table."

"Then talk fast," Harper said.

"Deal? What the hell is the deal you're talking about exactly? No one has had much time to elaborate," Stanley asked.

The deal the organization made was for Deena, and Deena alone. She knew that she was the one they wanted, in hopes that she could use the Shadow Energy to help track down others with her abilities. But now that Harper had it running through her as well, maybe it was time to renegotiate that deal.

Agent Rice butted in, obviously against Garrett's wishes. "They haven't explained yet? Agent Garrett wants you to come work for us."

"Work for you?" Stanley asked.

Garrett nodded. "We've worked out a deal. At least the start of one. Deena would help track down the less savory people with her kind of power."

"Got news for you, *we* are the less savory people," Harper said.

Everyone turned to look at Deena. Whether she liked it or not, she'd suddenly become the person in charge of the conversation, and she alone would dictate exactly what happened next. "So, what do you think?" Garrett asked, tilting his head to the side.

"If you're looking at me, I've already told you. I'll go along with it as long as it keeps us from being hunted like animals and experimented on like rats," Deena said. "But, things have changed for my sister. I think she may have the Shadow Energy in her as well now. The two of us can be more effective than I would be alone."

"Two Inks for the price of one? That might work," Rivers said.

There was silence as everyone started walking forward. Their footfalls echoed in the cavernous parking garage as they walked farther up the ramp.

"So, we'd be like Scooby Doo and drive around solving crimes?" Stanley asked. He was smiling and trying to placate everyone around him. "Or more like the A-Team. They had guns and explosives and shit."

Deena didn't like being the de facto leader, hated casting any sort of deciding vote. This whole thing had been her fault in many ways. No matter what had influenced her life and actions, she held the ultimate blame. If this was a way to free them from their past misdeeds, she couldn't refuse. "Either way, we'd have to get a kick-ass van."

"I think that means we're in," Stanley said. "Either that or Deena has a van fetish."

"Whoa. Who said anything about Stanley being involved in this? He's a federal witness…" Garrett said.

"Stanley comes or we don't." If Stanley wanted to come along, Deena would fight for him. He'd taken steps to help Harper, steps that Deena couldn't have pulled off herself. "And we only work with Agents Pel and Garrett." Deena watched Garrett turn to stare at the other men in suits. The men's faces both twisted slightly, brows furrowing. One of them finally nodded.

"Just out of curiosity, what was going to happen if we said no and decided to kill you all and leave your bodies in this parking garage?" Harper looked at Rivers as if she was sizing him up.

Rivers stopped walking and raised his left hand.

The group was startled by the sudden clang of loud noises. On the level above them, heavily armed men stepped from behind cover, pointing their guns at the little group. A number of officers slid into position from hiding places behind pale concrete columns and vehicles, training their rifles on the girls. All of them were decked out in tactical gear and riot helmets, padded breastplates and visors. Most were holding automatic rifles, but a few held weapons Deena couldn't identify and didn't want to know what they did. A flower delivery truck pulled up in front of them, slid open its doors and released ten more men in the same light-blue armored suits. Deena calculated the odds of any of them surviving the first volley. Her math wasn't great, but the chances were not good. Even if she knew her body could heal after a single gunshot wound, she was less sure it could handle multiple shots.

"I'm sorry. Did I say anything about any of you having a choice? That's my fault, 'cause I sure didn't mean to." Rivers glared at Deena and Harper. "We made a deal. This is the deal."

"If they started shooting, you'd bite it too," Harper said.

Rivers shrugged. "Think so?"

"Let's find out," Harper grabbed Garrett and pulled him close.

Deena reached out, just as Rice pulled her away. She clenched her teeth, fighting to keep her power in check. If she hurt anyone, the whole deal would be off.

"Let go of him," Pel unholstered her weapon. "Let's not make this ugly."

Harper held tight to Garrett, and Deena could see her arms begin to undulate with black lines moving along her skin. Harper's face showed her confusion at what was happening to her body. Her grip on Garrett loosened, but he didn't move. "Deena? What's happening to me? What did you do?"

Deena held up her hands to try to let her know it was OK. "Just calm down. You have to calm down. Don't get too excited."

Harper had completely let go of Garrett, but Deena could tell the agent was staying in place to block anyone from shooting Harper. He moved as she moved, keeping anyone from taking a clear shot. But when Harper fell to the ground, looking at her hands, Rivers took the opportunity to shove his fellow agent out of the way and point his gun directly in Harper's face.

"I told you this was a bad idea," Rivers said. "There's no way to control these people."

"Don't shoot." Deena pulled against Rice's grip.

Rivers' hands shook just a little as he spoke. "Deal's off. We are packing these Inks up and taking them back to the holding area."

Deena watched as Harper's face went from frantic to strangely calm. Harper's body got still and she placed her hands on the concrete floor of the garage. The dark lines on her arms quickly congealed in her fingertips and Shadow Energy began to form a puddle under her palms, which snaked out slowly to form long, gnarled, root-like lines stretching out in all directions. Harper looked up at Rivers and the garage grew quiet.

Rice had raised his hand at some point, indicating the armed men in the building should hold their fire. Deena watched as his face showed his resolve was wavering. "Don't," Deena said. "This is over. She won't be a threat."

"How the hell do you know that?" Rice asked.

From experience and from what she saw on Harper's face, Deena knew what was going on in Harper's mind. "Your agents told me what you found out about imprinting and what happens when the Energy first breaks the skin. It's like that matter has eyes and takes a good look at the first person nearby."

"And nothing before that? It lies dormant, just building itself up on aggression and adrenaline?" Pel asked.

Stanley couldn't take his eyes off Harper. "One of you makes it sound like a bug with eyes that look for a queen to follow, the other makes it sound like a cold or a cancer, growing stronger inside of her. Do any of you know what's going on? Really?"

Rivers looked like he wanted to respond, but didn't get the chance. Harper stood, and the tendrils reached out for him, stopping just short of his face. "I'm not going to hurt you. Just tell me what you want me to do."

"What?" Rivers asked.

"I get it now. I get the whole thing now, Deena. You weren't just being a selfish bitch. You *had* to do everything you did." Harper took a hard breath and the Shadow lines snapped back to her arms and disappeared completely except for a large blob on her forearm that resembled a fishhook.

His gun was still firmly pointed at Harper's head, but Rivers managed a cough. "What?"

Deena spoke up. "The thing inside her may have just chosen *you* as the person that Harper will follow blindly for the foreseeable future. She's certainly not going to hurt you now."

"You can put the gun down," Garrett said. "Before something happens. Something *bad.*"

Stanley pushed forward. "About that van? It's sounding real good to me right now. I'm thinking all black with a red stripe. Maybe one of those stretch limo Hummers?" He grabbed Deena by the arm and forced her forward. She let him lead.

"So, we do these things for you and our slate gets wiped clean, we're good guys with no strikes against us when it's all over?" Harper asked. She hadn't started forward when Stanley had and neither did Rivers.

Rivers made a show of looking around at all the guns trained on them and raised his hands in demonstration. "Little girl, there's no slate. There's no 'When it's all over'." He laughed. "You take this generous offer, do everything that's asked of you, jump when we say jump, and you get to breathe lovely fresh air. "You don't do it, you screw up, you look at someone wrong and we take each of you to trial with what can only be described as a mountain of evidence against you."

Deena wanted to stop him from talking, but she knew Harper needed to hear it.

"Oh, I forgot option C," he pointed to the men around them with weapons. "There's always a bullet in your head. You guys are chock full of options, aren't you?"

"Agent Rivers, look…" Deena began.

"No. You look. If you all want to make this some kind of television fantasy or something fine. I'll buy you a Great Dane or I'll shave Stanley's head into a Mohawk myself." Stanley's hand immediately flew to his head to protect his hair. "But don't have any illusions as to what this is all about. You will work for us. You will hunt down more of these people and you will help us put them away until we can figure out what this shit is inside of you."

It was quiet as the oversized white floral delivery van silently rolled closer. The side door slid methodically opened and Deena saw nothing but darkness inside. She looked to the side and noticed the others were staring at her, waiting for her to move. Her hand ached in the anticipation of something.

She stole a glance at Agents Garrett and Pel but couldn't read their faces.

Deena Riordan analyzed the situation and wondered how stupid this all would look to her old self. Risking her life, her future, on the word of some government agents she had no reason to trust. She looked at her sister and thought about what she'd become and what awaited her down the road. There weren't a whole lot of logical options. Sometimes relatively smart people had no other recourse than to make stupid choices. She could read the looks of anticipation and expectation on the faces of the people around her, just waiting for her lead.

Deena took a deep breath and stepped into the van.

70

Epilogue

"I'll want someone to get in here and clean up the rest of these stupid tennis balls," Morgan said as he kicked one of the bright yellow balls. His new assistant, Helena Barr, dutifully made a note on her tablet. Morgan stood at the huge window in what used to be Marsh's office. The view was amazing and Morgan took a moment to remember how many times he'd come in to find Marsh standing in the very same spot. It was an easy assumption that the man had been pausing for dramatic effect, but the view was so very amazing that he now understood it was quite possible Marsh had just been lost in the beauty of the city.

The sight was all the more breathtaking to Morgan knowing he'd just had state of the art bulletproof glass installed. He'd had the walls patched and painted to eliminate the bloodstains and holes that littered them. New carpet was on order.

Helena looked around. "I ordered those extra chairs for your office. It sort of seems like a lot. How many did you say? Eight?"

"Might as well make it an even dozen. I tend to have guests show up unannounced." Morgan looked around for any sign of his usual entourage, but they were absent. They'd been silent since he'd shot Marsh.

"Is there anything else, sir?" Helena asked.

"No. I think we can pick up this afternoon and start figuring our shit out."

Helena walked past the painter's scaffolding and equipment toward the door. She paused just short of the entrance. "Sir? Congratulations on stepping into Marsh's role. The board is thrilled to be working with you. You've been an important part of this organization for years. It's about time you received recognition for your service."

Morgan knew toadying and sucking up when he heard it, but he liked Helena. "Thank you. I only wish I'd been here to stop them from killing Mr. Marsh."

"It's a shame what that treacherous girl and her friends did to him. I hope you catch up with them and make them pay for what they did," Helena said.

"You and me both. I only regret that I had a hand in training that girl not so long ago." He neglected to mention that most of his tuition had been ignored or flatly denied by the girl. Much like he'd been neglecting to mention how Marsh had really died.

Once Helena left him, Morgan's hand went up to his eye and traced the circle of black dots that resulted from the explosion of shrapnel from his scope. The globule of Shadow Energy had combined with the glass pieces and imbedded themselves in a jagged simulation of a circle around his right eye permanently. It had been horribly painful for a few hours, but then, miraculously, felt fine by the next morning. He had no idea what it meant. He felt just the same as he always had, but the spots bore a remarkable resemblance to the one on Deena's arm. He couldn't find any sign he had the powers she did, but he thought maybe it would take time.

He half expected to see an apparition of Marsh sitting where his desk used to be, but Morgan found nothing. He thought for sure the ghosts would be all over him now, but they'd been silent. There was a twinge of doubt about how things would work out without them around, but they certainly had only been a hindrance. Of course, they'd be back. They couldn't stay away and let Morgan live in peace and quiet, now could they?

Morgan reached down and picked up a tennis ball. He bounced it a couple of times and nodded as he thought about the possibilities. The things to come brought a smile to his face. Everything was going to work out just fine.

About the Author

Matt Betts was born in Lima, Ohio, some years ago. Lima is just a stone's throw away from several other towns with excellent throwing stones. During and after college, Matt worked for a number of years in radio as an on-air personality, anchor and reporter. His fiction and poetry have appeared in various magazines, journals and anthologies.

Matt currently lives in Columbus, Ohio, with his wife and sons. He is hard at work on his next book. And watching old science fiction and horror movies. Mostly writing. And maybe reading comic books. Look, he's writing, OK? Jeez.

For more info visit: www.MattBetts.com.

www.ingramcontent.com/pod-product-compliance
Lightning Source LLC
Chambersburg PA
CBHW020650250626
47154CB00008B/2889